CINCH KNOT

A mystery thriller of Pigs,
Politics, and Petroleum.

The multinational plot to nuke the Trans Alaska Pipeline.

Ron Walden

P.O. Box 221974, Anchorage, Alaska 99522-1974

ISBN 1-888125-04-7

Library of Congress Catalog Card Number: 96-67380

Copyright 1996 by Ron Walden
—First Edition—

All rights reserved, including the right of reproduction in any form, or by any mechanical or electronic means including photocopying or recording, or by any information storage or retrieval system, in whole or in part in any form, and in any case not without the written permission of the author and publisher.

Manufactured in the United States of America.

Cinch Knot is a work of fiction. Any resemblance to actual persons, living or dead, is purely coincidental and unintentional. Except for the obvious inclusion of such broad categories of geography of Alaska, the Trans Alaska Pipeline and its environs, and other cities worldwide, the places are products of the author's imagination. Historical events surrounding the operation of the pipeline provide the backdrop for the story; but none of the story in this book should be construed as being a factual part of those events.

Cinch Knot is dedicated to the men and women who conceived, designed, engineered, constructed, and operate the Trans Alaska Pipeline. They represent every American, who have, and continue to give of themselves to ensure our country maintains a position of strength in protecting the worldwide environment and freedom of people everywhere, while still providing the highest standard of living history has recorded.

In the course of writing this book I received a great deal of help and advice from many people. I have tried to provide accurate technical information within the story. In accumulating this information, I called on so many individuals it would be impossible to acknowledge all, but every one of you has my thanks.

The personnel of the Alyeska Pipeline Service Company were wonderful in providing information. My thanks to the people of the APSC Public Information Office for their assistance, and for the written and video material they provided.

I also thank the Public Affairs Office at Elmendorf Air Force Base for arranging interviews with Captain Brad Davis, an F-15 pilot. He helped correct some errors in the book and provided tactical advice. I also extend my thanks Captain Troy Jackson of the Radar Section. He provided a great deal of information that added realism to the text.

I owe a debt of gratitude to the many security officers with whom I worked during my tenure on the pipeline. Many of the experiences quoted in this work are composites of stories told to me by those men and women. These people are still out there doing their jobs. They are professionals, providing a service in an environment too inhospitable for most of Mother Nature's creatures. Each of you have my sincere gratitude and admiration.

Introduction

Oil was discovered in the Prudhoe Bay oil field by exploratory drilling in 1968. The final permits to build the Trans Alaska Oil Pipeline were issued November 16, 1973 with the signing of the Trans Alaska Pipeline Construction Act by then, Secretary of the Interior, Rogers Morton. It took 5 years, 2 months, and 19 days to obtain the permits necessary to build the pipeline. Road construction to Prudhoe Bay was completed in the fall of 1974. On June 20, 1977, the first oil left Pump Station One to travel the 800 miles to Valdez. The pipeline was built at a cost of eight billion dollars.

The Trans Alaska Oil Pipeline, one of the all-time engineering and construction wonders of the world, stretches from the north coast of Alaska to the ice free port of Valdez on the Gulf of Alaska. A giant steel soda straw through which 20% of the United States domestic oil production flows. Thick black blood of modern civilization flows from the hundreds of wells drilled on the north arctic slope of Alaska.

The drilling area is divided into several lease tracts. During the early development of the field, it was shared by many oil and exploration companies. Today only a handful of companies are represented. The lions share of activity is conducted by British Petroleum Alaska Division (BP), Atlantic Richfield Company (ARCO), and Conoco. BP operates the west half of the Prudhoe Bay Field and the Endicott Field. ARCO operates the east half of the Prudhoe Bay Field, as well as the Lisburne and Kaparuk fields. Conoco is the sole operator in the Milne Point Field.

Crude oil produced by each well is transmitted through small pipelines into larger pipelines. This oil, flows through the small pipelines, across the tundra to metering valves where it is measured and tested for quality. It is at this point (Pump Station #1), it enters the Trans Alaska Pipeline and becomes the ward of the Alyeska Pipeline Service Company.

Three major mountain ranges are crossed by the pipeline. The Brooks Range is the highest point where the pipeline crosses Atigun Pass with an altitude of 4,739 feet. It crosses the Alaska range at Isabel Pass, 3,420 feet, and the Chugach range at Thompson Pass, 2,812 feet.

There are 34 major stream crossings and 800 small crossings. The pipe is above ground for a total of 420 miles and buried for 376 miles. The remaining 3 miles of pipeline are special animal crossings and areas where the pipe corridor is refrigerated under some highways to prevent damage to permafrost.

The pipe has an outside diameter of 48 inches. Wall thickness of the pipe varies with the pressures required inside. Low pressure areas (466 miles), have a wall thickness of .462 inches. High pressure areas (334 miles), have a wall thickness of .562 inches. The pipeline has a maximum operating pressure of 1,180 pounds per square inch.

At the height of construction, there were over 20,000 dedicated men and women working on the pipeline. Every day saw innovations in construction—building snow roads for construction pads and an aerial tram to lift 10 ton sections of pipe into position on mountain slopes so steep they had only been traversed by mountain climbers.

There are 12 pump stations on the pipeline. Two on these pump stations (Pump Stations Five and Eleven) are flow through stations only and do not actually pump any oil. Each pump station has two working pumps and one on standby. The pumps are powered by giant Rolls Royce turbine engines similar to the ones found on jumbo jet airliners. These pump engines also generate electrical power needed to run the pump station and its facilities.

Crude oil is pumped into the pipe at a pressure of over 800 pounds per square inch. Viscous properties of the thick crude make it necessary to inject the oil with an additive to reduce friction and the tumbling action of the crude inside the pipe. This friction heats the crude naturally to a temperature of between 70 and 80 degrees, cooled somewhat from the 120 degrees it had at the well head.

So begins an odyssey taking the thick, black fluid from the frozen north coast across tundra, rivers, mountains, and valleys to the Marine Terminal at Valdez. At the Marine Terminal it is stored in huge tanks until the next supertanker arrives. It will then be gravity fed through miles of pipes to the tanker berth where it is accepted aboard the vessel.

Valdez Marine Terminal is also the Operations Control Center (OCC). Every facet of the operation of the pipeline is electronically monitored and data transmitted by microwave and VHF radio to OCC. This is the nerve center of the pipeline. All automated safety controls, flow functions, emergency controls, and untold numbers of daily functions are tied to the OCC computers.

The daily throughput varies slightly with production, but averages between 1.9 million barrels and 2.1 million barrels per day. This is a tribute to the education, skill, and dedication of the people working for the Alyeska Pipeline Service Company. Their production and safety record cannot be matched by anyone in any industry, anywhere.

The Alyeska Pipeline Service Company is owned by a Consortium of oil companies, Amerada Hess Pipeline Corporation, ARCO Pipeline Company, Phillips Alaska Pipeline Corporation, BP Pipelines (Alaska) Inc., Exxon Pipeline Company, Unocal Pipeline Company, and Mobil Alaska Pipeline Company. The State of Alaska has been able to run its government, successfully, for many years on the revenues generated by taxes levied on the flow of oil through the Trans Alaska Pipeline.

Living in Alaska means living in a society, whose culture is based on the price of a barrel of oil. However, producers in Alaska do not dictate the market price of a barrel of oil. Many factors contribute to the value of crude oil, the largest of which is, of course, the OPEC council. Since they are the major producers and largest reserve holders, they have the power to dictate the price of oil worldwide. Their track record for reaching agreement on price and production quotas has been less than exemplary.

Unstable governments in the mid-east, roller-coaster oil prices, varying production quotas, loss of government tax incentives, oil depletion taxes, and a thousand other ills have contributed to making oil dependent societies a feast or famine existence. Declining oil prices are becoming a concern for everyone in America's northernmost state. The 450,000 residents of the state will somehow have to deal with a billion-dollar shortfall in state revenues. There are rumors, up and down the pipeline, of layoffs and cutbacks . . .

The Ultrasonic Pig
Its function and purpose

Any steel pipeline is subject to corrosion and the vanadium steel of the Alaska pipeline is no exception. When an unprotected metallic structure comes into contact with the ground, an electrochemical process may take place causing the metal to corrode. To minimize this process, a number of preventive measures were undertaken. The pipe was coated with a fusion bonded epoxy and wrapped with a specially designed polyethylene-based tape.

A cathodic protection system consisting of zinc ribbon anodes was welded to each side of the pipe at 500 to 1000 foot intervals. When coupled to the buried metal, the anodes are designed to corrode, instead of the pipe.

Test stations were installed approximately every three miles to measure and evaluate the system's performance.

There is usually very little corrosion inside the pipe. Most of the internal corrosion has been detected within the area of pump stations where the oil flows slowly and the water and anaerobic sulfur-reducing bacteria (SRBs) come into contact with the metal. Both water and SRBs are found in Alaska North Slope crude oil.

Alyeska Pipeline Service Company has run corrosion detection pigs in the pipeline since start-up. However, no corrosion was detected in the pipeline until 1988. It became apparent early in the operation of the pipeline that a better detection method must be found. In 1984, Alyeska commissioned the development of an advanced magnetic-flux system. This advanced system developed by Pipetronix Corporation (formerly IPEL of Canada) began to detect anomalies in 1988. These anomalies, or areas that had other than normal measurements, were found to have 40% metal loss. It was decided that further development in corrosion detection must be accomplished.

In 1988, with introduction of the ultrasonic pig, anomalies with a metal loss of 10% were detected. The ultrasonic pig was developed by the NKK company of Japan. The 6,600-pound pig is 10 feet long and constructed of titanium. It has amazing capabilities that only recent developments in micro-processing have allowed it to achieve. It has an onboard computer that stores and processes a tremendous amount of information. It travels down the pipeline at a rate of about 10 feet per second. Its instrumentation divides the interior of the pipe into 15mm by 15mm grids. There are 255 of these grids in the circumference of the pipe. That means that there are 255 transducers transmitting a signal every 15mm the full length of the pipe. The onboard computer receives the information and determines if there is indication of thinning of the pipe wall. If an anomaly is detected, the location of the irregularity is recorded on a commercial grade video recorder.

The pig is removed from the pipe at Pump Station Four and Pump Station Ten to replace the video tape and to charge the batteries operating the equipment.

Each time an inspection run is scheduled for the ultrasonic pig, it must be brought from Japan. At U.S. Customs in Anchorage, the pig is dismantled and inspected for contraband. This process of dismantling and reassembling the pig takes one month. The pig is then placed in its own container and shipped to the warehouse at Pump Station One for final installation of recorders and fresh batteries. All work on the pig is done by electronic technicians employed by NKK.

The information taken from the pig run is translated and evaluated by NKK in Japan and the results, in the form of computer printouts and graphs, are then sent to the Alyeska's, Bragaw Street offices in Anchorage for comparison to information from other pig runs.

It is a long and complicated process, but the oil companies guaranteed the pipeline to last for 30 years. This vigilant effort has discovered over 1,800 anomalies to date and precipitated the exhumation and repair of many miles of pipeline.

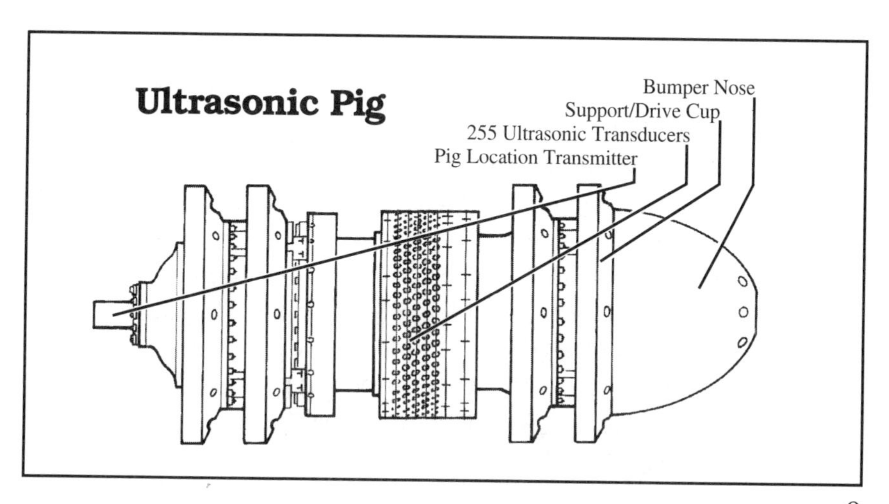

CHAPTER ONE

D*an Webster tried to open his eyes but they wouldn't cooperate. The unmistakable hospital odor told him where he was. Breathing, even shallow panting, was agonizing, hot, white pain, and into that pain images flashed: he remembered his moment of hesitation as his eyes narrowed on the front sight and his target; he could see his attacker's jaw tighten, the pistol muzzle flashing twice—but he recalled hearing no sound. "Is somebody there? Help me!" Pain again...and...flashes: air rushing from his lungs as he fell backward; squashed bugs stuck to the Blazer's bumper; and yellow dandelions in the green grass—then nothing. Somebody help me!" Were his words only in his head and not coming from his mouth? How did he get to the hospital he wondered. No one came. Pain and medication pulled the blackness around him and he drifted into darkness again.*

The Mountain House Cafe was a regular stop on Dan's patrol. Elizabeth Lucile Johnson was a waitress there. Even in her apron, with her hands full of coffee cups, she looked like a cheerleader: more cute than pretty, smooth skinned, slim, agile, and congenial. Beth finished her third year at college, majoring in accounting, and took up waitressing to get her through school. She found herself watching expectedly for the young deputy.

"Hi Dan. Busy night?" she asked, as she wiped the table and sat the coffee in front of him.

"It's pretty quiet tonight. I've had one burglary. It was Ernie. He'd parked his pickup in the wrong driveway and walked onto the back porch of his neighbor's house. Scared the neighbor lady out of her wits. I found him asleep in a pile of laundry. He thought he was home and complained that his wife wouldn't let him in the house." Dan grinned. "I took him home. Another case solved and goodness triumphs again." He rattled his knife and fork together.

Beth laughed with him and then looked at him seriously. "Do me a big favor, huh?"

"Sure."

"My brother borrowed my car last night and was supposed to bring it back before midnight. He called, said he'd been drinking and was spending the night at his girlfriend's." She looked at her watch.

"I get off at 6:30. Take me home, would you?"

Dan had been trying to work up the courage to ask for a date, and now the opportunity dropped into his lap.

"I have a briefing after my shift that'll last until about 6:30. I can get here around 6:45; if it's not too late. I'd be happy to take you home, I mean to yours, of course." Both smiled.

"That'll be just fine; about 6:45 then?"

There was a note from Sheriff McNabb on his desk when he returned to the station. Dan was to report to him at 1600 hours. Usually when a deputy got this kind of note from the sheriff, with no other information, it meant wear your cast iron shorts.

"I wonder which citizen thinks I was abusive?" Knots began to twist in his gut. "I suppose I'll find out this afternoon. I get to pick up Beth in a few minutes; life isn't all bad."

He saw Beth waiting in front of the truck stop; her hair reflected red highlights in the morning sun. "How can anyone look this good after working a 10-hour shift in a restaurant?" he thought.

"Dan, over here. Thanks for the rescue. I didn't know who else to ask. Certainly not some of the bums and deadbeats that come in here"

They had attended the same school. Dan, a couple years older had an impressive record in football and associated mostly with the school jocks. Beth had been a good student, loved math, was popular with the girls, but seldom dated. After high school, Dan joined the army, Beth spent winters at college in Sacramento and summers back home.

The trip to Beth's apartment was full of chitchat about each other. Dan's father had been killed in a logging accident while Dan was still in high school. Since his mother's death, shortly after his return from the army, Dan had been a solitary person, never had a girl friend, and spent most of his free time fishing for steelhead in the Trinity River. Just over 6 feet tall and muscular, he weighed about 175 pounds. Dan figured he'd be a cop forever.

Beth was paying her own way through college. She worked as many hours as possible at the truck stop in order to study without interruption while in school. Although she had her own apartment, she spent a great deal of time with her folks.

spent a great deal of time with her folks. Her mother was a full time housewife and her father worked in the sawmill as a foreman. Beth was witty, friendly, and generated good tips. She planned to apply for work in San Francisco upon graduation.

Their talk lasted long after the car stopped in front of her place. They made a date for the following Saturday night for dinner. Beth invited him in for a cup of coffee, but Dan declined, remembering his meeting with the sheriff.

Dan's first year in the sheriff's department had been spent as a deputy in the county jail. It was good experience. He met the town drunk and become good friends with him. Ernie, the drunk, was a likeable fellow who provided for his family, but, spent all his extra earnings and time at the Stardust Tavern shooting the bull and drinking Lucky Lager.

Although there was marijuana grown in the vicinity, there were few drug dealers on the streets. Drawing attention to themselves would have been bad for business. A dealer, usually from the city, setting up shop in his county, was caught within a few days. Dan spent many hours talking with these people, learning from them while they were in jail, awaiting court.

Dan did well his first year. Most new deputies whine every day about wanting to get into a car and "go get some bad guys." He, used his time at the jail as his matriculation in post graduate criminology. Street criminals, for the most part, are not very intelligent. Dan felt he needed to learn how they thought so he'd be able to anticipate criminal behavior in others. He found it much easier to anticipate actions of criminals than those of an attorney or a court. A few criminals, he learned are very intelligent and cunning, making them extremely difficult to apprehend and convict.

His last 3 1/2 months at the jail were spent as duty shift supervisor. Twelve deputies and 93 prisoners were his direct responsibility. It was good experience in the complexities of administration. He knew nothing of timekeeping and budget, but learning those considerations, made him establish a new inventory procedure for prisoner property. His innovations made Dan a frequent topic at weekly staff meetings.

Sheriff McNabb, from the old school, believed in rewarding good performance and gave Dan 8 weeks on the road OJT with Chief Deputy Morgan Duncan. Dan was now a full-fledged, badge packing, car driving, county deputy. Frequent duties consisted of taking reports from mothers about runaway daughters, cruising picnic areas for teen drinking parties near the river, and mediating local domestic disputes. Fourteen months smoothed the job into a mundane, day by day routine.

Sheriff McNabb was waiting for him. Dan knocked and the knots began twisting his gut again. He could usually talk himself out of a nervous stomach but not this time.

"Come in Dan. I'm just heading to the break room for a cup of coffee, walk with me. I've been so busy today I haven't stopped.

"By the way, I got a call from Ernie's neighbor this morning. That lady wants me to give you a medal for bravery. Last night when you went to her house, she was scared to death. She told me how you locked her in your patrol car while you investigated the burglary. Good move, Dan. It got her out of the house and made her feel safe. You have a real feel for people and you've done an excellent job for my department. I wish I had more officers with your second sight. I'm drafting a letter of commendation and keeping it in your file. It comes from the citizens of the county, and from me for a job well done.

"Close the door behind you, will you, Dan?" The Sheriff tossed his hat on a chair, took a sip of the fresh coffee and gave a satisfied sigh.

"Dan, this meeting is confidential. Keep it to yourself. Don't even discuss it with other members of this department. Comprende?" The Sheriff spoke a little Spanish and liked to show off occasionally. Usually, even the Mexicans working in the department shuddered at his attempts.

"Understood. This is a private conversation."

"The Feds, DEA (Drug Enforcement Agency), have asked me to lend them a man from this department to act as liaison between them and me. They want someone who can be trusted to keep his mouth closed and his mind open. I've got several officers with more experience, but this seems to be an operation suited to you. Are you interested?"

"You haven't told me what the Feds want me for. It sounds like someone's mounting a big operation, maybe a drug bust. Maybe you want someone to keep you informed, someone who knows the area. I'm guessing you don't want local folks getting harassed by some suit from the city."

"You're pretty astute for a hometown boy. So what do you think, are you interested?" The gleam in his eye was his answer. Dan could hardly hide his excitement.

"To tell you the truth, I've been trying to figure a way to ask you
for a change of duty assignment.

for a change of duty assignment. I want to get into investigations. The road is fun, and I get to meet lots of people, but after a while it loses its challenge. When do I start?"

"You started when we went for coffee. I want you to report tomorrow at 0800 hours dressed in civvies. You won't be in uniform, and you won't be part of the regular daily briefing. You report directly to me. If anyone asks what you are doing, you're in investigations. The shop will give you an unmarked Blazer. After you pick it up, drive down to Santa Rosa, to the Wine Country Motel. You'll meet an agent there named Roger Dorfmann. I've only met him once, but he seems like a square shooter. Dorfmann will fill you in on the operation and anything else you need to know. Here's a file on the case and some expense money.

"A word of caution, Dan, don't leave any messages for me. Give me all reports and requests in person. Have you got that? Security on this one is real important."

This was the career change Dan had been hoping for. "I'm still in the dark about a lot of things but I do understand some things. Thanks for your confidence in me, Sheriff. I'll keep you informed."

CHAPTER TWO

The next day, after picking up his new vehicle, Dan drove south out of the county. A little past noon, he arrived at the Wine Country Motel and met Agent Dorfmann in the coffee shop. Dan made his way to the table.

Dorfmann was a blond, round faced muscular built man. Like Dan, he had played football in high school. However, shorter than Dan, Roger was 5 feet 10 inches tall and built more like a weight lifter than a football player. He was born and raised in Virginia. His federal employee father assisted him with his education in law at the University of Idaho at Moscow. Roger wanted Yale, but the large tuition kept him out. Upon finishing law school, with a minor in business administration, he applied for and was accepted at the FBI academy.

Dan stood a moment until Dorfmann was through studying a file. "Mr. Dorfmann? Dan Webster." He stuck out his hand. "Sheriff McNabb sent me."

"Pleased to meet you. Call me Roger. Care for some lunch?" Like most people meeting Roger, Dan instantly liked and trusted him. They ate salad and chicken, then walked to the agent's room without any more conversation.

Bed, table, and dresser, were covered with maps, files, and reports; a motel room of a man dedicated to his task. "Find a place to sit, and I'll fill you in." Roger drew the curtains and turned the room a cold tea color.

"I asked the sheriff to keep all information to himself until I had a chance to meet you. The people we're going after are well connected, even to your Sheriff's Department. You should know, as a rule, after you take down one of your own officers...well, to put it bluntly, life can become hell for you. Still want in?"

Dan was positive, although he knew only fools are positive. The two men spent 4 days going over every aspect of the raid. They studied maps of the county, and compiled lists of names. They devised a strategy and calculated the number of men it would take to cover all areas.

Dan learned to respect Roger's ability during those 4 days and could see why he was assigned to lead this important raid.

could see why he was assigned to lead this important raid. He had a knack for quickly analyzing situations and selecting the best ways to handle them. Dan would later learn that Roger had no fear. He was the kind of partner everyone wanted; one you knew would always be there when you needed him.

Late Friday afternoon, Dan returned and went directly to the Sheriff's office. They poured a cup of coffee and locked themselves in. "Want to tell me about it, Dan?"

Sheriff McNabb was one generation out of Ireland with a shock of red hair visible for blocks. In the time it took the men of his department to get acquainted with him, they began calling him Red. The sheriff took it as a compliment.

"Sheriff, this is a real hot potato. "Dan began.

"You can call me Red," the Sheriff laughed, easing the building tension. "Even my mother does. I know this is a big bust, but you don't hafta to be so darn awful formal."

Dan smiled, slowed, and the two men talked as friends. "The feds have information about three farms in this area." Dan spread a map over the paperwork on the desk. "On these farms, is grown some big cash crops. We understand the owners are going to meet on one of the farms."

Dan poked the map with a pencil. "The word is, they're converting all their operations to indoor growing systems, the latest thing in growing high THC pot. Doing this allows them to have a year 'round crop instead of one large yearly crop. They're almost ready to start the new operations and this farm, we call it Farm One, is where the meeting'll be held. Our raid will hit all three farms at the same time. I'll be with Roger."

"Roger?"

"Yea. Agent Dorfmann, remember?"

"Dorfmann. Okay, okay. Sorry for the interruption."

"Anyway, I'll be at Farm One. Since everyone, except a handful of guards, will be at the meeting, there shouldn't be too much trouble shutting down the other two farms.

"Farm One is the main objective. The owner and financier will be there, along with his crook buddies. We know they're from Sacramento, but don't know their names yet. We do know they're very powerful, wealthy, and have friends in high places. Roger thinks they're in politics.

"One other thing, Roger has information that someone in this department is passing information to the growers. For a while Roger even thought it might be you. He's since changed his mind, but it's certain, someone is giving them protection. That's been the reason behind all the secrecy."

Red, turned livid when leaks within his department were suspected. He had been hoping the feds were wrong. Spies ruined hundreds of lives besides their own. The voters knew he was honest and progressive, and that his department kept their noses clean. He had spoken of reelection and knew he had support, especially if his office was clean. He had always been a cop first and a politician last, and a bad cop within his department would be a personal betrayal.

"Is there any information on who the jerk is?"

"No, sorry. If anyone knows, they're not talking," Dan sat and ran his fingers through his curly hair. "I'd like to take the weekend off, Red. The last four days have used me up. The raid's on for Monday, and there really isn't much I can do between now and then. Roger has my home phone number, and I'll be on the pager if you need me."

"Good idea. You deserve a lot more than just a day off. Now get out of here, and let me worry in private."

Beth's shift began at 8 PM, since it was almost that time now, Dan decided he might as well stop for a cup of coffee and confirm their date for tomorrow. Dan was beginning to feel like a high school kid on his first date. Something had awakened inside, something he had been missing, someone important to him who could make him feel good, take his mind off the job for a while, and value what he could offer. The restaurant was almost empty. Beth met him with a cup of coffee and the prettiest smile in Northern California.

"America, clean!" excuse me. "I didn't mean to holler that right in your ear."

"America clean, is what?"

"Apple pie, no ice cream. Some day, we'll spend all afternoon discussing restaurant vernacular. I thought you'd forgotten all about me." She teased.

"Years of police training have given me a good memory for detail. Of course I remember you, Harriet."

"Harriet? You be careful or I won't cook for you tomorrow night." she shook her finger at him. "You are coming over aren't you?"

He smiled. "Sure am; can't wait. I'm looking forward to it. See you tomorrow."

Beth's apartment had large windows along the south side and a vaulted ceiling. Along one wall was a small kitchen. A glass table set with candles and wine was pulled into the room. Soft music came from all around. Dan noticed there was enough room to dance. Maybe he'd take her in his arms later and hold her close. Dinner was wonderful: fried chicken, salad, and cheese cake for desert.

They spent the next Sunday together driving to the Redwoods and rode the narrow gauge train through the forest. Acting like a typical tourist, Dan bought her a silk pillow cover with California Redwoods embroidered on it. She gave him a coffee mug with the inscription, Enchanted Forest. Dan wondered if being with Beth could always be this carefree and uncomplicated. It would be a long drive home from the Redwood Forest, but Dan was in no hurry.

Monday, 0600 hours. Dan met Roger at the Pit Stop just south of town. Roger's men were in small groups having breakfast.

"Any changes?" Dan asked.

"No. Everything's still a go. I've briefed my men, and they know what to do. We have four vans—six men in each van. I thought I'd ride with you in your Blazer. One van will hit each of the upper valley farms. The other two vans, and you and I, will take Farm One, on Sutter Road. We'll hit all three farms at once. We can't go in earlier than 1000 hours because the two money men aren't expected there until then. You, I, and the team in the second van, will go in the front. The other team, in the first van, will cover the back. I expect a lot of guards and alarms. We'll have to move quickly. There's a lot of area for us to cover, and I don't want anyone getting away. Wear your vest. There's bound to be someone wanting to shoot it out. We can minimize risks if we move fast enough, but there are still too many variables for us to cover everything."

Dan thought a minute, "There's one thing. We're going to be using hand held radios with frequencies not on the repeater, and very a short range on the radios because of the trees and hills. Each team'll be able to hear their own members, but won't be able to contact other teams without going through the sheriff's frequency. If we use that frequency, a lot of people, with scanners, are going to hear." Roger acknowledged with a nod.

"Another thing, the sheriff has no clue who's the spy within the department. It could be anyone."

"Thanks, I'll give this information to the men. It's never easy when one of your own may be a bad apple."

Roger looked over his notes; then tucked them into a manila folder. "Okay, let's get into position."

"Did you bring your vest?" Roger asked.

"Yes...never leave home without it," Dan grinned.

Roger reached for a bag on the floor of the Blazer. "Here; wear this, so my guys'll recognize you and maybe not shoot you." From the bag he pulled a blue windbreaker with large gold letters, DEA, on the back. On the left side of the jacket chest was a gold Drug Enforcement Agency shield

"Great. Much appreciated. I needed a new coat too." They slapped each other on the back and knew they could count on each other.

"The other teams should be in place by now. Our objective is about 2 1/2 miles up this next road. I'll lead our team in. There's an old skid trail running behind the farm. The other van can take that. Time seems about right; we should all be in place and ready pretty quick."

Roger picked up his handheld radio. "Spotter, do you read me?"

A voice on the radio responded. "10-4."

"Come down to the road and meet us."

"10-4."

A quarter mile further, a man in a blue windbreaker with gold lettering stepped from the brush onto the shoulder of the road. He smiled at Roger. "Next time I'll wear my long johns; it's a might chilly." he said as the truck door opened.

"There's a thermos of coffee back there somewhere" Roger said.

"Dan; John Sutter; no relation to the guy for which this road's named. John; Dan Webster, local officer on this case."

"Pleased to meet you Dan. Coffee must have been your idea. Roger wouldn't think of it." A slight, friendly smile crossed his face.

John's dark, wavy hair and suntan complexion gave him a rugged outdoor look. Roger and John were friends, and had been since they attended the FBI academy together. Sutter, like Dorfmann, came from humble circumstances. He was born in Northern Florida where his father drove a truck and his mother clerked in a grocery store. John and Roger had other common background experiences. Both joined the army after high school, and both had law degrees, John receiving his from a college in Texas. John loved the combat and tactical training he received in the Special Forces and became an instructor at the Special Forces Training School for the length of his enlistment.

"You're not wearing boots today." Roger poked at his friend. "John rode broncs and roped calves during his college days," Roger explained to Dan.

explained to Dan. "Gave it up after breaking a bunch of bones. Still thinks he's a cowboy though; wears his hat, boots, and western dress to the office every day." Getting serious again, Roger asked John to report what he'd learned.

"The car you were expecting came in about 20 minutes ago—a blue Mercedes. There's three men in it, but, with tinted windows, I couldn't see their faces. The driver's a big man though; I could see that much, and the guy in the back seat had on a 10-gallon hat. The license number's in my notebook. There's a lot of traffic on this road early this morning. Mostly pick ups and vans. Seven vehicles in all. I saw 28 people, but there may've been some others in the back of one of the vans with no windows. I couldn't see inside. If they had any rifles, shotguns, or other large weapons, I couldn't see them. I haven't heard any dogs either.

"I found electronic detection devices on three sides of the perimeter. We're lucky there, too. While I was checking out the area, I saw a coyote run under the fence and through the microwave surveillance beam. Either the beam never detected the coyote, or it's adjusted high enough above ground level to allow small animals to pass. I think we can cross the fence by staying on our bellies until we pass the beam. John continued, "I saw them taking tables and chairs to the barn, so it looks as if that's the place."

Roger thought a minute. "That makes sense. If they're going to set up a demonstration there's more room in the barn. Nice work, John."

Roger spoke quietly into the radio. "Okay, get into position and stay out of sight. Check your time. Four minutes on my mark...now."

Several miles up Sutter Road, from where Roger and Dan were positioned, team one was counting down the time at the third farm. The team's six officers had seen no sign of movement since getting into position, and wondered if there was anyone left as guards. On a hand signal, the team leader, along with six men, moved quickly and cautiously toward the farmhouse and its large outbuilding. They reached the buildings without resistance. Two officers entered the outbuilding. There was no one inside.

The team leader moved quietly to the house and stepped onto the porch and peered into the window. He could see three men. One was reading a newspaper and having his morning coffee. One was sleeping on a couch on the far side of the room. The third was asleep in a reclining chair.

"Really guarding this outfit aren't you? You bums." he whispered to himself. He gave the signal to enter. Bursting through the front and rear doors simultaneously, and with guns pointing directly in the face of the suspects, the first officer in the room screamed "Federal officers, you are all under arrest."

The three startled to their feet, their eyes wide, faces turned white, but they gave no resistance. The raid was over.

The rest of the day would be spent inventorying seized property and drugs. The lead officer sat on the porch making notes in his book,

"It doesn't get any easier than this," he thought to himself. Easy or not, it would take the members of the team a full day to rid their bodies of the adrenaline in their veins.

Meanwhile, 3 miles away, at the second farm, the go signal was given at 1000 hours. The team could see one armed suspect walking in front of a small barn. Two officers were behind the barn, one on the far side of the house and one behind an old truck with no tires or wheels.

The team leader whispered to his partner, "Cover me."

He stepped into the open space near the gate. He shouted to the suspect in the yard, "Federal officers. You're under arrest. Drop your weapon and step into the open."

The suspect stopped, crouched down behind a rusty Ford tractor. He called to someone inside the barn. "Get out here! We got company." The small, man-sized barn door opened and another man emerged. He, too, jumped behind the tractor.

"I only see one." He desperately whispered. "There's gotta be more. What should we do? Wanna shoot it out?"

It was too late. A voice from behind them said, "Drop your weapons. Federal officers and you're under arrest." They dropped their weapons and lay face down on the ground as instructed.

The officer spoke again, "Is there anyone else?"

"Screw you, cop."

"Read them their rights," the team leader said as he passed the arresting officers.

Two officers entered the house and found it lacking furniture, appliances, or carpet. "Getting ready for a new growing system." they surmised to each other.

The barn was a different story. Living quarters, an office with accounting equipment: calculators, copiers, files, etc., were in a loft Everything would be logged for evidence, and later would provide information on the largest marijuana distribution ring in the USA.

One more suspect was in the loft. He was unarmed and very ill. He had been left behind to guard the farm because he was unable to attend the meeting.

the meeting. He'd never considered himself a criminal, after all, he didn't deal in drugs; just a book keeper. The team leader would have to call an ambulance to transport the accountant. It would be another week before he could be moved from hospital to jail.

It would take several days to inventory all material found in the makeshift office. The day would be used to inventory drugs and weapons.

1000 hours at Farm One. Dan, John, and Roger had the front. The Red team had driven along the old skid trail to the rear of the farm and taken their positions . The Green team split, with three men on the east and three on the west sides of the farm. The suspect vehicles were parked in a line at the front of the house. There were several people walking to and from the house and barn.

All officers had been able to get inside the fence, under the microwave detectors. Each officer waited for the go signal.

Roger gave the signal as Dan slammed the gas pedal. The Blazer dug into the dirt, throwing dust in great plumes, and raced up the drive toward the house. Dan switched the radio to it's external speaker.

"We are Federal officers," he shouted into the mike. "Come out with your hands up." He paused a moment, allowing his commands to be heard by those in the barn and house.

As is custom, he repeated the command, but this time more deliberate and forceful. "Throw out your weapons. We are Federal officers. Come out with your hands up."

It was distraction enough. The two teams were able to cross the open ground, obtain an attack advantage near the barn, and ready weapons. No resistance met team members as they rushed the house and barn. The careless guards set up defenses only toward the front of the house and barn.

The guard, who first spotted the Blazer, was now on his radio talking with someone. The Blazer skidded to a stop keeping the line of cars in front of the house between the Blazer and the guard. Dan, Roger, and John, kept as low as possible as they stepped out of the Blazer and took cover behind the first two cars. Gunfire from a semiautomatic pistol came from somewhere, and the windshield exploded from the Chevrolet protecting Roger.

Walking with an easy gate, and eyes constantly surveying his surroundings, John worked his way to the far end of the line of cars. From there, crossed the open area to the porch. No one fired on him. Two team members from the west side of the house joined him on the veranda. John pushed the door open; nothing happened. He squatted and took a quick look into the room. He saw no one. He and one young team member entered the house.

Roger and Dan motioned for the team members on the east side to advance. When the first team member stood to move, a shutter covered barn window opened, and the barrel of a rifle appeared. The bullet missed the crouching officers by inches.

The Green team member behind a small oak tree returned fire and was the better shot. A cry was heard and the rifle barrel disappeared from the window. He could see a gunman crouched behind an old hay wagon and yelled, "Drop it."

The gunman turned, raising his arm to fire. A Federal Officer's bullet hit him just above his first shirt button and he dropped.

A door in the barn opened and two men with Uzi automatic machine guns burst into the yard firing as they ran. The first team member was again the better trained. Both attackers went down. The officer dove for cover behind a hay wagon. He called again to the barn,

"Federal officers. Come out with your hands up."

Roger and Dan were startled by an explosion from the house. Smoke billowed out of the upper windows. The screen door flew open, and a man, handcuffed, wearing a plaid shirt and blue jeans was hurled across the porch and landed face first in the dust. Behind him, came John in a cloud of smoke. He called to Roger,

"Watch out for boobytraps," he coughed. "The Kid just got it from a boobytrapped door upstairs."

Two teams, each member carrying an AR-15 and Colt .45 auto, converged on the barn's large front door. From inside came the sound of a revving engine. Then, like a greyhound from a gate, came a brown Dodge van. The driver pointed an Uzi through the driver's window and began firing wildly. The officers jumped for cover. Two men fired from the van's open back doors.

Roger fired on the van. He took out both front tires and the driver lost control. The van pitched wildly to the right and rolled over in a huge cloud of dust and spraying gravel. The two men in the back of the van were thrown clear. Both, spitting dust, were handcuffed before they could recover from shock. The gunman on the passenger side of the van suffered a broken arm. The driver was less fortunate. When the truck began to roll, the door sprung open. The driver held the door with his left arm; centrifugal force threw him upward and partially out of the van. As the truck finished its roll, the door was forced shut again, nearly decapitating him.

The blue Mercedes snaked out of the barn and Dan made a run for the Blazer. The Mercedes swung around the wrecked Dodge, and Dan moved the Blazer into its path, and braked to a stop. The driver had no choice but to brake hard, skidding, and slamming the Mercedes into the driver's side of the Blazer. The impact, welded the two vehicles together and threw Dan against the dashboard.

The back door of the Mercedes opened, and Roger saw a very large man in a gray suit. "Get out of there. Now!" Roger ordered, his gun held in a straight arm press. State Senator Nels Bergstrom raised his head to pull himself from the car.

"Well, I'll be damned." Roger said.

The senator hauled his massive frame from the seat and another passenger became visible. Leo Sardoni, the west coast Mafia drug boss had blood running down his cheek.

"I'll be damned" he said again. "Out of the car!" Roger ordered.

As Dan struggled through the passenger door, of the Blazer, the barrel of a revolver appeared from the edge of the half-opened Mercedes door. Then a western style hat appeared as the driver stumbled to a standing position and aimed his revolver at Roger. Dan ran, gritting his teeth against the pain, drawing his weapon as he went.

"Roger!"

The driver heard him, and whirled around. Dan was surprised and confused and lost his advantage when he recognized the driver as Chief Deputy Morgan Duncan. Duncan turned and fired two shots into Dan's chest. The impact of the .357 bullets knocked him off his feet, skidding him in the dirt. A third shot, intended for his head, hit Dan in the left side of the neck. He didn't move once he hit the ground.

Roger reacted quickly. His only shot struck Duncan just below the left ear, killing him instantly.

The two suspects from the back seat of the car were now covered by John who had moved to the rear of the car. Roger ran around the car to find Dan lying in a pool of blood and gasping for breath. In the Sheriff's vehicle, Roger screamed into a mike.

"County one, County one, Do you read?"

"10-4, Roger"

"Three ambulances. Now! Quicker than now!! I have officers down. Don't bring them past the gate. This area's still too hot for civilians. We're a war zone here. Dan's down and hurt bad."

"Understood," Sheriff McNabb responded, "ETA 5 minutes."

Roger quickly searched and cuffed his prisoners, then returned to Dan.

"Take it easy, the ambulance is on the way." Dan, passed out. John ran to the gate and motioned for the driver to pull ahead.

"I'll take it from here. Still pretty hairy in there."

The driver and two medics jumped out and John drove the ambulance to where Roger was waiting with Dan. The two men placed Dan on the gurney and loaded it into the ambulance. John drove the vehicle back to where the driver and medics were waiting. The siren begin to scream.

Roger could hear occasional gunfire from the barn, but could see the teams beginning to move people out in handcuffs. He walked to the barn to confer with the Red and Green team leaders.

Red team leader, Sandy Crawford, summarized.

"There's only one more guy in the back of the barn; he's scared and shooting, but I think we can talk him out. I have one officer dead. He's a real mess, Roger. Damned booby trap. Three wounded, one from falling on a harrow. We have four dead suspects and six wounded. Here comes the other guy from the barn. I'd like to get my men to the hospital as soon as we can."

"John," Roger asked. "Get on the sheriff's radio and send in those other ambulances and the transport vans. Contact the other two farms and see how they're doing. I hate being out of contact with my men"

He turned back to Crawford and Davis, the team leaders.

"Your men did an outstanding job. Minimal injuries too. As soon as everyone is loaded up, have the rest of your men start the inventory. Thanks again for a good job."

Roger returned to the Blazer where John was standing. "What happened to the kid upstairs?"

"Whatever happened to the good old days, Roger? These drug people are getting more and more dangerous all the time. The kid never stood a chance. He opened a door to what looked like an office, and a grenade dropped down. Little Steve made a dive for cover but the grenade blew out the wall. He died instantly. This isn't just Marijuana farmers anymore, its organized crime. Steve was a good guy, had his whole life ahead; he deserved better. Was Dan hurt bad? It looked like he took two or three good ones."

"I don't know yet. We got the wounds packed good before he left." Roger said as he walked around the Blazer. "By the way, did you see who was in the back seat of that Mercedes?"

"I sure did. With big names like Bergstrom and Santoni, involved, we're going to have to be careful to dot all the I's and cross all the T's.

There's going to be some high priced, big city lawyers trying to take this case apart."

Roger looked at the Blazer.

"Help me get these cars apart, so I can go to the hospital. Take over here and supervise the inventory. You won't finish tonight; assign guards to watch, then finish tomorrow."

Roger met the Sheriff at the hospital.

"How is he, Red?"

"The vest saved him. He has two broken ribs, and a chunk of his neck is gone. He'll be okay, but, he's going to need time to heal."

Roger looked at the floor a moment. "Has anyone told you about your other deputy?"

"What other deputy?"

"His name tag said Morgan Duncan. I shot him. He was driving the car for the two big guys, Bergstrom and Santoni. He shot Dan."

Red gasp in disbelief. "Are you telling me the snitch in my office was my chief deputy?"

"Looks that way now, Sheriff. Sorry. I'll stay with this case for a few days. Keep me posted on Dan's progress, will you? I'll be back to see him in a couple of days. He's a good man, sheriff; don't lose him."

The door at the end of the hall burst open. A beautiful young woman in a waitress uniform ran toward the sheriff. "Where's Dan? Is it true he's been shot?"

"Calm down, Beth," the Sheriff held onto her shoulders. "He was shot, but he'll be Okay. He's going to be sore for a while, but he's going to be all right."

"What happened? How did it happen? Can I see him?" She wiped tears from her face. It was only now that she admitted to herself just how deeply she felt for Dan.

"Sit down. I'll tell you as much as I know. Can I get you some coffee; a soda?" The Sheriff motioned toward the lounge.

She wiped her eyes and took a deep breath. "No thanks. I just want to see Dan."

The Sheriff explained the raid and what little he knew. It was difficult for him. His thoughts kept returning to his chief deputy and friend. What was his reason for turning snitch?

Doctor Mathis came to the lounge and spoke to the sheriff.

"He's coming around now. He was lucky. The bullet proof vest saved his life. We dug two deeply imbedded bullets from it. The force of the impact broke his ribs. The wound on his neck has been sutured.

The bullet passed below the jaw bone and destroyed the tissue in a rather large path along the left side of his neck. There was profuse bleeding and destruction of flesh, but no main artery intervention. He may want to have cosmetic surgery for the scar later, but for now, we've done about all we can. He'll be sleepy, but you can see him for a minute. He's going to be fine." The doctor turned to the nurse; "Let them visit for just a minute." He walked down the hall, then turned. "He's a mighty lucky man."

Dan slowly rose from unconsciousness. He opened groggy eyes.

"Dan. It's Beth."

Dan tried to focus. "Beth." He tried to change positions and winced with pain.

"I heard you needed a nurse, so I applied." She attempted to smile, but tears came anyway. She wiped her eyes, "Are you sure you're all right?" her voice quivering with the question.

"I'm okay. I remember Duncan firing at me. The next thing I remember is waking up here. Did we get them? I hope they got Duncan. If they didn't, I want a piece of him when I get out of here."

CHAPTER THREE

On the third morning in the hospital, Dan finished breakfast and thought about going home. He smiled when the door opened and Roger came in with a small bouquet and a brown paper bag. He placed the flowers on the table by the door and walked to the bed. "Some people'll do anything to get out of doing paperwork. How're you feeling?"

"I'm dieing, Roger. Just got a few hours left. Think you could assign the paperwork detail to someone else?"

Roger laughed and shook his hand. "You don't get out of mucky work that easy. I can send it with you." Both men laughed.

"What's in the bag?"

Roger pulled out a blue jacket with gold lettering.

"I found one without bullet holes."

"Thanks friend, I'll try not to ruin this one."

"I don't quite know how to say this, Dan so I'll just come right out with it. I owe you my life. If you hadn't taken Morgan off me, I'd probably be dead. I'm in your debt. Thanks.

"Another thing, this was my last raid with DEA. I've transferred to a supervisory position with the FBI. As soon as the paperwork and the initial court proceedings for this case are out of the way, I'm being transferred to Phoenix."

"I was careless, Roger. In my surprise of seeing Morgan, I let emotions get in the way of good judgment. They tell me you're the one who took out Duncan. Makes us more than even, makes us good friends. Congratulations on your promotion. We'll miss your smiling face."

"Going home today? How about a lift?"

"No, thanks. Someone a lot prettier than you is coming with some clean clothes and a ride. I plan to be in the office Monday to finish the reports. I've written most of it out longhand; all I have to do is type it out. Come by the office Monday."

"I'll bring John Sutter; he wants to see you too. Says he owes you a cup of coffee."

Dan gathered his personal effects, washed up a little, and put on some cologne. Right now it seemed more important to be with Beth than to be out of the hospital. Home seemed good though; seemed like forever since he slept in his own bed and made his own coffee. The coffee here was less than great. He wanted to complete his reports too, before he reported to Red on Monday.

Beth was beautiful in her new dress, and new hairdo. Dan couldn't keep his eyes off her. Her eyes gleamed with the thoughts of getting him out of the hospital and home again.

"Are you ready?"

"Yeah, I'm ready, but not for the wheel chair the hospital insists on. Boy, you look terrific."

"Thank you, sir. You look rather good yourself."

The nurse came with a wheelchair. Beth loaded his personal belongings, along with one bouquet, into his lap.

"Would you give these flowers to the children's ward for me? Tell everyone at the nurses station thanks for being nice to me." Then turning again to Beth, "Now, let's get out of this place; it's full of sick people."

"I was so scared. I couldn't believe it when they told me you had been shot." Beth told Dan. "Forgive me for rambling, but I'm having trouble with my emotions lately. She hesitated..."I think I am falling in love with you."

He looked at her tenderly. "I've been doing a lot of thinking about us, too. I don't know if it's love, but I know I want to be with you all the time. I was like a kid at Christmas, when I knew you were coming to visit me."

She started the car, paused and turned to him. Their kiss was lengthy and mutual. As they drove to his home, they chatted about local current events. When they were only a few blocks from his house she said, nervously "I'm cooking dinner for you. The doctor said you could move around a little, but, I'd like to stay to make sure you stay put."

"Who else is coming to dinner?"

"Sheriff McNabb wants to talk to you and asked if it'd be okay for him to come over this evening. I thought it would be all right and asked him to dinner." she said.

"What could be so important to make him come to my house? I can't imagine anything that can't wait until Monday morning." He turned to Beth and smiled.

"Maybe I should have you schedule all my social events. How would you like to apply for the job as Dan Webster's personal secretary? The hours would be long, and the pay would be poor. Great fringe benefits though." She laughed as they turned into his drive.

"You must be getting well; you're getting frisky." She stopped the car. "You go inside, and I'll bring the stuff from the car." She looked into his eyes and said, "I'm really glad to have you home where I can take care of you."

It was just after six. Dan was in the back yard taking in the last bit of sunshine when he heard the screen door open behind him. Sheriff McNabb, with a beer in his hand, stepped off the back porch. He was not in uniform. As he approached, he reached out to shake Dan's hand.

"How are you feeling, son?"

Dan shook his hand,

"Pretty good. I'm glad to be home. It must be true what they say about God looking out for fools. My ribs are sore, but it could've been much worse. I'm ready now to finish those reports."

McNabb got serious.

"Niceties out of the way brings me to why I came over tonight. Since the raid, there has been big drop in morale within the department. Morgan was well liked and everyone is still in shock. Dan, I want you to help me reorganize the department. I'm going to run for reelection. There's been speculation about the person who'll take over since the raid. I'd like you to consider being my new Chief Deputy."

Dan was in shock. It took him a minute to answer. " You sure don't beat around the bush. Are you serious?"

"Dead serious, Dan. I need someone I can trust, you're it. I need someone with the ability to reorganize, and you have proven yourself there. You are good at managing people. There is no doubt in my mind; you are best qualified for the job. It'll be your job to review all cases, handle all personnel, and, in general, do all the things you've seen me doing. One of the reasons, I think, Morgan was able to do what he did was because I was too busy with my reelection and didn't pay enough attention to the general operation of the department. I feel guilty about that."

Red stood and walked to a large tree and leaned against its rough trunk. "I don't want my people neglected anymore. There's too much strength lost in the department when one of the officers turns sour. I'm going to be dealing more with the County Commissioners, writing grants, and focusing on other administrative duties. Perhaps this new administrative structure will allow a more efficient department. I really do need your help, Dan. Think about it and don't say no."

Dan's mind ran a thousand directions. "It's a big step, but I will consider it."

There was small talk around the dinner table, both Dan and Red laughed over old war stories. Beth sat quietly and enjoyed getting to know these two fine men. The sheriff left about nine. Beth washed the dishes while Dan sat quietly at the kitchen table thinking.

"Want to share?" She flicked a towel at him.

"There are so many things happening in my life right now, it's hard to sift through. And you're not helping any either."

Beth sat down and took his hand away from his coffee cup.

"What am I doing to confuse the situation?"

"You're becoming such a big part of my life, I can't imagine being without you. I want to be with you every minute, and . . ." he laughed. "I keep building this house for you, and every time I do, it gets bigger. I'll be out of money before I propose. I'd call that love, wouldn't you?"

Beth blushed a rose pink and whispered, "We'll talk about it later. You and Red did a lot of talking tonight. He really likes you, you know."

"He's asked me to become his Chief Deputy. What's more, he wants me, as the new Chief Deputy, to run the entire department. I'm not sure I'm ready to take on all that responsibility. What do you think, am I up to the job?"

"Oh, Dan! You underestimate yourself. You can handle it, and do an excellent job. Red knows you can handle it, or he wouldn't have asked you. Besides, it'd take you away from all those gunfights. If you plan to stay in law enforcement, then it would be a good career step. Maybe with the raise, you can build that house you keep dreaming about. I think it's exciting. I'm happy for you." She kissed him on the cheek and then kissed his hand. He reached out for her and she slipped away.

"Beth, will you stay with me tonight?"

She turned to him and quietly said, "I'll stay."

Monday morning, Dan was in the office early. He accepted the Chief Deputy position. Roger Dorfmann and John Sutter came to the office. After passing the time of day and some joking and small talk, they became engrossed in the ton of paperwork surrounding the bust.

Months passed before the first of 29 drug cases went to court, but the success rate in court was phenomenal. Only one of the indictments was dealt down by the federal attorneys. The attorneys for the accountant made a deal with the government for immunity from prosecution in exchange for his testimony regarding the financial end of the drug dealing operation.

Their success of arraignment, however, did not extend to the top.

The two men suspected of masterminding and funding the operation were never indicted. Legal maneuvering became a model for future criminal cases where high priced, low conscienced, lawyers represented very rich and influential clients.

At one point in the evidentiary hearings, lawyers were arguing definition of three letter words written into law. It was a legal circus. In the end, Senator Nels Bergstrom wasn't indicted. The Senator's lawyers had convinced the judge to throw out all hard evidence. This left the Grand Jury with no choice but to dismiss charges against the senator. They were left with only hearsay evidence and couldn't get an indictment.

The Senator claimed he was there to investigate a drug operation, and, was not only allowed to complete his term in office, was reelected.

Mafia boss, Leo Sardoni, never made it to court. Rumor was his bosses were troubled with the publicity. Two months after his name first hit the papers, he was boating on Lake Shasta. Leo liked fast boats. Witnesses at the scene stated Leo's boat was traveling at more than 60 miles per hour when it disintegrated in a ball of fire and a plume of black smoke.

Roger Dorfmann eventually became the FBI Anchorage bureau chief. John Sutter became a district supervisor for the DEA in Phoenix.

Under Dan's leadership, the Sheriffs Department served the public for many years without scandal. Dan and Red became best friends. Red was the best man at Dan and Beth's wedding. Together, they overcame the turbulence of the Vietnam protest years.

Twenty-two months after Dan and Beth were married, about the same time the court cases from the raid were ending, Beth gave birth to a son, Roger Sutter Webster. Dan told the sheriff, "Beth wouldn't let me name him Angus."

The couple became leaders in the community and moved to a larger home. Most people in the county expected Dan to run for Sheriff when Red retired. But Dan realized long before, though he was a good supervisor and administrator, he didn't have the desire or disposition for politics.

In the early spring of 1976, the sheriff told Dan, he didn't intend to run for reelection. He wanted Dan to register and run for the office. It was the end of an era in Northern California.

Being a presidential election year, the ballot for sheriff was overshadowed in the press. It never was much of a contest. Only one candidate had any law enforcement experience, a tall, thin, Randolph

Scott-like man by the name of James T. Brooks. He was a brilliant politician and loved to quote statistics. Jim Brooks had been a Lieutenant on the Sacramento Police Department for many years, especially in charge of statistical data and public relations.

Dan found the very skills and attributes which propelled him to his position in the department, would now cause conflicts between him and the new sheriff. Brooks wanted every move an officer made documented and entered in his statistical computer. The officers began to have less time to work with residents of the county. They were becoming response oriented; responding only to call-in reports and investigating, but not necessarily solving crimes. The incidences of crime in the county increased.

One warm July night, a patrol officer found Ernie sleeping in his pickup just south of town. The officer woke him up. After administering a field sobriety test, arrested him for driving while intoxicated. Ernie was brought to the jail and booked. Ernie whined for a cup of coffee. The booking officer became agitated.

"Shut up about coffee, Ernie, You ain't getting one 'till morning." Ernie became loud and insisted he be given coffee.

"I've always had coffee here. I need coffee. I can think better with a cup of coffee. One cup of coffee ain't gonna hurt anyone. Give me a cup of coffee!"

A heated discussion resulted, bringing the officer's temperament to a boiling point. He called another officer for assistance, and the two dragged Ernie into a holding cell. He was pushed around some, then ignored for the rest of the night.

When day shift came on duty and took the first count, they found Ernie on the floor, dead. His hands were bloody from beating on the door. A heart attack, and then a call for help. The on-duty officers had ignored his calls.

Dan investigated the incident and submitted his report to Sheriff Brooks. He recommended termination and criminal negligence charges against the two officers involved. The sheriff told Dan he could not accept the report.

"It casts a shadow over the reputation of this department, and I will not let that happen. I'll verbally reprimand these men; you'll amend your report and that'll be the end of it. Do you understand?"

Dan tried to contain the emotion inside himself, but words poured from his mouth like fire from a dragon.

"I understand everything, better than you might imagine. You're so worried about your image, you're willing to sacrifice this entire department. I've stood by and watched you destroy the public confidence in this office. I'll be damned if I'll be party to your abuse of public trust. I'm going to do everything I can to see that Ernie's family sues for negligence. I'm resigning as of now. My formal letter of resignation will be on your desk this afternoon."

He slammed the office door. Everyone in the work room heard his angry words. Some of them clapped or pounded their desks. He went to his office, tossed his personal belongings into an empty box, changed clothing, left his uniform hanging in his locker, and called Beth.

"Beth, come and get me, can you? I've quit the force and now I just want out of this place." She saved her questions until she could talk to him face to face. When he came out the officer exit in the rear of the sheriff's headquarters, he was dressed in civilian clothing, his face was livid red, and he was carrying a paper box.

"Take me to the newspaper office," he said, and slammed the door.

The editor of the local paper had written articles grumbling about sheriff Brooks. When Dan told his story and gave him a copy of the investigative report, he knew exactly how he would handle it.

Dan handled it by beginning to drink.

He and Beth sat on the patio one afternoon discussing their life together. Young Roger, was in school and their second son, Timothy, would soon enter kindergarten. The house was their only real debt. Beth skillfully managed their money, and even had a small saving account. Their life, up to this point, had been a fairy tale with a happy ending.

"Dan, Call him. Roger has a lot of contacts and he may know of a job opening."

"Okay! Okay. I'll call him. I sure don't want to, but you've nagged me long enough!"

Beth kept the hurt of his words to herself. She tried to understand what sitting around meant for him.

"Dan Webster here. Is Roger around?"

"One moment." Came the reply.

"Dan! So you didn't go off the edge of the world after all."

"Damn near, Roger. Like walking on a razor's edge."

"Hey, what's up. Kids okay? Beth? Come on talk to me. Or would you rather meet someplace?"

"No. No. Family's okay. What I need more than anything is a job. Something to do. I'm going crazy and taking Beth with me—just sitting around."

"I'll get back with you." Roger hung up.

Roger checked around and found Trans Alaska Pipeline was hiring security guards. Roger contacted the head of the security company for Trans, an old State Trooper friend. Roger called Dan.

"Meet me, Dan. I've got to go to California and I'll be in your neighborhood around noon. Meet me at the Squealer. I'll buy us a couple of dogs with everything."

They ate the peppery Big Chief hot dogs and washed them down with milk. They laughed about old times and Dan told Roger about the kids. "I'm telling you, we couldn't convince him he was just tanned. He thought he was dark all over." Both men laughed uproariously. "Then he looked at his pale little butt in the mirror and crumpled to his knees and said, "Oh, no. I'm two sided." Dan struggled through laughing to tell Roger about his namesake.

When their guffawing settled down, Roger said, "Well, old buddy, You have an interview appointment, in Anchorage, Alaska this next week. So get your Ulu and your Parka and fly away."

Dan interviewed and was hired. He moved his family to the Kenai Peninsula, about 70 air miles south of Anchorage and a wonderful place to live. Weather was moderate, schools were the best, people were friendly, and hunting and fishing were legendary. He bought a home on an airstrip on Mackey Lakes, and he soon learned to fly.

He'd worked for the company 14 years, before he turned down a supervisory job. There were only three people who'd been with the company longer. He was happy working two weeks in Prudhoe and spending two weeks on the Kenai. He kicked the drinking habit during the first two years in Alaska. Now, Dan was well respected, and occasionally was asked to teach classes in the head office.

His son, Roger, was in his first year of college and Timothy was a Senior in high school, and football team captain. He smiled when he thought about those days with the California force.

CHAPTER FOUR

Wednesday. Dan tried to sleep as the jet cruised its way toward Prudhoe Bay and Deadhorse Airport. This was crew change day. He got up at 4 AM and had driven to the Kenai Airport for his early morning shuttle flight to Anchorage to make Alaska Airlines' North Slope flight.

The big difference between crew changes now and those of the "good old days" was he no longer made the flight with a hangover. Age, years of depression, and too much drinking had given him a look of intensity. His face now angular and stoic. His hair beginning to show flecks of gray.

For the past 12 years, Dan had been employed by Pipeline Security of America. PSA held security contracts for the Trans Alaska Pipeline. PSA corporation started small but had, over the years, built an outstanding reputation for commitment and professionalism, achieved only by hiring skilled professionals, ex-law enforcement people, and by maintaining an ongoing training program.

Security on the pipeline requires police skills, human relationships, good judgment, along with knowledge of company policy and law. A guard might be required to arrest an individual and hold him for an extended period waiting for backup. Weather could prevent assistance from arriving for a week or more. The job required special people with special talents—Dan qualified.

As the jet cruised north, through blue skies and over craggy, snow covered, ridges, he tried to rest. The early days, as a deputy sheriff, kept invading his mind. Nine years in that sparsely populated county in Northern California had given him the experience to be where he was today, a pipeline security guard.

"The sky is clear and the temperature is 33 degrees; wind is out of the north at 25 miles per hour. We will be landing at Dead Horse in about 10 minutes. Please check that your seat belts are fastened. Thank you for flying Alaska Airlines."

The announcement brought Dan back to the present. He zipped his parka and pulled the hood onto his head.

Three officers worked his schedule. The youngest, Rod Brassington, met Dan at the door of the plane. He slapped Dan on the back and said, "Welcome back to Shangrila. Glad to be back, I bet?"

"Always," They walked down the stairs from the plane together. Dan liked Rod. He was a rawboned, good natured, 6 foot 4 inch ex-policeman from San Jose, California. Rod always had a smile and a joke or a prank to pull. He had a knack for lightening everyone's load. Rod was good for morale.

Like Rod, Kenny Newby, was also a good medic, and a good officer. He met Dan and Rod at the baggage pickup station. The entire staff at the pump station relied on his medical ability. For the summer months, there was a construction crew on site repairing corroded pipe. It was Kenny's job to treat illness or injury of the maintenance crew. The permanent staff was treated at the BP hospital 3 miles away, but Kenny was called first for any minor illness or injury.

"Are you ready for two glorious weeks in paradise?"

"I told him it was Shangrila." All three laughed and walked from the Deadhorse Airport terminal building.

Two men met them outside. They were just leaving their shift. One man would stay behind to maintain security until the new shift arrived. He would then change into civilian clothing and catch the company crew bus to the airport 6 miles away. Shift change briefing was a haphazard affair. Millman gave Dan a quick rundown; the rest would be covered in the written pass-on.

"Hi, Dan. How were your weeks off?" Millman asked.

"Great." Dan said, "Anything new here?"

"No. The dig crew is still working. It's hard to keep up with who's going in and out of the gate—construction people racing around. They've been good about stopping at the gate, but sometimes they forget. We're getting about 300 gate entries a day now. Oh yeah! I almost forgot. The pig crew is on station. They came in a couple of days ago. They're with the same company, TMC, but they're all new people working on this pig run. They're getting the pig ready and have worked a bunch of hours, so we haven't seen much of them.

"A grizzly walked through yesterday. He didn't stop though—just sniffed at the dumpster—kept on walking. One other thing. The Sarge'll be at Pump Station Four all week. They have a couple of days of Oil Spill Contingency Plan meetings, and then he'll wait there until the pig has passed Pump Station Four and is out of our district."

Millman's partner had already made his way to the boarding gate and found a seat in the lobby.

and found a seat in the lobby. Millman waved to the three men and finally said, "Have a good one."

The red pickup was warm, and the sun was bright as they began the drive to the pump station. Rod and Kenny were on duty until 6 this evening when Dan took over. He worked the night shift alone, 12 hours. It was boring on nights, but the first couple of nights were customarily filled with reading pass-on and memos.

The first stop was at the BP east checkpoint. Purcell Security company had the contract at BP. Dan stopped the pickup at the window. He didn't recognize the guard.

"He must be new," Dan thought. It only took 1 minute to check the badges against the computer and get admission past the checkpoint.

In the summer time, the drive from the airport to the pump station was a good place to see wildlife. The tundra was alive in the summer. Geese nested everywhere. Ducks of every kind raised their young in this area. Arctic fox made the rounds of nests, stealing young when the parents were away. An occasional grizzly could be sighted. There was a small herd of muskox just south of here and could sometimes be seen passing through. Caribou were everywhere.

Rod reached for his bag when the truck turned off the main Spine Road and onto the short road leading to the main gate at the Pump station. "I'll change uniform here. Take my other bag to the room, Kenny, would you?"

"Sure. I'll change and be back in a few minutes," Kenny said.

Arlon Hebert stepped out of the gatehouse, clipboard in hand.

"Welcome back," Hebert said, as he made check marks on the clipboard, accounting for the three new men on the station.

Rod went inside and began changing into his uniform. When he took control of the gate, Arlon changed into civilian clothing and was ready to catch the bus 10 minutes from now. He would get to the airport just as the flight to Anchorage was loading. It was the same ritual every 2 weeks the year around.

Pump station staff had a similar routine. Their shift change was Tuesday. They'd change each week rather than the two-week schedule for security people. Although it varied slightly, the regular population of the PLQ (personnel living quarters) was 36. The pump station used nine technicians on each shift. There were also cooks, housekeeping personnel, mechanics, and administrative people. This was the most complicated of the pump stations and required the greatest number of technicians to keep track of equipment in the metering buildings.

There was just time to catch a couple hours sleep and a shower. Dinner would be served at 5:30. Dan shared his room with Rod. There were two bunks, two closets, a desk, and a TV. The bathroom was shared with those in the next room. Although small, the rooms were comfortable. Housekeeping did a wonderful job keeping the rooms clean. There was a rule about taking your boots off at the front door. No boots were to be worn inside the PLQ, thus avoiding tracking oil or mud onto the carpet. There were also rules about noise, making it possible for the night shift crew to sleep during the daytime.

The catering staff knew Dan had to be on duty by 1800 hours and so allowed him to come in a few minutes early to eat. He had finished his dinner, and was about to have his second cup of coffee and a piece of apple pie, when the technicians began coming through the line with their trays. A short black man brought his tray to Dan's table and sat down. Charley Bickford was chief technician on night shift this week.

"Hello, Dan, just coming on?" Charley asked, stirring his iced tea.

"Nights. How's your family, Charley? Doesn't your son graduate from college this year?"

You could see the pride in his smile.

"Graduated 2 weeks ago. Has a job, too. He's going to be teaching school in Bethel starting in September. He's going to be a deckhand on a salmon drift boat this summer. His mama's proud of him."

"And, his papa isn't? Let's see, didn't your last daughter graduate from high school this year?"

Charley smiled again. "Last one. Going to college this fall. Going to University of Alaska at Fairbanks. She wants to be a teacher, too."

Dan drank the last of his coffee and was picking up his tray when Gwen Stevens sat down at the table.

"Well look at these brutes."

"You'd better be glad we're not brutes. Got to go. Duty calls."

"Dan, is it all right if I come by the gatehouse later and talk to you for a minute?" Gwen asked.

"Sure, I'll be there all night."

"Thanks, I'll make my rounds about 2300 hours."

Dan cleaned his tray and told Jimmy the cook "good dinner." He went to the front mud room where he sat and pulled on his boots. He walked the 100 yards to the gatehouse. Mosquitoes weren't bad tonight. An arctic fox scampered out from under the PLQ, running ahead of him toward the gate. Once outside the gate, it ran into the grass under the pipeline that brought crude from the Lisburne field.

When Dan entered the gatehouse, both Rod and Kenny were there waiting for him.

"There's fresh coffee, Dan. What's for dinner?" Rod asked.

"Steak tonight. Try the apple pie too, it's really good. Jimmy has salmon and baked chicken if you don't want steak. Anything going on I need to know about?"

"Nope. The project's construction folks have quit for the night. Should be a quiet night for you. The Sarge left a list of training stuff to do, if you get time." He smiled. Sarge called from Pump Station Four and wants you to handle things here this week. He's going to be out at the project site and away from the phone...that's about it. Oh! Kenny added, "I brought some new country music tapes. They are there by the tape player. I guess that's about all. Rod and I will see you in the morning," The two men began gathering their belongings.

"See you in the morning," Dan said, pouring a cup of coffee. He turned his attention to the mental checklist of items he would need for his duties.

There was minimal vehicle traffic this evening. ARCO laboratory technicians had come by to pick up samples from the lab. There was also a carryall with four surveyors who were going fishing. The surveyors had returned at 2214 hours, bragging about their good luck.

Dan managed to get most of the training material read and had checked and inventoried all the required equipment. He'd been busy and not noticed the lateness of the hour. He reached into the file drawer and brought out a new pack of Gate Log forms. It was time to begin heading up the gate logs for the next day. The logs, forms, and reports began and ended at midnight. All personnel on station at midnight must be entered on the gate logs for the day beginning at midnight. During construction project times, it became a very time-consuming job. He put a new Hank Williams Jr. tape in the machine and began to write.

He, intent on his task, hadn't seen the technician's truck stop at the man-gate. Gwen was opening the door to the gatehouse when Dan became aware of her presence. It was 2325 and she was making the rounds taking readings and changing recording instrument charts.

Gwen Stevens was one of the most unusual people on the pipeline. The first thing people noticed was her physical beauty. She had the body of a playboy bunny and the face of an angel. She was easygoing and a fun person to be around. She had been born on a farm near Vermilion, South Dakota. Her father was a teacher and moved the family to Benson, Minnesota when Gwen was just a baby. Gwen's mother was a traditional Midwestern housewife. Her father wanted her to become a teacher, and she studied hard to please him. As she grew older, she knew she wanted to go to college and break away from the life her mother endured.

Gwen had never been very domestic and would run off to a party whenever she had the chance. She was always pretty. That gave her an advantage at cheerleader tryouts and other school activities. She was popular and a good student. She had graduated from high school on the honor roll, Valedictorian, with an intense interest in science.

With the help of her science teacher and her father, she was accepted at MIT. Again, she was a good student and very popular. She majored in electrical engineering. In her senior year, she met a nuclear engineering student. They were married a few months later. Both Gwen and her husband, Martin, managed to stay in school and finish their Master degrees. They each studied and worked hard to finish together. They were in love, and made plans for the future, if it ever got here.

Martin was working at a nuclear generating plant near Boston and Gwen was working for Westinghouse in the city. Her project was to develop a computer to diagnose blood disorders. The couple was a picture of success and happiness.

It was their fourth wedding anniversary, they had each had a few drinks, the roads were frosty. Martin didn't see the stop sign until it was too late. He ran into the intersection and was hit by a station wagon driven by an old man. Martin and the old man were pronounced dead at the scene. Gwen was taken to Boston General Hospital, in shock.

It took her many months to fully recover. She loved Martin, and it took her many years to get over her great loss. Her life fell apart after the accident. She lost interest in her job and soon resigned. She spent the summer in Minnesota with her parents, suffering from a great mental hangover. She became more and more depressed.

Her old science teacher was to be the one to convince her to "get on with her life." It took several months of talking and coaxing before she agreed to a job interview with Trans Alaska Pipeline Company. The interviewer thought her overqualified for the position, but she was hired. She'd probably be promoted to Pump Station Supervisor within the next year. She lived quietly these days. She only attended an occasional party and then only with close friends. She had two Irish Setters, constant companions when she was off the pipeline.

Chapter 5

Dan stopped his work, stood, and shook the kinks out of his tired back. "How about a cup of coffee, Gwen?" He poured his own, and seeing her nod her head, poured one for her. "What's up?"

"There's something in the warehouse I want to show you. Before I tell you what it is, I want you to promise to take this seriously; this is not a joke. And I want you to keep this a secret. It looks like a big conspiracy at this point. I don't know who is involved, but I do know it means big bucks. I need your help to investigate. Will you help me?"

Dan watched as she explained. Seriousness on that pretty face was not to be ignored. She was beautiful even though her hair was pushed up under a hard hat, and the blue coveralls she wore were tied in the middle with a webbed tool belt. The sad shadow in her eyes reminded him of a lost little girl

"I haven't been a real cop for a long time," he told her. "You know I'll help you any way I can, though. What's this all about?"

"It's about what I found in the new pig." She paused, trying to judge if he would take her seriously when she told him what she suspected. "Dan, that new pig on the warehouse floor is an atomic bomb."

"You're kidding me, right? What the hell would an atomic bomb be doing inside an ultrasonic pig?"

"That's what I want you to help me find out. The pig alone is worth five million dollars. It stands to reason that anyone with the money to build an atomic bomb and to blow up a five million dollar piece of equipment in the process, has got to be very rich, and the reasons have to be very big. It scares me. Please, Dan, Just look at it and tell me I'm wrong, If I'm not, then...."

"Okay, I'll look. Meet me in the warehouse at 0215 when I make my walk-through? Gwen, I could look inside that pig and not know what I'm looking at."

"I knew I could count on you." She sighed with relief, sipped the last of her coffee and tossed the cup in the trash. "I'll meet you there at 0215 and show you what I found. If you'd never had special education in nuclear electronics, you'd not know what you were looking at. But, believe me, this is a very sophisticated device. I know." She went out the door and back to her truck.

Dan returned to the task of changing the gate log sheets and entering reports into the computer. At midnight, the computer began sending the midnight alcohol report that kept track of how many people in the northern division were tested for alcohol consumption. He placed the information with all his reports, and signed off the logs for the day just ending. He then initiated logs for the new day and double checked his work. He peeked over the edge of his coffee cup at the wall clock. In a few minutes, he'd turn control of the gate over to the pump station control room, and he'd make his nightly security and fire hazard patrol of buildings and equipment in and around the pump station property. This nightly security check ordinarily took about an hour and a half.

In his mind, Dan reviewed what he knew about pipeline pigs. He didn't know why they were called pigs, but it was a universal term used on pipelines everywhere for the bullet shape objects made to travel inside a pipeline for cleaning, or, in the case of the ultrasonic pig, measuring thickness of pipe walls to tell if they had been weakened by corrosion.

Dan took a last drink of his cold coffee. By this time of night, it began to taste really bad. He picked up the phone and dialed the three digit code for the control room.

Charley answered the phone,

"Control room." It was the voice of a man being interrupted from an important duty.

"Hi, Charley, it's Dan. It's 0135 and I'm beginning my security check. Can you monitor the gate, by camera, for me?"

"Yeah, I am just finishing my daily report for yesterday. Anything going on out there?" Charley was more friendly now.

"No. Just that mother arctic fox and her kits. Those four kits have been sitting outside the gatehouse door. I think dayshift must give them a handout. After my security check, I'm going to stop at the PLQ for a snack. I should be back by 0300. I'll be on your control room radio channel if you need me, and I'll stop by on the way through. Thanks Charley." Dan cradled the phone, picked up his blue hardhat, set the door alarm, and locked the gatehouse.

Dan enjoyed summertime perimeter checks. He seemed to walk in the fizzle of a 12-hour sunset. White front geese, Canadian geese

Canadian geese
and several kinds of ducks nested in the tall grass and ponds behind the buildings outside the perimeter fence. A flock of rock ptarmigan, a few white feathers still showing, giving them a speckled look, landed near gate number five at the rear of the pump station.

Mother fox came around the corner of a large metal building, hunting for a meal. There was not much chance of catching one of the fleet, quail-size birds, picking gravel, in this open area. With a surprising burst of speed, the white fox dashed directly at the flock. They all burst into the air at the same time, into an arcing departure pattern. One bird must have been paying more attention to the fox than flying and arced too wide, striking the perimeter fence about 7 feet above the ground. The fox ran directly to where the bird had fallen. One bite of the head and the bird was dead. Mama fox picked up the bird, and holding her head high in triumph, trotted off to share her prize with her young.

Where the pipe comes out of the ground from the pump station, there is a sign designating this spot MILEPOST 0. Tour buses bring their passengers here to take pictures. Six caribou were feeding under the elevated pipe and sign. They paid little attention to the red crew-cab pickup making its rounds.

Dan finished his exterior patrol and returned to the gate. He called Charley on the radio, asking him to access the main vehicle gate allowing him to enter the fenced facility. He checked the buildings and equipment areas, following his normal routine.

It was 0218 when Dan walked onto the warehouse. Gwen was there, in the back of the shop, working on an electronic metering device. She had a look of relief when she saw Dan. Dan looked around the large shop area; he was the only other person there. The pig, a gleaming metal cylinder, was on a special stand in the center of the shop area. The rear cover plate was off and the interior was exposed. There were several large crates with locked lids in a semicircle around the stand. A table nearby contained tools and testing equipment.

Gwen retrieved a dropcord from the work table and turned on the light. She placed it inside the pig and illuminated an electronic world of science that could have looked comfortable on the Starship Enterprise.

Dan looked inside and shook his head.

"I have to be honest with you Gwen; I haven't the slightest idea what I am looking at. Turning the television on is the outer limit of my electronic expertise. To me, this machine looks just like it did last time it was here. Show me what has you so spooked?"

"I'll try to explain. Yesterday when I looked inside here, I was fascinated by the changes in the design. See up there, toward the center, on the left. That thing that looks like a control panel. I noticed that entire center section had been completely redesigned. The circuitry in this area is so miniaturized and more efficient it piqued my curiosity. I began to mentally follow circuits and admire the changes. This is the most efficient and advanced pig I have ever seen.

"Then I discovered something strange. See that wiring harness coming from the cover plate in the front?" She paused while Dan looked inside and nodded recognition. "That circuit was never in the old pig. And it doesn't integrate with the new system on the left side. It's a whole different kind of electronics. I've seen similar electronics only one other time. When I was at MIT, my husband and I were part of a team experimenting in the design of detonation devices for nuclear warheads on ballistic missiles. My husband was the expert in nuclear electronics, but I learned only enough to recognize what's here." She pointed to another area with the drop cord light. "I thought the fissionable material may be in the nose, up there ahead of that bulkhead where the wire harness comes through. I checked and there is no radiation detectable on the outside of the nose, but there is a very low reading inside at the bulkhead. I made some crude sketches of the wiring and have looked at it to see if there could be another possibility, but the only answer I can come up with is a nuclear device."

Dan still did not know what he was looking at. "Can this thing explode now?"

"No. That's strange too. There's no detonator inside. The cannon plug for it is there though. See that flat cannon plug with about 40 or 50 pins? That goes to the regular pig computer. That round one on the right, in the rib...yes there...is connected to the wiring harness and circuitry going to the nose of the pig, ahead of the bulkhead." There was strain coming into her voice.

With the noise from the turbine engines running the pumps, the two had not heard the footsteps behind them. It startled them when the voice with an oriental accent asked, "What are you doing?" The two stood and faced the scowling man in the gray visitor hardhat.

Dan tried to appear relaxed, but he didn't think it was working.

"I was making a security check and saw the pig sitting here. I just stopped to look inside. Gwen here says it's the latest thing. I'm Dan Webster. You...just visiting?"

"Mr. Yamazawa." He bowed slightly without taking his eyes from them.

them. "I am TMC foreman on this pig contract. I must inform you, this machine contains very confidential instrumentation—the property of TMC. My company would be very upset to learn that Trans Alaska Pipeline Company had sent people to inspect inside our unit. For your welfare and the interest of my company, I must demand that you leave this area and not return."

"I'm sorry if I upset you, but my duties demand I look everywhere inside this pump station and that includes this shop. My duties aren't meant to interfere with your work or compromise your trade secrets, but I'll do my job whether you like it or not, Mr. Yamazawa. Come on Gwen we have other things to do." Dan walked from the shop with Gwen in the lead. Dan's truck was parked just outside the shop door.

"Get in." He slammed her door and walked to the driver side of the pickup. As they drove slowly under a yard light Dan could see Gwen was wide eyed and tense. He reached to touch her hand and could feel her trembling.

Her voice was weak when she spoke. "I have never been this scared. Now do you believe me that something is going on?"

"If I was skeptical before, I'm convinced. You're right about a lot of things. I still don't know about nuclear bombs, but I'll take your word that you understand it. What I do know though, is that Mr. Yamazawa made his threat clear, and he did it with enough authority that I'm convinced you were right about the power of the people involved. There's no way to know how deeply involved the management is or how many people. One thing is for certain, we can't use the regular telephone communication system. It goes to the Bragaw Street office, and there's no way to know who's listening. You got any ideas?" Dan could see she was calming down now.

"No, I don't, but there is one thing I know, I don't feel safe here. I'm taking a commercial flight out of Deadhorse as early as possible."

"Before you just run off, let me try to figure out what to do next...to maybe work out a plan." Dan thought a minute. "When you get off, go to your room and change into civilian clothing and eat breakfast. Give me that much time anyway." Thoughts kept tumbling through his head. "Meet me at the gatehouse about 0700. Dress warm and bring a coat."

"Dan, please, I . . ."

Dan wasn't listening. His training in the police force had taken over and a plan was forming. "Bring those drawings you made." He patted her arm. "I have friends who can help us, but we've got to get off the north slope to see them. We're too remote up here and if anything happened . . ., well, we have no backup. We could disappear and they could tell any story they wanted. Whoever 'they' are."

"Dan, stop you're going to fast. I can't, I can't...."

"Gwen. You're the only one who knows about the device. You recognized it. I'll be the first one to get you out of here if we find it's too dangerous." Gwen looked long and hard at Dan. She felt with his expertise, they would be safe enough, for a while, anyway. She sighed, as she stepped from the truck.

"Tomorrow is going to be a very long day."

Gwen waved to Dan and began to climb the steel stairs to the compressor building, the anxiety and fear still with her.

Dan drove back to the gatehouse and called Charley in the control room. "Sorry I took so long. I got tied up on some other stuff. Go ahead and switch the gate control back to me now."

"No problem. It's all yours, see ya later."

It was not going to be easy to get off the north slope without a lot of people knowing about it, and Dan wanted to go as quietly and quickly as possible. He would try to get confirmation on his little bit of information. He picked up the phone and called the maintenance shop. The night mechanic answered.

"Hi Dooley, have you got a spare pickup I can borrow for today? I need to go to Deadhorse, but . . ."

"I ain't supposed to lend equipment out, but if you need one, I can let you use one from the projects. They have so many trucks they can't remember where they all are." Dooley laughed.

"It's okay to keep it overnight, then?"

"Awright. Who is she?"

"You know better than that."

"Well. Sure keep the truck. Just don't put any dents in it."

Next, Dan called the hanger at the Deadhorse airport. The early shift was just coming in and would be drinking coffee, waiting for the early morning helicopter flight to arrive for fuel. The phone rang several times then a sleepy voice came on the line.

"ERA Services, Williams."

"Hello, this is Dan Webster with Pipeline Security. Would you do me a favor and look outside and see if Steve Ortmann's Cessna 185 is on the ramp?"

"It's not here, Steve left last night to go to Fairbanks."

"What about the Cessna 206," Dan asked.

"It's not here either; his brother took it to Colville River. The only thing here is the PA-14, that's the Piper Family Cruiser. What's the deal?"

"I have permission from Steve to fly his planes when I need them. I have an emergency to take care of, and I need a plane. Would you top the tanks on the PA-14 and check it over to be sure it is okay to fly? I'll be there about 7:30 this morning. And, remember, this is a security flight."

The attendant felt important to be in on a security operation.

"He just had the 100 hour inspection done on the plane; that's why it's here, so I know it's airworthy. I'll fuel it, check the oil, and give it a preflight inspection for you."

"Thanks," Dan said as he hung up the phone.

There were several telephone lists under the plastic cover on the desktop. He located the number for Deadhorse Flight Service and dialed the number.

"Flight Service." Came a reply.

"What's the weather from Deadhorse to Bettles to Fairbanks?"

"Should be a bluebird day all the way to Fairbanks. There will be high scattered at 20,000. Winds from the north at 10 miles per hour until about noon, and they are expccted to change to southerly at about 5 to 8 miles per hour. There may be some low scattered in the area of high peaks over the Brooks Range. The altimeter at this time is 29.98 and rising. Looks like great flying weather on the north slope. What is your aircraft number?" Flight Service personnel at Deadhorse usually had time to be friendly.

"November 4289 Hotel. Thanks for some good weather for a change." Dan tried to joke with the briefer.

"That's Steve Ortmann's airplane. Is he going to let you fly his pride and joy?" he asked, good naturedly.

"Yep, I guess he figures if I ding his airplane, he can come get mine in exchange. There are about 40 PA-14s still flying and he and I each own one. Thanks again for the briefing. Talk to you later." He hung up the phone and began to make fresh coffee for the officers coming on duty.

He tried to think. Did he have everything covered? Were the assumptions they were being made correct ones? Did Gwen really know about nuclear electronics? One thing was for certain, if he was wrong, he'd be unemployed by tomorrow. But the gamble was too great; if they were right, and did nothing, many lives could be lost.

"What the hell, go for it," he thought.

Chapter 6

O550 hours, and the sun was high. Except for a faint fog bank just visible to the north over the Arctic Ocean, there wasn't a cloud in the sky.

Out the window Dan could see a long tail jeager bird diving on something in the tall grass on the edge of a pond. Two officers in blue and gray uniforms with blue security hardhats were walking from the PLQ toward the gatehouse. They were joking with each other as they came into the shack.

"I hope you made better coffee this morning," Rod teased as he entered. The two officers went to the back office to get their duty belts and weapons. "How was your night, Dan?"

"It's been quiet until about a half hour ago. The place starts hopping when project crews begin to arrive. Nothing unusual though. I'm going to make a schedule change, though. I have to go south for a day, maybe two. I hate to change shifts like this but I have to. Kenny, I want you to stay on days and be available to tend the sick and wounded on projects. Just give the gate to control if you have to leave for any reason. Rod, will you stay for a while this morning and help get the project crew signed in and then get some rest and come in tonight to cover my shift? It's important. If anyone asks, just tell them I had to go to Pump Station Three and Four. The pig is scheduled to go into the pipe at 1400 hours. Most of the administrative people and the pig crew will leave shortly after that and things will be less frantic around here."

"What brought all this on?" Rod asked.

"I can't tell you just yet. Sorry Rod, I'll let you know as soon as I can." Dan wanted to trust his compatriots, but he knew the danger of information leaks.

"Kenny, can I see you in the back office a minute?"

Kenny gave Rod a curious look and followed Dan into the office. Inside the office, Dan turned and closed the door.

"I need your help, Kenny."

"What the hell is going on, Dan? You know I would do anything to help you, but I don't like all this secret stuff."

to help you but, I don't like all this secret stuff. What do you need?" Kenny seemed irritated.

"I need you to call the Pump Station Supervisor and tell him that you saw Gwen Stevens this morning and that you medi-vacced her out to Anchorage. You can make up some medical reason. It is important that no one know that we left together or where we went. I know you don't like doing this without all the information, but I can't give you any more right now. If the Sarge calls and wants to know where I am, just tell him that I will call him as soon as possible. I can't stress enough that I don't want anyone to know we're gone. Will you do that for me?"

Kenny studied Dan for a moment then said, "Yeah, I'll do it. I guess I know you well enough to know that you are not being foolish with Gwen. But I hope you've thought about what happens when all this gets out. Some one is going down the tube, and I don't want it to be me."

"Thanks, Kenny. I'll see to it that you don't get any blame." The two men left the back office and walked into the bright security office. Dan removed his duty belt and hung it on a hook. He put his weapon in the locker and passed the keys to Rod.

"I'm going to get some breakfast and change clothes, then I'll be back." He picked up his hard hat and walked to the PLQ.

It was 0645 when Dan returned to the guardhouse. Both men were still there, and it was obvious they were discussing the situation.

Rod was the one to speak.

"We've been talking about whatever it is you're doing, and we want you to know we're behind you. We just want you to know you can count on us for anything, okay?"

Dan was relieved, "Thanks guys, right now you don't know how much that means to me. I'm going to have to get a move on. Rod, give me a ride over to the vehicle shop?"

Dooley was just walking out the door when Dan and Rod pulled into the parking lot. Dan got out and waved to him. Dooley didn't say a word but tossed him a set of keys and pointed to an unmarked blue pickup. Dan started the truck, rolled down the window and asked Dooley if he wanted a ride as far as the main gate.

"No thanks, it's such a nice morning I think I'll walk."

Gwen was walking toward the main gate when he backed the blue truck into the parking spot. He thought a minute and then stepped out of the truck and entered the guardhouse. He got the keys from Rod and opened the weapon's cabinet. He took his duty weapon and two speed loaders. He closed the cabinet and returned the keys to Rod. Rod raised his eyebrows and tightened his lips. He knew this was extremely important for Dan.

Rod opened the main vehicle gate enough to allow Gwen to exit the fenced facility. She waved at Rod as she passed the window in front of his desk. She could see Dan striding down the metal stairs on the north side of the guardhouse. They met at the blue pickup. Dan waved to his two friends as he opened the truck door and said "Good morning" to his traveling companion.

"We'll see," she replied.

She was wearing a plaid shirt and blue jeans. Her blond hair was combed out and hung to her shoulders. Dan reached for the key, paused, and looked at her.

"Last chance. Still sure about this?"

"Last night I was unsure and terribly frightened. But this morning, I'm very sure. Since I left you, I reviewed my drawings. Something seemed familiar about the wiring coming from the bulkhead. Then it hit me. That wiring harness was taken from a soviet nuclear warhead. I don't know from what kind of delivery system, but it's a low yield type that has been around for a long time. Dan. This is really scary."

Dan didn't stop at the intersection with Spine Road—just checked traffic and sped onto the wide dirt road.

"There's one question we haven't thought about. Where do you think they'll detonate this thing? It's going to have opportunity to travel the full length of the pipeline. We have no way of knowing where it'll blow."

"I've thought about it a little, but there's not enough information." Gwen brushed her hair back and secured it with a barrette from her shirt pocket. "We don't know who's behind it. We don't know their motives. We don't know where the device is destined. It doesn't look like the detonator will be installed here. Which means it can only be installed at three other places: Pump Station number Four, Ten, or at the exit point at the Marine Terminal at Valdez. Those are the only places the pig can be taken from the pipeline. We can trap the pig anywhere on the line, though."

"What do you mean 'trap the pig?'" Dan asked as he began to slow for the checkpoint. He rolled down the window to be able to speak to the guard. When exiting the checkpoint, the guard would only require the driver's badge number and name and the vehicle number. In less than half a minute they were on the road again.

"One of the things security checks, when it makes pad checks or pipeline checks, is the RGVs (Remote Gate Valves). The pig is propelled through the pipeline by the movement of the oil. It would be possible to close one of the RGVs on each side of the pig and trap it in a given place. At least we would be able to stop it in a remote area where no one would be injured when it's detonated." Gwen was sure this plan was the most prudent, considering the amount of verified information available to them. The problem then became, who could they trust with the authority to shut down the pipeline.

Dan drove directly to the main terminal parking lot of the Dead-horse Airport. He stopped the truck and pulled the keys from the ignition, opened the ashtray and dropped them in. He looked around the parking lot. There was no one.

"Let's go," he said.

They left the parking lot and walked along the airport fence behind the few buildings on the west side of the terminal area. It took only about 2 minutes to walk to the last building in the row, a large Quonset-shaped hangar. Then, through the open vehicle gate, they opened the office door in the hangar. There was no one in the office. Dan opened the door leading to the hangar bay. As he opened the door, he felt cool fresh air and smelled the familiar aroma of avgas. A man was standing by the engine cowling of the PA-14 parked in front of the main hangar door. It was quiet at the airport this morning and the man heard the office door closing. He turned to see who was there.

"Hi, are you Williams?" Dan inquired.

"Yup, are you the one taking Steve's Family Cruiser?"

"Yes, is she ready?"

"She's ready to go, but I need to have you sign that you took the plane. You know, your name and badge number. I hate to ask, but if something happens, I don't want to be the one they blame." Williams thought this precaution would make everything legal.

Dan wrote the information on a piece of note pad. He was leaving the office again when he turned and asked Williams for a map. He probably wouldn't need it, but just in case.

He met Gwen at the airplane. It was a quick but thorough preflight check. Walking counterclockwise around the perimeter of the aircraft, he checked hinge pins and strut bolts. He opened the gas caps to visually inspect the fuel level. He checked the tailwheel and flying control wires. He checked the brakes and the propeller. He snapped open the small door on top of the cowling, unscrewed the oil dipstick to read the level. He replaced it and re-latched the small cowl door. All seemed to be in order.

It was quite a trick to get into the small airplane. Dan entered first, through the single door on the right side of the airplane. He fastened the seatbelt and pulled it tight. He then picked up the end of the passenger seatbelt, placed it in his lap and motioned for Gwen to climb aboard: right foot on the step, left foot stepping over the seat, right hand grasping the tube above the instrument panel. This being a taildragger, it was like pulling herself up a hill by the strength of her arms—the front of the aircraft is 3 feet higher than the tail. Once in the seat, she fastened her seatbelt and Dan reached behind her to close the door.

He reached for the headset hanging on the compass. As he slipped the earphones over his ears, he began his cockpit check: fuel to left tank, magneto to left mag, master switch on, mixture full rich, throttle open 1 inch. Clear the prop and press the starter. The 150 horsepower Lycoming engine sprang to life on the second revolution of the propeller. Magneto to both and set the throttle to idle the engine at 800 RPM. Oil pressure is in the green. Everything was running smoothly.

Dan turned the communication radio on and dialed it to 119.2, the Automated Traffic Information Service (ATIS). He listened carefully to the entire recording which gave weather information and advisories important when flying in the area. The information was the same as he had received in his earlier briefing. He then changed the radio frequency to 134.4 for departure.

"Piper 4259 Hotel on 134.4 with Quebec (the code for the ATIS message being broadcast this hour)," Dan said as he pressed the mike switch attached to the stick.

"59 Hotel, Deadhorse departure."

"Yes sir, request information and permission to taxi for departure to the south."

"Taxi to runway 22, wind from the north at 6, altimeter 29.93," the voice on the radio gave Dan the current conditions.

Dan eased the throttle ahead, and the plane began to move.

"Request midfield departure."

"Approved, take off at pilot's discretion; no other traffic reported in the area. Have a nice flight."

"Thank you, Deadhorse." Dan checked his mags while taxiing. They would have to be quitting before he would turn around now. He did not slow when he reached the runway, but turned so the little airplane straddled the line in the center of runway 22. He added power

He added power smoothly and watched the airspeed build. The indicator read 40 mph when he reached between the seats to pull the flap handle up one notch. One instant a creature of the earth and the next a free and soaring eagle, out of the grasp of man and his earthbound limitations.

The airspeed climbed to 70 miles per hour, and Dan slowly raised the flaps. He rolled into a left bank, making a turn to a course 45° away from the runway heading. At 500 feet he eased the nose to level and pulled the throttle back to 2350 rpm. This would give an indicated 110 miles per hour, but with the wind forecast to be on their nose later, they should average about 100 mph to Bettles, and on to Fairbanks. Dan cranked the trim handle ahead to put the craft on step, which meant the most efficient flying attitude.

Piper November 4259 Hotel had been in the air for only 3 minutes when Dan made his turn to the south. He could see the pipeline and the Dalton Highway stretching south across the tundra. He gave a courtesy call to Flight Service.

"Deadhorse, Piper 59 Hotel is leaving your area at this time. Thank you."

"Roger, have a good flight. Yesterday the muskox herd was seen just west of the pipeline about 10 miles south of Pump Station Two. Wish I were flying today myself."

Dan reached to the instrument panel and turned off the radio. He disconnected the headset from the jack-plugs on the panel and took the earphones from his head and placed them on the rear seat.

He turned to Gwen. "Warm enough?"

She had not spoken since entering the aircraft. "I'm fine," she said, "but little airplanes scare me."

"Just relax, sleep if you can. We'll be flying just west of the pipeline corridor. It would be easier to fly through Atigun Pass, but since we don't want to tell people where we are, we will stay west and fly into Bettles for fuel. I'm going to stay low and cross the mountains at about 5,000 feet. The peaks in that area are about 8,000 feet so we'll be flying between some big rocks. It'll be about 3 hours to Bettles, so you might as well enjoy the trip." Dan felt good when he was flying. He had always told Beth it was his stress reliever. Dan's PA-14 allowed him to fish streams and lakes on the Alaska Peninsula not regularly reached by other anglers. He was fascinated by flying to remote areas and observing wildlife, plants, and flowers.

Gwen was becoming more relaxed and began to enjoy the sight of the caribou herds below. She was the first to spot the musk ox herd a few miles south of Pump Station Two. From this small insulated vantage point, where the world seemed at peace, it was difficult to believe her life had become so complicated.

Both occupants of the tiny plane needed to stretch their legs and take a break by the time the Bettles landing strip appeared over the nose. Dan had turned the radio to 122.2 and replaced the headset.

"Bettles Flight Service, Piper November 4259 Hotel."

"59 Hotel, go ahead."

"Yes sir; we are 5 miles north for landing, request information."

"59 Hotel, estimating 10,000 scattered, wind calm, altimeter 29.95. No other traffic reported." The voice had an Alaska native accent.

"Please report entering the pattern."

"Thank you, Bettles. I will be straight in on 19." The little Piper was approaching the field now, slowing to 70 mph. He could see that the services were all at the north end of the runway, so he made a plan to land short: full flaps, nose down to three degrees below the horizon, slow to 50 mph, threshold lights just ahead, pull off the power, ease the stick back a little to obtain the proper landing attitude, let the wheels kiss the gravel runway at 40 miles per hour. He had made it look easy.

Dan parked near the only visible fuel tank. He reached behind Gwen opened the door. The air was cool. She pulled her left knee onto the seat and found the step with her right foot. Getting out was easier than getting in. Out of the airplane, Dan stretched and shook himself to ease the stiffness in his muscles. A cute native girl about 15 years old approached.

"You're not Steve." She said. "You fly Steve's plane? I thought you Steve."

"Steve let me use his plane. Can I get some gas?" The girl was grinning now and Dan returned the smile.

"Steve think this plane his baby. He must like you a lot. I gas the plane; if you want to eat, you go to there. Mom has fresh cinnamon rolls and good coffee." She pointed to the cabin behind the fuel tanks.

Gwen's appetite for fresh cinnamon roll was amazing. The roll was at least 6 inches across and 3 inches high. It was covered with melting butter and the aroma of heaven. She ate it all. Dan had only coffee. They each finished off their second cup of coffee when the girl came into the cabin. Gwen smiled at the girl and asked,

"Does Steve like you or the cinnamon rolls best?"

"He like cinnamon roll but I like him." She laughed and hid her smile behind her shoulder. She then turned to Dan, "The gas, it's $41. I charge Steve?"

The girl's mother, behind the counter (which was really just a kitchen table), added the total for food and gas.

"That's $45.50 total," she said.

Dan left a $50 bill on the table and the two walked out of the cabin restaurant. There was only one outhouse and Dan took first turn, then walked to the plane to check the oil and to make a quick preflight check. He had just finished checking the fuel tanks for signs of water when Gwen returned. It was now just after one o'clock.

"Bettles, Piper 59 Hotel," he called.

"59 Hotel, go ahead."

"I'll be departing south, runway 19; any changes since I landed?"

"No. It's still the same, wind calm, altimeter 29.95. You headed to Fairbanks?"

"Yes, how is it down that way?" Dan asked.

"It is going to be hot south of the Yukon River, maybe 80°, that will cause some moderate turbulence below 1,500 feet. Other than that it should be great. Have a nice trip."

"59 Hotel departing runway 19 at this time. By the way, you folks have the best looking gas attendant and the best cook north of the Yukon, right here in Bettles. I'll have to come back when I can stay a few days. Thanks again." Dan liked the people in the bush and wished he had more time to spend with them.

They would be leaving the Brooks Range soon and the country would become flat again. Dan checked the time. Unless something unforeseen happens, they should be on the ground in Fairbanks before 1630 hours. He was thankful for the GPS (global position system) Ortmann had installed in the airplane. It took all the guesswork out of navigation here in the north where a compass may not tell the truth. The cabin of the small craft was hot as they flew across the Yukon River Valley, the Tanana Valley, and into Fairbanks.

Because of the engine noise of the small aircraft, it is difficult to carry on a conversation while flying. Consequently, the problem at hand had been reviewed, mentally, many times during the past several hours. There just wasn't enough information. Neither Dan nor Gwen could decide who was behind, what had to be, an enormous conspiracy.

Dan had given much thought to the purpose of the bomb. It was probably a low yield warhead from a Soviet missile. The detonator had not been installed when it was placed in the pipeline at Pump

Station One. If the purpose was to destroy a pump station, why not Pump Station One? The pipeline is routed several miles to the east of Fairbanks; therefore, detonating it near there would have little effect on the city and it's residents. It would not take a nuclear device to simply blow up a pipeline section. So what's the purpose of the device?

The destination of the pig and, coincidentally, its contents, was the Valdez Marine Terminal. But the device seemed too small to destroy the terminal, which is spread over a 1000 acre hillside area. What is the target?

Suddenly, it was like a flash of light in his mind; the purpose was not to destroy the pipeline but to disable it—to shut it down. Some terrorist or extortionist wanted the pipeline shut down. Probably a terrorist, an extortionist's motives would be to threaten, and he could do that with conventional explosives. That was it. A nuclear device would destroy the terminal end of the pipeline and the Operations Control Center. This would stop operation of the pipeline for an extended period of time without destroying the entire terminal.

Dan was very tired. He had received clearance to land on runway 19 Left. His reactions were getting slow, and he did not make a smooth landing. He had recovered from the first big bounce, but was having trouble keeping the nose pointed down the center of the runway. As the speed bled off and more weight settled on the tailwheel, the craft became more manageable. He switched to ground control frequency and asked for directions to transient parking.

He found an empty tiedown spot and pulled the mixture to stop the engine. The heat was stifling. He opened the door and held Gwen's arm for support while she performed the gymnastics necessary to exit the little plane.

"I'll tie down the plane and then check in at the terminal and pay the tiedown fees. You take my credit card and rent us a car. I'll meet you in front car rental counter." He climbed from the plane and dug a credit card from his wallet. "I won't be long."

"It'll be good to walk around and shake out some kinks," she said, as she reached into the airplane for her jacket. "See you inside."

Chapter 7

Dan finished tying down the airplane. Inside, he filled out the form for a tiedown. He put money inside the envelope and dropped it into the slot provided. He met Gwen at the car rental desk and signed for the auto. The two walked to the parking lot and found the car. Dan tossed her the keys and said, "Here, take the keys, you drive."

She started the sedan.

"Where are we going?"

"Take a left at the street and head into town. We have to stop at a store and get a toothbrush and comb." Dan was tired, but he realized she must be even more exhausted.

She found a small filling station with a grocery store and stopped in the parking lot. They purchased personal toilet articles.

"Do you want a newspaper?" She pointed to the newsstand.

"No. Get one if you want, but I'm too tired to read."

They carried the bags to the car and drove toward the city center. Dan was not very familiar with Fairbanks and told Gwen to turn left at an intersection with the Steese Highway. There would be motels on this street.

The big yellow sign read Captain Barratt Motel; they pulled into the lot and walked to the desk. The dining room was just off the lobby and the aroma of food stimulated their senses. Dan asked for two rooms. The desk clerk was sorry, but it was the tourist season and all the rooms were reserved. Perhaps if they waited until six o'clock there would be a cancellation.

Dan leaned over the counter and whispered to the clerk, "I'm with Pipeline Security. I'm here on official business. Surely you have a room with two beds for the Trans Alaska Pipeline Corporation," Dan bluffed.

The clerk didn't know how much weight TAPS had with the hotel management, but this man had the look of official business and there would surely be a no-show anyway.

"Of course, Sir," the clerk apologized, "Will you be paying for the room or will you be charging it to the company."

"Charge it to the Company." What the hell, they could take it out of his termination check if he got fired.

The two found the room and went inside. Gwen searched the two sacks for a comb and lipstick—then went to the bathroom to wash up. She was shaking when she looked into the mirror. Fatigue, stress, and fear had taken their toll. A shower would help a lot she thought.

Dan found the FBI man's card in his wallet and dialed the number. He looked at his watch, "Come on Roger, be there."

The phone rang several times before a stern voice came on the line, "FBI." It was Roger Dorfmann's voice. The sound of that voice was like sun breaking through a Prudhoe winter day.

"Roger, this is Dan Webster."

"Dan, good to hear from you. How are Beth and the boys?"

"They're fine, Roger. But I need your help. I can't talk on the phone. Can you come to Fairbanks? I need your help, right away."

Roger had known Dan for over 20 years and in all that time he had never heard fear in his voice—until now.

"Alaska Airlines has a flight in the morning, pick me up at the airport at 9:30 in the morning. Do you want me to bring anything?"

Dan reached into the small of his back and pulled the heavy Smith and Wesson from his belt. "No, I have everything I need. Thanks, Roger, see you in the morning." He hung up the phone.

Dan heard the shower running.

"I'll have time," he thought. He picked up the phone and dialed his home number. A voice came on the line after only two rings. Hearing her voice made him feel good.

"Hi honey. How are you?"

"Oh! Dan. I thought you might call tonight. How's it going?"

"That's what I called to tell you. I am not at the pump station. I'm in Fairbanks. There's a problem on the line that I can't discuss on the phone, but I wanted you to know I'm okay. I am here with that female tech I told you about, Gwen Stevens. I called Roger and he is meeting us here in the morning. I don't know where I'll be for the next few days, so you won't be able to call me. I'll call you. Promise."

"What's wrong Dan; is it dangerous?"

"No, there isn't anyone shooting at me if that's what you are worried about. I love you, honey. I promise to be careful. It's just an investigation. But I don't know who is involved, so if anyone calls about me, all you know is that I am at work."

"I worry so much about you getting hurt again. Please be careful.

I love you." In spite of what Dan said, she was getting an uneasy feeling.

"I promise. I love you, too. I have to go now, but I'll call you as soon as I can. Roger'll know where I am if you need me. Say 'hi' to the boys. Bye." Dan had not wanted to worry her, but he knew she would worry even more if she didn't know where he was.

The bathroom door opened.

"Your turn."

"Thanks, are you getting hungry? I'll get a quick shower, and we can go down for a bite to eat. I called my friend with the FBI, and he will be here in the morning. If it's any comfort to you, we're not alone any more." He smiled at her and disappeared into the steamy bathroom.

Fifteen minutes later, the two walked the hall back to the lobby and the dining room. They put their names on the list for a table and sat down at the bar.

"You are going to like my friend Roger. He's a real character. Did I tell you he saved my life once?" He sipped his drink.

"No, you didn't. How did that happen." She drank lite beer.

"It was when I was a deputy sheriff and he was with DEA. We were making a raid on a marijuana farm and there was a big shootout. I stopped a car from escaping and jumped out of my vehicle to arrest the passengers. The driver got out of the car, and it was one of our deputies. I was so dumbfounded, I let him get the drop on me. He shot me, that's this scar under my left ear, and would have killed me but for Roger. Roger got the guy before he could finish me. That was over 20 years ago. As they say, time goes by fast when you're having fun." Dan had not told this story to anyone on the pipeline before, and he didn't understand why now.

They finished with dinner and returned to the room. The food and drinks had made him very sleepy. Dan sat on the edge of the bed and unbuttoned his shirt. Gwen went into the bathroom and returned in a couple of minutes with a large bath towel wrapped around her. She slid under the blankets of the other bed then tossed out the towel.

"Good night." The light was barely off and the two were asleep.

Dan awakened at 6 to hear her moving around. She went into the bathroom and he slipped his pants on—then turned on the Today Show on television.

"...according to military sources. Again, repeating the news bulletin form news central. An armed force with sophisticated military equipment attacked the Saudi palace in Riyadh and captured the Saudi Royal Family. Simultaneously, another force attacked Kuwait

City and captured the Prince and the Royal family. The attacking force had the markings of the, now defunct, USSR. Sources close to the military say the military doesn't know who the attackers are. The State Department has told us they will issue a statement at noon, Eastern Standard Time. That's about 45 minutes from now. There have been no reports on casualties or what the attackers intend to do with the members of the two royal families. We will bring you more information when it is available. We return you now to our regularly scheduled programming."

The bathroom door opened and Gwen appeared. "Good morning. Rested?" She asked, smiling.

"You bet. I really slept. I'll go clean up and we can get some breakfast. We have to pick up Roger at 9:30. Have you heard the news? Sounds like another war starting in the middle east," He informed her as he walked into the other room.

After breakfast of coffee, juice two sunny eggs, and toast, they stopped at the desk and told the clerk they'd need the room for another night. On the drive to the airport, they discussed what they knew and reviewed the possibilities. There was nothing new they could add to the information they would give to Roger.

Alaska Airlines flight from Anchorage was on time, and Roger Dorfmann walked down the ramp carrying a small athletic bag. He smiled when he saw Dan. They shook hands and slapped each other's backs. Roger kept in shape by going to the gym every morning to exercise for an hour. There were flecks of gray in his blond hair, but the look of youth had not left him. Neither had the impish gleam in his eyes.

"Dan, old friend. I use the term loosely. What's going on? You okay?"

"I'm fine, Mr. Atlas of the North. Have you had breakfast?" Dan asked, playfully.

"Yes, they served it on the plane." Roger chuckled.

Gwen had moved closer,

"Roger, I want you to meet Gwen Stevens. She's the one who brought this situation to my attention. She's a technician for Trans Alaska Pipeline Service Company."

"Pleased to meet you, Gwen" Roger said as he turned again to speak to Dan. "Do you have a place we can talk?"

"Yes, we have a room at the Captain Barratt. Any other baggage?"

"Nope. I'm ready if you are."

The three drove the few minutes back to the motel. Roger spent the time getting acquainted with Gwen. When they entered the lobby,

When they entered the lobby,
Dan stopped at the desk and asked to have two pots of coffee sent to the room. Once in the room Roger asked,

"Okay, what's this all about? I know you wouldn't have called me unless it was important?"

Dan looked at Gwen, "Go ahead, lay it out for him."

"Are you familiar with pipeline pig operations?" Gwen sat in one of the chairs and reached for her bag. She took out the sketches and diagrams she carried.

"I know they are used for cleaning and inspection of the inside the pipeline, but I have no technical knowledge," Roger replied.

"You know what a pig is?" She asked again, handing him a diagram.

"Generally speaking, yes."

"As Dan told you, I am a technician with TAPS. My training is in electrical engineering. When I came to work this week, they were preparing the Smart Pig for the scheduled run down the pipe. I was curious about the new pig and found electronic circuits inside I could not account for. I made these drawings and spent time studying them."

Gwen spread the paper work on the coffee table. "I was once married to a nuclear engineer, and I worked with him on nuclear projects. I began to recognize the circuitry in the pig as similar to that from a nuclear warhead. Later, I remembered where I had seen some of this wiring." She pointed to a schematic of what appeared to be an electrical box. "It came from a Soviet low yield tactical weapons warhead. When Dan came on duty I told him about it and here we are." She watched to see if Roger was taking this seriously. Roger gave out a low whistle.

Dan spoke.

"That's a somewhat Readers Digest version, but that's the story. I had my suspicions confirmed when we were looking at the pig. The head technician for TMC found us and made some threats. He was not happy with us for looking inside the pig. This has to be big, Roger, for anyone to fit an atomic warhead into a five million dollar pipeline pig. We didn't know who to trust, so I called you. I think we're onto something that's bigger than us both, so I called you. Maybe the three of us can surround it."

"I assumed neither of you have lost your marbles and that you're both dead serious, excuse the pun. When is this pig scheduled to start down the pipeline?" Roger asked.

"It was supposed to be put into the pig launch chamber yesterday at 1430. It should arrive at Pump Station Four sometime this evening.

They'll take it from the pipe, clean it up, recharge the batteries, replace the recording tapes, and put it back into the pipe in the morning." Gwen volunteered.

"If it goes all the way to Valdez, it should be there next Tuesday." Dan said, thinking for a moment, then turning to Gwen to ask, "What about the Pig Box and all the equipment and tools we saw at the warehouse. Won't they have to truck that equipment down to support the pig operation?"

"You're right, they will." Gwen said.

Several hours passed while information and suppositions were evaluated and weighed by the trio. Roger didn't understand nuclear physics, but he knew someone who did.

Roger picked up the phone and dialed his office. "Hello, Miss Dill. This is Roger Dorfmann. Look in your file and give me the number for Sam DeGrosso at Elmendorf Air Force Base." There was a pause- then Roger began to write the number. "Thank you Miss Dill. If you need me, you can call the Fairbanks office."

He pressed the button in the cradle of the telephone and released it again. Then while dialing he said, "Sam is a civilian with the Air Force. He heads the nuclear division at Elmendorf. He also has ties with the CIA...Yes, this is Roger Dorfmann, May I speak with Sam DeGrosso. Tell him it's urgent."

"Hello, Sam." Roger was using his official voice. "Roger Dorfmann with the FBI . . ., Fine . . ., I have something here, some sketches, I want you to take a look at. I need your opinion as soon as possible. Do you have a fax number where I can send them to you?" He listened a moment, then wrote a number on the pad. "About 15 minutes. I'll have to drive to the office, here to send them. Do you have that number? Thanks Sam."

At the Fairbanks Field Office of the FBI, Roger asked for access to the secure fax machine. Roger was supervisor for operations in Alaska and the office began to secretly buzz with, "I-didn't-know-the-boss-was-coming?" whispers. Roger ignored it and went about his business. A surprise visit by the boss from time to time would keep the office on its toes.

The second sheet of copy was just sent and the third was beginning when the phone rang. It was DeGrosso.

"Roger, this is Sam. Hold the rest of those drawings. I want to see the originals. I will be there in less than 2 hours, if I can get the base ops King Air. Can you meet me at Eielson?"

"Sure. Can I assume that these drawings contain what we suspected?" Roger wanted preliminary confirmation.

"Yes, and there are some things you may not know. I don't want to discuss it on the phone...the secretary just told me I have the King Air. See you in less than 2 hours."

The two strangers were introduced to the staff in the office. Current case load was discussed with Roger. There was a meeting in the conference room to discuss technical points in a missing person investigation. Roger tended his official business for over an hour while Gwen and Dan waited. The two were becoming impatient, checking watches, and pacing the floor when an office door opened and Roger emerged.

"Okay. We can go now." Roger said as he walked past Dan.

Visitor passes were issued to the three at the gate to Eielson Air Force Base. Roger directed Dan to the base operations terminal as he drove through the base streets. They could see a Beechcraft King Air with U.S. Air Force markings, designated the C21A, taxiing to the terminal. Dan parked in the loading zone in front of the terminal. They all went inside to await the scientist/CIA man.

Sam DeGrosso was a short, solidly built man, with a quick gait, wearing gray slacks and a tan London Fog jacket. His black hair was graying. He stopped at the operations desk and spoke to the clerk. He finished his business at the desk, turned, and recognized Roger immediately. His expression remained stern as he approached.

"Hello Roger, good to see you again. Let's go down the hall. There's an empty office we can use." He turned and began to walk ahead of them.

They passed an open door. Sam spoke to the airman inside and was given directions to a vacant office. The four entered and closed the door. Sam was about to speak when there was a knock on the door. Sam opened the door to see the airman he had spoken with earlier.

"Can I get you any coffee or juice, sir?" he said.

"No, thank you. I would appreciate it though if you would ensure our privacy. We do not want to be disturbed. If we need anything, we'll call." Sam then closed the door. He turned back to the small group again and apologized, "Sorry to be so abrupt, but what you have here may have international significance."

Roger spoke,

"Sam, this is Dan Webster. He's with Pipeline Security." The two men shook hands.

"And this is Gwen Stevens. She's a technician with Trans Alaska Pipeline Service Company, and who made the sketches I sent you."

"Pleased to meet you both," Sam said, "I've heard Roger speak of you before, Dan." He turned to Gwen. "Are you really the one that did these drawings? They are very good and, I might add, very accurate. Where did you see this?"

She related her story about her curiosity of the new micro circuitry inside the ultrasonic pig. She told how she had recognized the wiring leading from the front bulkhead of the pig as that of a nuclear device. She told how she had enlisted Dan to help her get word to someone about what she had found.

Dan volunteered his supposition about the device inside the pig having a destination of Valdez and the Marine Terminal. He gave a thumbnail sketch of the operation of the Operations Control Center (OCC). After telling how this destruction would disrupt the flow of oil without devastation of the pipeline or the main terminal, he said, "But we still don't have a clue about who is responsible."

Sam had been taking notes. He thumbed through them and finally looked up and said, "I can't think of anything else I need from you two. I want to assure you that action will be taken as soon as I get back to my office. You two have done a remarkable job of keeping this a secret. I'm flying back to Anchorage to get started on this. Roger, would you handle the company and start the ball rolling to get this thing into our possession before it can be armed?"

"Sure. I'll be available through the Fairbanks office if you need anything more tonight." Roger said. "If there's nothing more here tonight, we'll leave and start on this the first thing in the morning."

Sam looked at the pile of papers in front of him for a moment before responding,

"Nothing I can think of right now; I'll be talking with you in the morning, thanks Roger."

The three picked up their jackets and were about to open the door when Sam spoke again.

"I want you to know that what you have discovered is of vital national importance. I'll try to get clearance tonight to allow you to know the whole story. Meanwhile, I want you two to know that, though you may never get a medal for it, you are heroes."

Chapter 8

The best idea was Roger's. The three would fly back to Anchorage with Sam in the Air Force King Air. Dan would stay with Roger, and Gwen could stay at her place. In the morning, there would be a meeting with TAPS company brass to discuss a course of action. Roger would have one of his local agents pick up the rental car and return it to the airport.

They stopped for a late supper at the Cattle Company enroute from Elmendorf Air Force Base. While at the restaurant, Roger called a private number to make an appointment for an early meeting the next morning.

It was almost midnight when Roger and Dan sipped a cup of tea at Roger's house. Both men were tired and had little to say. Roger led Dan to his room and told him where to find clean towels.

"See you in the morning," Roger said.

It seemed to Dan that he had only just closed his eyes when Roger yanked at his covers. "Sun shining, bud. Lift that sleepy head." Dan showered while Roger found him a change of clothing. By the time he was dressed, coffee was hot

"Good morning." Roger looked up from the table and smiled.

"Well, you're half right." Dan ran his fingers through his damp hair. "A couple of hours sleep would've felt better. Have you heard from Gwen?"

"I called her a few minutes ago. We'll go by her place and pick her up as soon as you finish your coffee. George Lords wants to see us at eight. I called Sam and he'll meet us there."

A very tall blond in a blue dress met the four and showed them to a conference room. A tray of pastries and fresh coffee was on a small table. There were large photographs of the pipeline covering the walls. Behind the conference table, the wall had eight by ten framed pictures of company executives. It was exactly eight o'clock when George arrived; with him was Bill Scott, Director of Operations for Pipeline Security Corporation.

George was a man well respected in the law enforcement community. He had been the director of the Department of Public Safety for the State of Alaska. He had been an Alaska State Trooper and was generally known throughout the state as a good cop. He was now the head of the TAPS security and aviation divisions.

TAPS had suffered through a period of scandal caused by leaks of sensitive information. An investigation had been authorized by the president of the company to find the source of the leaks. The Trans Alaska Pipeline Service Company president had given George the authority to hire Metzgar Security, a private security company, to do the investigation.

Metzgar Security set up a dummy company and attempted to obtain confidential information and learn the sources from which it had been routed. The investigation found a powerful entrepreneur, a senator and several TAPS company employees the culprits.

Once the investigation was made public, the mudslinging began in earnest. A congressional investigation was called to determine the propriety of the investigation by Tran Alaska Pipeline Service Company. George gave a calm and professional testimony. He gave the company position and explained its directives regarding the investigation. Although TAPS was embarrassed by the publicity, George was able to convince the investigating committee that his company's roll had been undertaken with honorable intentions. It was decided the investigation had been intended to stop leaks of confidential information and had not been intended to defame public officials.

Bill Scott, like George Lords, was a retired Alaska Department of Public Safety Commissioner. He had also worked his way up from the bottom. He came to the troopers from the small town of Cordova, Alaska. He too was considered a good, respected cop. His present position was General Operations Manager for Pipeline Security Company.

George sat at the head of the table, a yellow legal pad positioned in front of him. He looked up and surveyed the group in front of him.

"Good morning. Do we all know everyone here?"

Introductions and credentials were given. Each of those present gave his name, where he worked, and his qualifications.

"Roger, you said this urgent meeting was about security. I have asked Bill to join me. The Company President is out of town, but I've contacted him and he has authorized me to act as I see necessary in any situation involving security."

"I'm going to defer to Sam; he has the best knowledge and current information, and will be able explain the entire situation. Go ahead Sam."

Sam gave the account methodically and without any frills.

"I received a call from Roger stating there had been some suspicious circuitry found inside the ultrasonic pig. He faxed me some drawings accurate enough that I flew to Fairbanks to meet with him, Dan, and Gwen. Gwen, your technician, found wiring from a nuclear device hidden inside the pig. The strange part is they tried to economize and use the original wiring harness leading out of the front bulkhead, otherwise we would've never detected the device. This wiring harness is unique and the color codes are distinctive. I suspect it wasn't replaced because of time restrictions. I also suspect whoever's responsible for the device never expected any engineer capable of recognizing it, since it was brought through customs without being recognized.

"The immediate concern, of course," Sam continued, "is where and when will the device be armed and detonated. It seems to me, that as long as the TMC technicians are following the pig, it's safe. Dan thinks the destination is the pipeline terminal and the OCC at Valdez. I agree with him."

Sam pressed on. "What I am about to tell you cannot leave this room...." He paused and looked directly at each person at the table to be sure they understood. "This is a matter of National Security." He reached into a brief case and spread a hand full of papers and file folders on the table.

"Several months ago, before the demise of the Soviet Union, my agency followed a Soviet general to Paris. This general was in charge of the operation and security of the Trans Soviet Pipeline. He also had a rather large command of forces and equipment at his disposal. We kept tabs on him because he was powerful, influential, and ranked high in Soviet government.

"We didn't know why this general, General Lianid Lisishkin, was traveling to Paris. Boy, did we get a surprise! This guy met with an American billionaire and a Japanese financier. Both of these men, Nels Bergstrom and Gaishi Yamamata...."

"Wait." Dan interrupted, "did you say Nels Bergstrom?"

"Yes, he's a big money man from Arizona. He used to be a Senator in California."

Dan looked at Roger. "I've heard of him. Sorry to interrupt, please continue, Sam."

Sam continued, "We never got firsthand information on what took place in that meeting, but we have a good suspicion. All three men are deep into oil, oil production, and oil stock. All three men have other interests, too. Bergstrom has been in and out of the marijuana and cocaine business for years. The Japanese guy, Yamamata, has ties with the Yakuza, the Japanese Mafia. He also finances several electronic companies. These people represent big money." He picked up another piece of paper.

"My office in Washington tells me the men presenting themselves as TMC technicians don't work for TMC at all. We suspect that these men are working for Yamamata.

"You may have been following the news about the abduction of the Saudi and the Kuwaiti royal families. My office told me that the operation was carried out by the forces of General Kisishkin. When the Soviet Union broke up, he was able to hide away an army in southern Armenia. We also have information that his stockpile of nuclear warheads was one short at the last inventory. We suspect that he shipped it to Yamamata's people in Japan.

"The United Nations is meeting today to plan a course of action against the General. They are not aware of the missing warhead. My office is working on arresting Mr. Yamamata. That leaves us with the immediate concern of the warhead inside the ultrasonic pig," Sam said in conclusion.

"I would like to suggest a plan if I may." Roger said.

"You people are the experts in the spy field. We are open to suggestions," George said.

Roger glanced quickly around the table before speaking.

"I will take Sam and Gwen to Valdez and arrest the TMC impostors. There, we'll deal with the device, disarm and impound it. I'd like Mr. Scott to authorize Dan to go to Arizona to work with our officers there to arrest Nels Bergstrom. It's going to be a big job to get evidence to convict him of conspiracy to terrorism."

"I'll take care of your assignment, Dan. You're supposed to be at Pump Station One, correct?" Bill Scott said in a quiet tone. "We have one other problem though. We are running short on time for the arrival of the pig in Valdez. What time is it due to arrive, George?"

"At 1630 this afternoon. Where would you three like for our helicopter to pick you up and what time?" George was writing on his yellow legal pad.

Sam offered the first response.

"I'll get clearance for you to land at Elmendorf. We'll be ready, at the base operations terminal at noon."

"Is there anything else then?" George asked.

"I have one thing. I'll instruct my Captain to cooperate fully with you in this operation.

you in this operation. Will you want the State Troopers to assist in the arrest of the technicians in Valdez?" Scott asked.

Roger thought a moment; "Yes, we'll need two or three troopers.

George stood, "If there is nothing else, then we'll adjourn. We've a lot of work ahead of us. And let's keep in mind that if we fail, there will be a terrible loss of life and an environmental disaster making the Exxon Valdez look a kid's game. Keep me informed at every turn. Let's do this thing right, folks."

In the parking lot, Roger turned and spoke to the small group. "Let's meet at my office. We can go over final plans there."

As they reconvened in Roger's private office, Dan thought this to be an unlikely group to be facing an atomic bomb and an international plot with world wide consequences. Each took a seat in the office, each with their own questions.

Roger was the first to speak. "Dan. I'll have someone in the Phoenix office meet you at the airport. You won't be able to get that big revolver on the airplane, so I'll have our office there supply you with a weapon and a shoulder rig. John Sutter is head of the DEA office in Phoenix. He'll be interested in knowing our old friend is still in business. I have a call through to him now. If at all possible, I'd like to have him with you when you go after this guy."

"Thanks, Roger. We've waited a long time to get another chance at Bergstrom. This time we'll get him. And it will be good to see John again." Dan commented.

"You two speak of Bergstrom as if you've been involved with him in the past. Where'd you know him?" Sam asked.

Dan tilted his head slightly to the right and said, "See this scar? A souvenir from the last meeting we had with Senator Nels Bergstrom. Now it's my turn to give him a little surprise."

Roger looked at Dan.

"Just remember he is even richer and more powerful than when we lost the case to his fancy lawyers 22 years ago. Don't let revenge blow this case, Dan."

"Don't worry, Roger. I'm not as green or wet behind the ears as I was then. I'll do it all according to the law. I promise, we will not lose to this fat scumbag again."

"I've had my secretary get you a temporary commission through my office. Leave your revolver here, and I'll lock it in the gun safe. Miss Dill will take you down to be photographed for the I.D. card. Do that while we finish here. We'll meet in my office in 30 minutes."

Dan drew the big Smith and Wesson from its place in the small of his back. He opened the cylinder and handed the gun to Roger then opened the door and proceeded down the hall with Miss Dill.

Sam gave Roger a questioning look. "Are you sure you want him involved on that end? He's very personally involved."

Roger gave a small wry smile.

"Dan's about the best all around cop I know. He knows where the boundaries are, and he'll stay within'em. He deserves a chance at this one. I don't think his wife will like me much for giving it to him, though."

Roger returned to the subject back to the job at hand.

"Gwen, you and Sam will have to disarm the device. I'll meet with the security people and the troopers to set up a secure area and handle the arrest. It's going to be up to you to give the technical information to get the pig out of the pipe and to deactivate it. Will you be able to handle that?"

"I think so, but I'll need a lot of help from Sam."

Sam was looking at the floor and thinking. He looked up and said, "We've got to get to that pig before the arming device is installed. Once the timer is turned on, there'll be no way to stop it. Everything ahead of the bulkhead will be radioactive and there'll be no safe way to open it with the equipment available to us. If the arming device is installed, it's going to detonate. You'll have to get to those technicians before they can install it. We'd better get a move on. The helicopter'll be here soon."

The trio left the office with grim resolve. If they failed, there would be a nuclear explosion at the Valdez Terminal and they would be at ground zero. Dan was returning with Miss Dill.

"She has me booked on the late flight tonight. I'm going to call Beth and have her bring me a bag with clothes and shaving gear. She's not going to be happy with us, Roger. Try to keep her posted on the progress of the case and let her know I'm OK, will you?"

Gwen put her arms around Dan. "Thanks for everything. I'll see you when you get back."

"Keep an eye on that old bachelor over there. I've known him for many years, and no lady has been able to stand him for very long." Dan said, pointing a thumb at Roger. Good luck to you too, Sam." Dan called as the three departed.

Dan used the phone in Roger's office to call Beth. He would have her take one of the hourly commuter flights from Kenai to Anchorage and meet her at the airport, and attempt to explain what was about to happen.

happen. He knew there would be no way to diminish her anxiety, but he would try to convince her his involvement was essential. It had never occurred to him to lie to her. No one could love another person more than Dan loved Beth; he hated bringing her greatest fear back. He also knew no matter how much he explained, Beth would be crying when he boarded the plane for Phoenix tonight.

Chapter 9

Since talking with Dan 3 days ago, Beth had become more and more apprehensive. Dan had called from Fairbanks. An added dimension of fear grabbed her at the most unexpected time of day; when she was reading was the worse. She'd stop and review his call. He wasn't at the pump station, but rather, on a mission he could not, or would not, explain. He was so vague, she couldn't shake the feeling he was in great danger. The terrible memory of his getting shot, had been safely tucked away—until now.

Dan had been in administration and was usually home at a regular time each day. He'd investigated many shootings, but had never actually had to be there when the bullets were flying.

The year and a half before he left the Sheriff's department was very hard for him. He began to drink heavily. Dan had always been a people person. He tried his best to help each individual in the county. He answered even the most trivial calls. "People get scared and need assurance of a uniformed officer." He told her. It had been this type of police work that had kept crime level at an extreme low during Red McNabb's administration.

When James T. Brooks was elected Sheriff, Dan felt out of place in the department. He lost the authority to assign and supervise his men. Officers no longer stopped at the Sunshine Souvenir Store and chatted with Netty Saltsmith, and asked if any strangers were hanging around the area. Checking for teen parties along the river was no longer a priority and several of the county's teens had been severely injured following these parties. In short, the entire personality of the department had changed, and Dan never coped well.

The drinking had always been a private affair with Dan. It started with a drink after work to ease the stress created by his job. It escalated, over the years, to drinking himself to sleep each night. It began to tell on his body. His health began to show small signs of succumbing to the long term effects of alcohol. The death of Ernie the drunk in the county jail left Dan even more frustrated than before. He investigated the death, made recommendations and submitted reports. All of which was the final straw for him. He had spent a lot of time with Ernie's family during that time. Ernie had been a friend for many years, and Dan could neither condone, nor forgive the negligence of the Sheriff, the officers, or the philosophy that had caused his death. Dan drank even more.

During this period, Beth worked for a successful accounting office in town. She studied evenings, and attended night classes at the college. She finished her Masters in Business, passed the exams, and received her CPA. She also became the mother of two wonderful boys during this time. She never lost her schoolgirl appearance nor her bubbly personality.

The love this couple shared was the envy of everyone. They went everywhere together. The boys were happy and mischievous. They never missed one of the boy's ball games, whether soccer or T-ball. Beth was President of the PTA. When the grade school had its Christmas play, the boys were on stage dressed as animals and sang to baby Jesus. How proud they were then. Beth thought she couldn't ever forgive Sheriff Jim Brooks for what he had done to her life.

Dan began to taper his drinking after moving to Alaska and became a Security Guard. But after a couple of years, he settled into the work and was happier. Flying had a lot to do with it. Once he started, he was hooked. He flew places other people only read about. He bought his own plane. And his interest in flying continued to build.

Beth became supervisor of accounting for the Borough School District working for Dale Berkins, a prince of a man, who made life wonderful at the office. She took all office supervisory difficulties of a burgeoning district off his shoulders, yet found time to resolve inner-office problems and encourage her subordinates to upgrade their skills. She taught weekly night classes in accounting and computer skills.

Now, young Roger was in college and his younger brother, Timothy, was a senior in high school. Both boys were working this summer at Lake Clark Lodge. Both were well liked and respected by the lodge owners and the U.S. Park Rangers. Roger developed an interest in becoming a Parks Ranger and work in the Brooks Lake or Lake Clark/Iliamna area.

Both boys loved to fly and Roger had already received his Private license. He was now studying for his Commercial and Instrument ratings. Tim would have to wait another year before he could get his Private. Both were good pilots though and could fly their dad's PA-14.

Dan met the 12:30 flight. He could see Beth walking into the terminal carrying his large black athletic bag. He met her just inside the door and took her in his arms. He knew she hated the mystery. He thought long and hard how to tell her he was going after Bergstrom. He held onto her and kissed her.

"Please Dan, Aren't you going to tell me what's going on?"

"Soon, honey. How about some lunch, maybe at the International Inn? There's a good restaurant there?"

They didn't talk during the walk to the parking garage. Once inside the car though, Dan took her in his arms again and whispered, "I love you, my dear, sweet Beth."

She melted into his strong arms. "I love you. I always miss you."

It was only a 5 minute drive to the motel. Dan ordered lunch sent to the room. He thought he could tell her over a good lunch. He began with Gwen finding strange wiring inside the pig and of being caught, and threatened by a phony TMC technician. He told of meeting Roger and Sam.

"Why are you hesitating, Dan?" Beth looked at him as he stood at the window. "Is there something you'd rather not tell me?"

Beth, I have never lied to you. I have considered you my best friend. I guess this is the hardest part. I know what your fear has done to you over the years and I don't want to aggravate that." He came back to the tiny table holding their half eaten scattered lunch. He took her hand. "When I say this to you, I don't want you to coax me out of going."

"Now you're really scaring me."

"I am flying to Phoenix tonight to meet with John Sutter and some other federal officers to arrest Bergstrom for International Terrorism. I have no idea when I'll be back. If all goes well it should end in a few hours." He tried to sound as casual as possible.

"Bergstrom? The name sounds familiar—No! Dan, not the man who shot...I don't want to sound like the hysterical wife, but I can't help it. The last time you were nearly killed. I don't want to be a widow. Why is it necessary for them to send you to Arizona? Doesn't the government have enough agents to arrest him?"

He pulled her close. "Hey, hey now. I'm not going out there to get hurt. I just have a job to do, and I need you. It's just unfinished business, honey. If it will make you feel any better, I'll get you a ticket and take you with me. Call your boss and take some time off. Let's get this done and behind us once and for all."

"I can't do that, Dan!"

"Why not? Come with me. When this is done, I'll take a couple of extra days and we'll visit your folks in California."

Arizona would be unbearably hot this time of year, but she would be close to Dan.

"You'll have to buy me some new clothes," she said as she picked up the telephone and began to dial her office.

"Just like a woman to bargain for new clothes." Dan sat back on the sofa and put his hands behind his head.

How many years had it been since they made love in the afternoon. It seemed years. Always, daily problems and pursuits occupied the afternoons. It was different now. It seemed natural to hold each other and press into each other's warmth. They were as much in love today as when they were married and their passions ran as deep, serene, and controlled.

Later, while Beth was in the shower, Dan called for a pot of coffee sent to the room. "Wouldn't it be great if life could always be this uncomplicated?" He whispered as he joined Beth.

"Hmmm. Coffee's good isn't it?" He grinned and winked at his wife.

"I think Roger has eyes for Gwen. He hasn't said anything, but I saw the look in his eyes."

"Roger has avoided serious commitment for a long time. It'll take someone very special to rope him," Beth commented, as she snuggled into Dan.

"He could do a lot worse. She's pretty, educated, and has a good job. She'll probably be the next pump station supervisor. She's a really neat person; you'll like her. After this thing is over, maybe we can have the two of them down for a weekend."

"Oh. You old cupid, you." and she playfully slapped is leg.

His voice turned serious: "I hope they don't have any problems this afternoon. They have a dangerous assignment."

"What do you mean?"

"Now honey. They're headed to Valdez to arrest the people involved in a plot to destroy the OCC and cause damage to the terminal facility. I don't want you to tell anyone this, but the reason for all the secrecy is that Gwen found a nuclear warhead inside the ultrasonic pig. It wasn't armed, and we hope to arrest the people involved before they can arm it." Dan could see the panic building in her eyes again.

"Do you mean, atomic, atomic bomb? What kind of people are they? Oh Dan, if these people can afford to build something like that, they are super wealthy and have no conscience." She knew her pleading would do no good. Dan had always thought he was John Wayne, and he was in the right. But to Beth, being right didn't seem to be enough to endanger his life.

"I owe Bergstrom for what he did during the California raid. It's my chance to make things right for good men who were killed and wounded there. I have an obligation to little Steve. I owe Bergstrom for nearly getting me killed and putting me in a position where I had to draw down on a friend."

"You've been a cop for a long time, Dan. You know, even better than I, that revenge is a motivator that'll get you hurt or killed."

"I know, and you're right. I promise to be careful."

They finished their coffee and lay back on the bed. They'll have a long night of flying ahead. The Alaska Airlines flight to Seattle with a 2 1/2 hour layover, then on to Phoenix.

"John Sutter will be at the airport to meet us. It'll be good to see him again." Dan remembered his four fishing trips in Alaska. John loved Alaska. He liked flying to remote rivers and catching Grayling. Dan laughed when he thought about John attacking the fish with the same commando style he used for criminals. John had stayed on with the DEA and remained in Phoenix because his wife was a local girl and wanted to keep it that way.

They had a boy and a girl. The boy, Steve, was all-state middle weight wrestling champ. The girl was Goldwater High School cheerleader captain. She was also a straight "A" student. As a freshman, she had seen some bad times because of a newspaper article showing a picture of her father arresting some drug dealers. Her fellow students began to call her "Narc" and tormented her. With some encouragement from her father, she was able to turn it around and start an antidrug movement in the high school. She received a commendation from the Governor and was recognized by the Arizona Teachers Association for her efforts.

It was just after 1100 hours when Sam, Roger, and Gwen stopped at his workshop on Elmendorf AFB. Sam had called ahead and the canvas satchel full of tools was ready for them when they arrived. "Gwen, we have a couple of minutes, would you like to look around the shop?"

"I'd love it," she responded. "Are you sure we have time?"

"We only have time for the nickel tour, but we can have a cup of coffee and look around, if you're interested."

Roger was not interested in tours. He'd leave that to the two scientists. He was a cop and had other things on his mind. He took an address book from his wallet and walked to the phone. He called the Alaska State Trooper office in Glennallen. He asked to speak with the Sergeant, Greg Milner.

"Hello, Greg. This is Roger Dorfmann. I need you and two of your troopers to meet me at the Valdez airport about 1330. It's important, and secret, Greg." Roger could have ordered him to be there under jurisdiction of the U.S. Government, but he knew it would be more acceptable to the young sergeant if he asked. Roger had been friends with Greg's parents for many years and had known Greg since he was in Junior High School.

"What have you got, Roger? Will we need CIRT (Crisis Intervention Response Team) equipment?"

"No, I hope it's just a simple arrest. There should be six suspects, and they shouldn't be armed. But you know how these things go; better wear your vest. I'll give you a better briefing when we get there. Thanks Greg." Roger hung up the receiver.

The telephone rang almost immediately after Roger hung it up. Airman First Class Anthony Souza answered the ring.

"Electronics Shop, Airman Souza speaking. How may I help you?"

After a short pause, he responded again, "I'll tell him, Sir." He hung up the phone and turned to Sam, "Sir, that was operations; your helicopter's about 10 minutes out."

"Thanks, Tony." Sam looked around the shop. "I guess we have all we need. Let's go." At the door he turned and spoke to the airman. "Tony. You drive my car back to the shop, please."

The red Bolkow helicopter was just landing as they entered the building. Sam checked in with the duty officer. Seeing his companions, he motioned, "Roger, Gwen, over here." The three walked to the door leading to the ramp and the waiting helicopter. "It will take an hour and a half to reach Valdez." The pilot of the red Security helicopter asked for and was given clearance to depart from the terminal ramp.

"God. Please, keep us all safe today," Roger uttered quietly as the helicopter began to rise from the concrete flight line ramp.

Chapter 10

Valdez airport is located in a mountain valley, surrounded on three sides by breathtaking snowcapped mountains. The view from the helicopter was spectacular. Sam counted nine moose grazing along the stream banks and in willow patches just west of the airport. Sun was shining on the glaciers and gleaming off many glacier-fed streams. Eagles were soaring in the summer thermals. "How can anything so beautiful be such a menace to aircraft?" Sam thought, as the helicopter maneuvered into the wind for landing. Three troopers were standing near a Cessna 185 parked at the terminal.

The three removed their headsets and stepped out of the craft and walked to meet the three troopers. The helicopter pilot began his cool down. "Standby here and keep your radio tuned to the Trans Alaska Pipeline Service Company security frequency, just in case we need you." Roger instructed.

Captain of the Valdez district security for TAPS, Mike Deitz stepped from the TAPS tourist office.

"I have a conference room set up in here," he said.

As they entered the conference room, Roger asked Deitz, "How much time do we have?"

"The truck with the pig box and the other equipment arrived this morning. There were two technicians in the truck. The chief tech and the rest are due to arrive by helicopter at 1530 hours. That gives us about an hour and a half. The pig is due to arrive in the pig trap at about 1800 hours."

"Will the helicopter with the techs land at the Pipeline Terminal or here at the airport?" Roger asked.

"They'll land at the Pipeline Terminal helicopter pad."

Sam asked, "Do you have a map of the Terminal? We'll need to know the roads and the locations of all buildings and facilities."

Deitz reached behind his chair and offered a large roll of maps and drawings. He took the large rubber band from the roll and flattened the papers on the conference table. An ash tray was placed on two of the corners and a book on a third to keep the maps from coiling up again.

Sam looked from the table to an aerial photo hanging on the wall. Both gave a good view of the terminal layout. There are three levels. The first was the water and loading berths. The second level was the pipeline entry level. There were ballast holding tanks and metering buildings on that level as well as the OCC, Operations Control Center. On the third and highest level were 18 crude oil holding tanks and the power plant.

Sam studied the blueprints and drawings now covering the table. He thumbed through the sheets. He folded the others back carefully and began to study the detail on the sheets before him.

Gwen too was studying the schematic drawings of the Terminal Facility. She spoke to Sam as she pointed to the East Manifold and Monitoring building.

"This is where the pig trap is located. The truck with support equipment for the pig will be parked here. But look at this," she was pointing to the buildings on the map marked "Operations Control Center."

"What is it?" Roger asked. The men studied the map on the wall.

Sam caught on first.

"This is one very sharp lady, Roger. She's noticed where the OCC is in relation to the pig trap. You have to understand the kind of weapon we are dealing with,"

"What do you mean?" Roger asked.

"Given the size of the weapon we're dealing with, there are only a few possibilities. First of all there are only three types of devices for this use. The first is the old Plutonium fission bomb, like the one used on Japan in World War II. This type is very dirty and cause radioactive fallout and residual radiation, harmful to living things.

"The second type is the Neutron device which doesn't destroy property, only living things. It can destroy an army and leave all the equipment still intact. It's designed to eliminate personnel with high gamma radiation, though that doesn't seem to be intended here.

"The third, and the one I think this is, is a Hydrogen device, designed for battlefield use. It has great destructive capability with a minimum of residual radiation and fallout. This is the one we are dealing with because it was used in missile warheads, roughly the size of the nose of the pig. We used them in the Phoenix, Hawk, and Nike missile. The Soviets copied technology from us. They paid a great deal of money to get our designs and used the drawings down to the last bolt. That's how we know so much about these types of Soviet warheads, They're our designs." Sam paused.

Roger was still puzzled. "So you think this is a hydrogen warhead, but I still don't understand what it has to do with the maps. Wouldn't it destroy the whole Terminal Facility?"

Gwen spoke now.

"Correct me if I'm wrong, Sam. A device of this size has a quarter of a mile destruction zone. The OCC office is about a half mile from the pig trap. There are also three large ballast water holding tanks between the pig trap and the OCC buildings. These tanks are large enough to cause a "shadow effect." That means that the OCC buildings would be somewhat protected from the destructive blast of the warhead. There would be a great deal of damage but the target, or at least we think it's the target, would not sustain a great deal of damage."

Sam spoke again.

"What all this means, in terms of logistics, is that the pig, or at least the device inside it, must be moved from the East Manifold and Metering Building to somewhere near the OCC building. In a way, that's good news. It means the arming and detonating switch is not on a Mercury Triggering Device which would activate the detonator if the triggering device is moved or tilted or even shaken."

Roger tapped his finger on the table and slipped into deep thought. "Okay then, let's get a priority list established. As I see it, our first concern is to arrest the two technicians who drove the truck with the support equipment and are now on station. Second we have to find the arming device. Third we must await the arrival of our technicians who are coming by helicopter. We'll arrest them the instant they hit the ground. We have to remove the pig from the pipeline and secure it until a disposal team can remove the warhead. All this is going to spread us pretty thin."

"Captain, can you get us a van to transport suspects?" Greg asked.

"Of course. I also have several good men to guard the pig once it's out of the pipeline," Deitz replied.

"Is there an office we can use for a command headquarters?" Roger asked Deitz.

"I've set up a communications and telephone center at Operations Control Center. The Terminal Supervisor has set aside the conference room and will give us anything we need,"

"Sounds like you're way ahead of us."

"Need to be. You guys are pretty quick."

"Where is the truck and the two Japanese technicians now?" Roger smiled.

"I don't know for sure. I'll have one of my officers find them and make sure they're at the pig trap with the truck when we arrive. I'll make that call now," Deitz reached for a telephone.

"Is everyone clear on what they're supposed to do? We can't allow these guys to have any communication until we have all of them in custody. We don't want any of them slipping away, and we don't want them dropping into any contingency plan." Roger looked around the table, "Does anyone have any questions or anything to add?"

Roger looked at the notes he had made; then he announced, "Okay, it's time to get going. Be careful, I don't want anyone hurt. Good luck."

Deitz, Dorfmann, and Milner were in the TAPS crew cab pickup. The other two troopers, Sam, and Gwen, walked over to the other side of the parking lot to a red GMC Suburban. Sam opened the rear door and tossed in the canvas bag of tools, electrical testers, and Geiger counter. He then walked around the truck and opened the driver's door. He would drive, but not knowing the area, he would follow Deitz. It was a 10 minute drive from the office at the airport to the Security Gate of the Trans Alaska Pipeline Company, Valdez Marine Terminal Facility. There was little conversation during the trip. Each participant was reviewing his roll in the upcoming operation and each recognized an adrenaline rush.

The two vehicles stopped at the main gate canopy. The two officers on duty came to the observation window. Captain Deitz left the truck and went into the gatehouse. He gave the officers a list six people accompanying him. While officer Reardon wrote names in the logbook and listed visitor badge numbers, Deitz called the OCC conference room and ordered the six standby officers to report to the East Manifold and Metering Building. Deitz walked to the suburban. He gave the driver and Sam three visitor badges. He then returned to his own truck and handed out the badges.

"The troopers in uniform wouldn't have any trouble, but you in civilian clothing will be stopped and asked for ID. These visitor passes will eliminate that. Officers are on the way to meet us. They can secure the building and guard the pig after the arrests." Deitz started the truck and began the half mile drive to the East Manifold Building where the pig trap is located.

It was only a few hundred yards to the first junction where one road led to the terminal area where the crude filled oil pipes dispersed its black gold. The second road turned right and led to Tanker Berth

Numbers One and Three Tanker. The giant tanker, Exxon Alaska, was tied to Berth Number One. A floating boom was deployed around the tanker to assure trapping any contaminates which could accidentally fall into the water during loading. A red, rotating beacon atop the loading Berth signaled crude oil was being loaded on the huge tanker.

The two vehicles turned left for a quarter mile—then right. The first turn on the right was the large East Manifold and Metering Building. The red flatbed truck with the pig box and other assorted equipment was parked next to the west side of the building. No one was visible.

"When I called from the gatehouse, the officers told me the two technicians were here. Gwen, you have a TAPS employee badge. Go inside and get them out here on some pretext, okay?" The Captain asked.

"I can say I need something from the truck." Gwen said nervously.

Just then another red crew cab pickup pulled into the lot. There were six officers dressed in blue and gray uniforms and blue hard hats inside. Captain Deitz walked to the truck.

"Two of you move these other vehicles out of sight. The rest of you stay out of sight behind the building until we need you. Give me one of your portable radios, don't use the TAPS frequency, use the security frequency, channel five." Deitz gave short concise orders.

He saw Gwen enter the pig receiving station as he walked to where Roger was standing. The vehicles were moving out of sight. The uniformed officers were out of sight. Roger planted himself flat against the wall of the building behind the door the two Japanese technicians would exit. Taking a last look around, Deitz said, "I think we're ready."

Roger motioned for everyone to be still. It seemed like a very long wait. With the noises of the terminal equipment operating and the insulation of the building, it was impossible to hear what was happening inside the building. Suddenly the door began to open and Roger could hear someone speaking Japanese. As the two foreigners stepped through the door, Gwen pulled the door closed and slid the deadbolt into place leaving her inside and the two suspects outside with the officers. She watched the action outside from a window. The two slightly built men were speaking in Japanese to each other and did not see the officers until Roger, holding his badge in view, said, "Put your hands up. You are under arrest. I am a Federal Officer. You are under arrest. Do you understand?"

"We understand English, but why are we under arrest?"

The three uniformed troopers were covering the situation with handguns drawn. Sergeant Milner spoke to his officers,

"Cuff these two and search them."

The one who had spoken before and appeared to be the senior technician of the two, turned to face Roger.

"Tell us why we are arrested. We have done nothing wrong. We are only visitors in your country. Ouch. Loosen cuffs please."

"Put their personal effects in these bags." Roger directed.

"The charges will be read to you in detail later. For now we are arresting you for terrorist acts against a company incorporated in the United States of America," Roger explained.

Gwen unlocked and opened the door.

"Can I speak with you a minute, Roger?"

The two stepped away from the others.

"If you can, get the keys to the equipment boxes on the truck." she said quietly. "Sam and I can get started looking for that arming device."

"Good idea," Roger said, and turned to speak to Sergeant Milner.

"Greg, I need any keys you took from these men."

Captain Deitz was holding the radio close to his ear. He dropped his arm and called to Roger, "Roger, the helicopter is 10 minutes out."

Roger nodded his acknowledgment.

"Captain."

Captain Deitz joined the FBI agent and the Trooper Sergeant.

"Captain, I want to put two of your men on guard here at the pig receiving station. I also want one of your men and one of Greg's troopers to take the two prisoners to the OCC and hold them until we can transport them to jail in Anchorage."

The Captain turned away and began to make assignments.

Roger, Deitz and Milner were in the same Security vehicle. Deitz looked at Roger and said, "I have an idea for getting the others."

"I'm open for suggestions; you know this place better than we do. What's your idea?" Roger asked.

"The helipad is across the terminal area from the pig receiving station. It's policy that Security check the helicopter passengers for proper identification; then someone from TAPS will pick them up and drive them to their assigned work area. Let's stay with the policy. We pick them up and drive to an area where the rest of the officers are waiting. That way, we can control the entire arrest and not endanger anyone. We can make the arrest just off the helicopter pad. We have to stop at OCC. I can have one of my men get a pair of TAPS coveralls from there."

"Sounds like a good plan to me. You'll have to show us where to meet the other truck. One more thing. We should get that helicopter out of here fast. We don't want to give them an escape route." Roger was uneasy and did not like being in unfamiliar territory.

The helicopter was approaching, and the officers could hear him asking OCC for a clearance to land. OCC obliged and the helicopter circled into the wind to make his landing. A uniformed Security Guard took the pickup as Deitz and his two passengers got out. Another officer pulled on blue coveralls with the TAPS logo over the left breast pocket. The two designated officers had been briefed and were climbing into their vehicles. The remaining four stood beside the road to wait. Waiting was always the hardest part.

The two officers parked on the edge of the helicopter landing pad and waited while the red aircraft settled onto its skids. Almost immediately, the side door slid open. Four men stepped from the open door. The last to exit turned and closed the door behind him. The officer in the blue coveralls stood with the truck between himself and the four suspects; making sure they could not see him, he waved to get the attention of the helicopter pilot. When the pilot spotted him, he motioned for the helicopter to take off. He unzipped the coveralls to show his uniform, the pilot got the message and lifted the helicopter into the wind and circled to a departure to the north.

The uniformed officer checked the identification badges of the arriving personnel to make sure they were authorized on the Terminal property, and their badges had the proper stamps showing they had been properly instructed in safety procedures. He wrote their names and badge numbers in a notebook and wished them a good day. He also made note, the only baggage they had with them was one black brief case. He returned to his pickup and drove off the helipad and back to the waiting officers. The four oriental men walked to the GMC Suburban and told the driver they would need a ride to the East Manifold and Metering Building.

The high banks of the helipad had prevented anyone there from seeing the group waiting beside the road just below the pad. The members of the group were speaking to each other in Japanese and had not been suspicious The driver stopped near a group of men and a security truck. The driver pulled the key from the ignition and stepped out of the vehicle. Roger, Greg, and one of the uniformed security officers were on the driver side. The Captain and the other two officers were at the door on the passenger side.

Roger presented his badge and ordered, "Come out of the truck with your hands up. Federal Agents. You're under arrest. I repeat, you're under arrest. Come out of the vehicle with your hands up. Do you understand?"

"Yes, we understand. What is this all about?" Mr. Yamazawa asked as he stepped to the ground from the truck.

Greg and his trooper held their weapons on the group while the uniformed security officers placed handcuffs on each of the suspects. Greg and his officer began to search the four.

"Mr. Yamazawa, I am Roger Dorfmann. I'm a Federal Agent with the FBI. You and your associates are under arrest for the act of terrorism. I'm not sure you understand, but I'd like to tell you if you're found guilty, you could be given the death penalty. What I am saying, Mr. Yamazawa is, you're in very deep trouble."

Roger stepped to where Sergeant Milner was helping his men. "Greg, let's finish searching these men and get them to the OCC conference room. If you have a tape recorder, I'd like to have you record the reading of their rights."

"Sure can. We're just finishing here. Has Yamazawa said anything?" Milner asked.

"No. I haven't asked him any questions yet, and I walked away before he could. I want these guys to understand their rights before I question them. These foreigners sometimes lose their ability to speak and understand English when they get to court. I have seen it many times, and I don't want to lose this one on a technicality."

"At least we stopped the destruction of the Valdez Terminal. If Sam and Gwen come up with that arming device, we'll have done our job here. How soon do you want to transport these people?" Greg felt good that the arrests were made without incident.

"I don't know the whole story yet, but you can be sure this is only the tip of the iceberg. We'll go over to see how Sam and Gwen are doing as soon as we get the rights read to these guys. After, we will let them stew for a while. We can go over and see how the search is doing. We'll have to arrange for transport in, maybe . . ., 3 hours should be enough." He checked his watch. "I don't think they'll talk without a lawyer, but we might get lucky." Roger, too, felt good about the arrest being without incident. His old cop instincts told him he couldn't relax just yet.

Once at the OCC building, the suspects were escorted inside. Greg gave instructions to one of his troopers and handed him a small

Panasonic Micro-Cassette recorder. The six offenders were seated at the conference table as the officer began to read the Miranda warning from a card. After reading the list of guaranteed rights to the suspects, each was asked to give his name and to answer whether he understood his rights if he had any questions, and, each was asked if he wanted a lawyer present during this initial questioning. All understood and no lawyer was requested.

Sergeant Milner spoke softly to Agent Dorfmann, "I can call Sergeant Schoen in Soldotna and see if he'd be available to transport this bunch in the Trooper's Piper Navajo. It seats nine plus the pilot and copilot."

"Make the call. It's 1835 now and we'll be ready to transport by 2100. In the daylight it should be an easy trip. Book them at the Cook Inlet Pretrial Facility in Anchorage."

As Greg disappeared into another office to call, Roger spoke to Captain Deitz.

"Tell your men I appreciate the outstanding job they did today. They performed like clock work and in a professional manner. If you'll give me a list of their names, I'll have my office draft a letter for each of their files."

"Thanks for the compliment. The men'll be pleased, " Deitz said.

"Greg and I are going to see how the search is going. Want to join us?"

"Yeah, sure" The captain walked to the window and looked out. The deep blue water of the bay was near calm and glinted in the sun. The bay, bordered with lush greenery, mirrored the jagged snow capped peaks. Across the bay, the city of Valdez was clustered against the mountains. After the Exxon Valdez incident, the city recovered and carried on. He felt good about being part of preventing another catastrophe and wondered what motivated a person to indulge in wanton destruction of such beauty.

Chapter 11

As the three senior officers approached the Pig Receiving Station, they saw two uniformed security guards standing at the door. The red flatbed truck was parked where it had been before, only the large pig box had been left. Contents of various boxes and containers were spread on the ground. Sam was searching the cab of the truck when Roger and the others arrived.

"Find anything?" Roger asked.

"Nothing." Sam shook his head in frustration. "I even looked to see if other tool boxes or parts could be assembled to make the device. Did the other technicians have anything possibly connected with all or part of the arming device?"

"No. The only thing they brought with them was a brief case with, what appears to be, legitimate papers inside," Roger reported. "Where is Gwen?"

"Inside," Sam said, pointing to the door, flanked by security guards. "The pig arrived about a half hour ago. We weren't finding anything here, so she went inside to help retrieve the pig from the trap."

"We'll be inside if you need us. Let me know right away if you find anything at all suspicious." Roger turned to go, but Sam grabbed his arm.

"Okay, but right now I'd have to say the arming device is missing. I'll go through all this stuff again to make sure. Give me a shout when they're ready to open the pig. I want to get in there with my test equipment as soon as I can. They may have installed the arming switch when the pig was out of the pipeline at Pump Station Ten. I think that's only a remote possibility, but an option nonetheless." Sam had not yet finished speaking when he returned to his task.

The three walked to the guarded door. They presented their identification to the guards and stepped inside. Mike Deitz lagged behind for a few minutes to confer with his guards. He had hand picked his men for this job and knew them well.

Waylon "Tex" Smith was a thin, sandy haired, young, ex-cop from Houston. He had left the Houston Police Department after he was investigated for shooting a 17 year old Hispanic boy. The boy had shot a liquor store owner during a robbery. Tex and his partner accidently came upon the robbery. They'd seen the young robber run away with a gun in his hand. Tex's partner got out of the patrol car and ordered the kid to drop his weapon. The kid turned, yelled "chinga tu, cop," and fired two shots. The first stuck the windshield of the patrol car while the second disintegrated the elbow of his partner's right arm. Tex stepped out of the car, using the door for protection; he shouted, "Freeze right there, drop the gun." The young robber turned and took aim. Tex fired, striking the youngster in the chest. He died before the paramedics arrived. The investigation proved it was a justified shooting, but Tex found it impossible to work the streets after that night. It had taken him a long time to deal with self incrimination over the death of the Mexican boy.

The other guard was a red head by the name of Sean Dillon. Deitz suspected Sean had received his early training while with the Irish Republican Army. A prankster and jokester, he was fun to have around. He had the best powers of observation Deitz had ever seen.

"Hi, Captain," Dillon said, "Looks like a good night for swatting Alaska 'skeeters!"

"Hello fellas," Deitz greeted. "I've set up a 4-hour schedule. I want this truck and the pig guarded within an inch of your lives. Information is tight, but rest assured this is a situation of grave importance."

"I don't like that word grave, Cap." chided Sean. "Except for Sam and Gwen, you must keep everyone, and I mean everyone, away from here once the pig is out of the pipe and cleaned. Do you understand?"

"Yes sir, we understand," Tex Smith said. "Tell our relief to wear warm coats. It's warm now, but it'll cool off."

Deitz smiled and slapped Sean on the back, "I'll pass that along. I'll try to get some coffee out here to you, too. Stay alert and be careful. I mean alert, Sean."

Inside, he found five technicians working with Roger and Gwen. Gwen was busy helping the regular crew of techs remove the pig from the pipeline. The end of the large pipe was open. The metal door usually bolted over the end of the pipe, had now been removed making the pig visible. It was resting on a carriage. The technicians were backing the pig out of the pipe. It would be some time before the object could be cleaned with a pressure washer, and the rear bulkhead removed thus allowing access to the electronic equipment inside.

"She's got this under control. Let's go back to the OCC and have a talk with our friends," Roger said as he turned to leave.

Back in the conference room at the Operations Control Center, they each poured a cup of coffee. Roger stared at Mr. Yamazawa, then, addressing Greg he said, "Let's take him into the other office. I think it's time we had a talk."

In the office, Mr. Yamazawa was placed in a comfortable office chair. Roger sat behind the desk. Deitz and Milner each sat intimidatingly on a corner of the desk looking down on him.

"Mr. Yamazawa, I am with the FBI. I have found that you are involved in a conspiracy against the Trans Alaska Pipeline. I am not asking for a confession; I already have enough evidence to get you the death penalty. There are, however, several questions. I need answers.

"I will not make any statement. I am a foreign national and demand that I be treated with respect," Yamazawa spat out.

Roger continued, unabashed, "You say you're a foreign national, for whom do you work?"

"I am Field Supervisor for TMC Electronics Limited of Japan."

"We've checked with TMC. The company said you had no business being here. It seems the names fit, but the faces are wrong. Any explanation?"

"I do not know who you talked with at my company, but I assure you they have made a terrible mistake. I am Field Supervisor for TMC Limited of Japan."

"Somewhere in Japan you or your associates switched the TMC pig for the one we have here. Where's the real one now?"

"We have detected radiation emitting from the forward bulkhead in the pig. We know there is a nuclear bomb inside. Where is the arming device?"

"You are mistaken. If you detected radiation, it came from the ultrasonic transducers. There's a residual magnetic influence that would trigger a reading similar to nuclear radiation." Yamazawa seemed confident in his explanation.

"Who do you work for?" Roger asked again.

"I am Field Supervisor for TMC Electronics Limited of Japan," came the calm reply.

"Take him back with the others." Roger was becoming irritated.

"Sergeant Schoen will be here with the airplane to transport these people in about a half hour. Do you want to question them any more before we transport?" Sergeant Milner asked after Yamazawa had been taken from the room.

"No. I don't think we're going to get anything from him. I can't figure how this Yamazawa can be so confident. He knows we have him cold. Can it be he has that much confidence in the power of those who employ him?" Rogers frustration level climbed again.

The beige color Piper Navajo, N6SF, lovingly called Six Sugar Fox, was parked in front of the terminal building. The two TAPS vehicles drove through the cargo gate and onto the flight ramp. Alaska State Trooper Sergeant Arlon Schoen was waiting beside the aircraft. Arlon was not only one of the finest pilots in the state, but he was, also, one of the best cops around. He was a rare individual who could act instinctively and always make the right decision. The ladies thought he was just tall, dark, and handsome.

Roger said hello to Schoen, then turned to Greg. "Good luck kid. When you get these guys to Cook Inlet Pretrial, tell the Corrections people to keep track of who they call, especially overseas calls."

Mike Deitz and Roger Dorfmann stood on the flight ramp and watched as the Piper made its departure.

"I had TAPS make reservations for you and your two partners at the Westward Hotel, near the boat harbor." Deitz said.

"It's been a long day. I'm be ready to get something to eat, a hot shower and some sleep. I'll drive back and see what's going on at the Manifold Building. If Sam and Gwen haven't found anything, I'll have them call it a night. They must be beat, too."

It was a slow drive back to the Terminal Facility. After checking in with Security at the gate, the two trucks motored directly to the East Manifold Building. The guards were still outside the building. Inside, the pig had been cleaned and the rear bulkhead removed. The regular technicians had left the area and only Sam and Gwen remained.

Sam had his head inside the opening at the rear of the huge instrument. The pig was nestled in a form fitted cradle. The rear bulkhead plate was resting against the far wall.

"What is the cone protruding from the bulkhead cover over there?"

"It's a radio transmitter, Roger. It's used as a locator. As the pig travels down the pipeline, we keep track of where it is by locating the signal sent by that small black box. In fact, we call it the locator beacon," Gwen explained.

"Did you find anything inside?" Roger asked.

"Sure did," Sam said as he backed out of the cramped space. "Gwen was right. There's definitely a nuclear device in the nose. She was also right about the type. I've just run some electrical tests on the harness, and it all checks out. What we didn't find was the arming

"What we didn't find was the arming device that plugs into a Cannon Plug right there." He pointed to a large round electrical plug with 25 or 30 connecting pins.

"Is there anything else we can do tonight?" Roger asked.

"Can't think of anything," Sam replied. "We're going to need a lot of help finding the arming device if we can't figure out where it is. This is a big place, and it'll take a lot of people for a search."

"The Captain has assigned guards here all night and as long as the unit is secure, let's call it a day. We will all think clearer after a good night's sleep. The pressure is off now, and we can work on our schedule."

"Sounds good to me," Sam said. "I'm beat."

"It sounds good to me, too. I don't know about you three, but I'm hungry. I'm not used to going 16 hours between meals," Gwen said, trying to brighten the mood.

Captain Mike Deitz laughed. "You three go ahead. Roger knows where your rooms are. I have to check with the duty Sergeant at the OCC. I have a meal and room waiting for me here." He was writing in a small notebook. "This is the phone number for the supervisor at the OCC; he'll know how to get in touch with me at all hours. I'll meet you at the conference room at the OCC in the morning...how about 0900?" and he ripped off the sheet and handed it to Sam.

The hotel was quiet when they checked in. The clerk was courteous and they were given three rooms on the first floor with the same view of the entrance to the Valdez Small Boat Harbor.

Roger and Sam were each sipping a drink when Gwen arrived in the dining room. The waitress led her to their table near a window overlooking the harbor. It was rather quiet here. Most patrons had left the dining room, and a few tourists, still awake, had retired to the bar.

"Would you like a drink?" Roger noticed her well pressed clothes and smoothly brushed hair. One simple wave along the back told him she had worn a barrette most of the day. He was glad she had brushed it loose.

"Yes, thank you. Bring me a lite beer," she said to the waitress as she sat down at the table.

Halibut steak, vegetables and cheese cake assuaged their hunger. The three left work behind and became better acquainted; they had already become friends. "Where did you put all that food, little lady?"

"You carrying your own doggy bag for later?"

The two men teased Gwen about her appetizer, a loaf of bread, salad, halibut steak and potatoes, and two beers. She was laughing with them and sipping coffee.

"I wouldn't be so hungry if you guys would stop the mystery and intrigue for a minute and buy me lunch. Even a simple snack would do." She kept watching Roger from the corner of her eye. She was impressed, and strongly attracted to him.

They finished dinner and sauntered to their rooms. Roger had just turned the television on when someone knocked at the door. Gwen was standing in the hall, holding a tray with two cups of coffee.

"May I come in for a few minutes?"

"Certainly, a man would have to be a fool to turn down a cup of coffee delivered to his room," Roger said, smiling. "and by such a beautiful lady too."

"I didn't want to watch TV and I needed to relax a little before I can sleep. Do you mind talking for a while?"

"Not at all. In fact I'm a little keyed up myself. I'm glad you came." Roger would have been embarrassed to tell her just how glad he was. He had been trying to think of a way to become better acquainted.

They talked for almost 2 hours. They talked about her marriage to the nuclear scientist and about how Roger had met Dan Webster. They talked about her job and her future. They talked about his job and his future. Finally she looked at her watch; it was late.

"Are you really going to run in the morning?"

"Yes, I have to stay in shape. It will be a short run though, I don't have the right shoes to make my regular run."

Gwen stood and walked to the door, "Would you mind if I ran with you in the morning?"

"I'd like that. Say, 7 then?" he took her hand.

"I'll be at your door at 7," she said as she left.

Roger looked at his watch; it was a quarter past 12. Dan would be on the plane now, on his way to Phoenix. It had been a long and eventful day. He thought about Dan for a moment. Had it been a mistake to send Dan to Arizona? Would he be a cop or an avenger when he met Bergstrom again? He was too tired to reevaluate his judgment. He kicked his shoes off, lay back on the bed and was asleep almost instantly.

Roger didn't know how long the telephone had been ringing when he awakened. He knew he had a headache and he wanted to go back to sleep. The phone continued to ring. He looked at his watch, 2 AM. Who the hell would be calling him at this hour. He reached for the receiver, "Yeah, this is Dorfmann."

"Roger, this is Mike Deitz. You had better get Sam and Gwen and get over here as quickly as you can.

get over here as quickly as you can. We've found the arming device. But we also have one big problem. I need you here right away."

"Okay, Mike, we'll be right there," Roger said as he hung up the phone. He was not totally awake yet, and shook his head.

He stepped into the hall and knocked on the next door. Sam sleepily stared at him. "What is it, Roger."

"Deitz said they found the arming device, but there was some kind of a problem and he needs us right away. Better get dressed."

"Great. Okay, okay, be with you in a minute."

Roger knocked on Gwen's door. After what seemed an hour, "Yes, who is it?" came through the door.

"It's Roger. We've got to go back to the facility. They have found the arming device."

"Give me 2 minutes."

The three discussed all the possibilities on the drive back to the Marine Terminal.

"Gwen, are you shivering?" Roger asked.

"Must be the sudden change from a warm bed to the chilly night. How come these kind of things happen only in the middle of the night?"

"It couldn't be all that bad if we now have the black box we've been looking for." Continued Roger.

"Maybe Deitz just got overexuberant, not hysterical mind you, upon finding the last piece. In any event we'll soon find out. We're almost there." Roger slipped his coat over Gwen's grateful shoulders.

"Hmmm," she whispered.

Chapter 12

At this latitude and time of year, it never really gets dark. When weather is clear, there is a constant dusky glow at the horizon. The sky is never full of stars. In Valdez, where the Swiss Alps-like mountains ring the bay and the surrounding lowlands, it's darker. It was now 15 minutes before 3 in the morning. A driver could see the road well enough to drive without headlights, difficult though, to see a pedestrian or a moose on the roadway. Roger was driving faster than he liked but, the call was urgent.

Several vehicles with motors running, and headlight illuminating the door of the Pig Receiving Station, were in a half circle. People were milling about. He skidded to a stop and jumped from the truck.

"What the hell is happening?"

"Haven't the foggiest." Sam shook his head.

Captain Deitz was angrily striding toward them.

Roger met him near the front of the truck. "What is it, Mike? What's happening here?"

"Someone killed two of my men, Damn it!" Deitz paused, shifted from foot to foot, looked at the ground, raised his head and continued, "Someone came in here between 0110 and 0130. It looks like they shot Patton first, the other officer, Randy Winkleman, drew his weapon, but didn't have time to get off a shot. Both men were hit in the chest. Whoever did this is a pro. Troopers are investigating, but there isn't much here to go on." He pounded his fist on the hood of the truck. "These were good men. I've known them a long time."

Roger couldn't say anything, He put his hand on Sam's shoulder and stood quietly.

After a minute, Deitz gathered his wits and explained, "We have another problem, maybe a bigger problem. Whoever shot my men also had the arming device, installed it, loaded the pig on the truck, and parked it behind the OCC building. My patrol spotted the truck. He came here to check with the guards, he found them dead. Anyway, I looked inside the pig at what looks like a countdown clock. If it is, then there's only a little over 2 hours before that thing explodes."

"How could someone get in here, shoot two seasoned officers, and arm an A bomb?" Roger shouted in frustration! "That's exactly what we put those men here to prevent." his voice echoing off the buildings. In an instant, Roger took in the sea of faces watching him. The gravity of the moment was forming in his mind. He might be looking at the killer. He wasn't sure who he could trust.

Almost as quick as his anger flashed, Roger calmed and the cop inside him quickly took over. "Tough news about your men. Any suspects or idea of how and when it happened?" He asked.

"No. My patrol officer saw only two technicians taking readings at the Vapor Recovery buildings. No one else has been seen, outside, since midnight."

"Sorry about your officers, Mike," Sam said. "Let's get to the truck and see if the thing really is armed and if we can stop the countdown."

They found the red flatbed truck on the south side of the Operations Control Center parked near the building at the base of the communications tower. Sam picked up his canvas tool bag and jumped from the pickup as it came to a stop beside the flatbed. He wasted no time climbing to the truck bed and working his way to the rear of the pig. The pig box had been taken off the truck and the pig loaded on it. It was resting in its cradle. "Good thing they didn't put it into a shipping container." Sam whispered to himself. At least this way he had access to all sides of the pig. The rear bulkhead was open.

Sam climbed into the opening. He had only been inside about 3 minutes when he began to curse. "Damn it, Damn it all to Hell."

"What's the problem, Sam?"

Sam jumped from the rear of the truck. "We can't stop this thing. It's going to detonate in 2 hours and 22 minutes."

"Disconnect the arming device or detonator! Just unplug the black box. Sam, c'mon. There's got to be a way to...."

"Roger. Listen. Whoever made this thing knew what they were doing. The box itself is sealed tight, welded on all corners. There are two openings: the cannon plug and the clock. If electrical current is interrupted at either of those points, it will detonate immediately. The only option we have is to haul it some place where it won't do any harm."

"And just where would that be. Sam? C'mon, Gwen. Help me out here. Where's one of your smart ideas?" Roger asked, nervously.

Gwen took two or three steps backward and shook her head. I...I just can't think."

Roger reached into the red pickup and retrieved the portable communications radio. He spoke calmly into the radio, "Captain Deitz. Deitz. This is Roger. Meet us in the OCC office right away"

"Affirmative," crackled over the radio.

In the office, Sam explained the situation to the captain. "Is there anywhere we can take this thing and let it detonate? Keep in mind that it has a total devastation area of a quarter mile and a sure kill area of almost a mile. We need somewhere at least five miles from known inhabitants," Sam explained.

Deitz was thinking. "This valley is very small and crowded, especially this time of year. It's too heavy for the helicopters we have available here. What about taking it out to sea?"

"Do you have the boat available to do that?" Roger asked.

The Captain reached for a large binder on a bookshelf behind the desk. The binder was marked Trans Alaska Pipeline Service Company, Oil Spill Contingency Plan.

"Here it is," he said as he picked up the phone and began to dial. He waited for an answer; "Hello, this is Captain Deitz with TAPS Security. I need the vessel "Alaskan Star" at the onshore dock, like an hour ago." He paused and listened. "I know. I know. Okay, hurry."

"I have to make two more calls. I have to notify the Coast Guard to get everyone out of the area, and I'll get our helicopter out to cover the area and be sure everyone is out."

Gwen was looking at a photo charting the route tankers follow in and out of the fjord.

"How long would it take for your boat to get to, lets say, Bligh Reef?" she asked.

"A little under an hour. It's about 30 miles from the onshore dock to Bligh Reef. What you got in mind?" Deitz asked.

Her audience looked at the chart on the wall. "Bligh Reef is a hazard to tanker navigation. Look at this chart. See the tanker lanes?" She traced the black lines with a pencil. "They make a turn to the west to avoid Bligh Reef."

Sam studied the chart more closely. "That's where the Exxon Valdez went aground?"

"You got it," Gwen continued, "It is a very small reef, but it's in the tanker lane. If we took this device out to the reef and placed it on the apex. See, near the navigation light. I think we could take the top off the island and make a safer route. It's also an uninhabited area. No ones around there for miles. When the Coast Guard clears all boats

When the coast guard clears all boats
from the area, it should be safe to place the pig there." She turned from the photo and looked at the men. "There'll be hell to pay from the environmentalists and there'll surely be an investigation, but that will happen no matter where it detonates. Importantly there will be no loss of human life, minimal loss of wildlife." She waited for a reaction. "C'mon, guys, don't take all day."

Roger looked at Sam. "You're the expert here, Sam; will it work?"

"Given the amount of time we're dealing with, and for the potential for loss of life, I think it's a great plan. Wish I'd of thought of it, myself."

"Okay then," Deitz said. "If you'll take the truck with the device down to the loading dock, I'll notify Mr. Lords. Do you know how to get to the onshore dock?"

"You'll have to help us there." Roger said.

Deitz pointed to the north end of the building. "Take the road to the right, at the end of the OCC building. After you cross the pipes you'll see the loading Berths. Turn right again and follow the road to the dock. You'll see a small stationery loading crane. Park there and I'll have someone come down to run the crane."

"I can operate the machinery, Captain" Gwen offered.

The OCC operator was speaking on the radio, "Captain Deitz, the Alaskan Star is reporting 5 minutes out."

Sam looked at his watch, "One hour and forty-three minutes. It's going to be close."

"See you on the dock," Mike said as he picked up the telephone to call George Lords.

They began counting each minute; 4 minutes to start the truck and drive to the dock. Two minutes to jockey into position. The Alaskan Star was just tying up at the dock when the flatbed truck stopped under the small yellow crane mounted on the loading dock. The tide was high, almost at slack, making it easy to maneuver the boat. It also raised the elevation of the boat 11 feet, in relation to the crane.

Gwen stepped from the truck and into the small glass cab of the loading crane. She turned the switches that energized the electric motors for the hydraulic pumps. The pig weighed 6,600 pounds; she raised the arm of the small crane to decrease leverage the heavy, titanium cylinder placed on the boom.

The clevis was still in the lifting eye, from work done earlier. Sam climbed to the back of the truck and waited for Gwen to drop the cable with the large steel hook. Five more minutes. The hook lowered slowly toward him, and Sam guided the hook into the lifting eye. He gave Gwen a signal telling her to lift the cable and take the weight of the electronic pig.

Roger, meanwhile, was talking with the crew of the boat that looked like a small landing craft with a square bow. They were standing by and ready to receive the pig. They placed two large 12 inch by 12 inch timbers, each 8 feet long, across the front deck. Near the wheel house, at the rear of the craft, was a large steel davit, originally designed for loading crab pots, now used for moving freight around the deck. There was also a small hydraulic hoist, similar to the one being operated by Gwen, but way too small to lift an object as heavy as the pig.

"Heads up. Roger, watch it." Sam called a warning as Gwen began to swing the load out over the boat. As the shiny metal pig cleared the side of the dock, she began to lower it onto the large timber skids. A deck hand motioned to stop lowering and to move toward the center of the boat deck. Gwen complied. Then he closed his fist signaling her to stop the lateral movement. He then gave her a thumb down to lower the pig. She lowered it slowly until she could see slack in the cable. The deck hand drove large wedges under the sides of the device to prevent it from rolling off the skids. He then hooked a chain into a ring on the deck and tossed the loose end over the pig, walked around to the other side, and hooked that end. He pulled a chain binder from a rack on the side of the boat and tightened the chain, then disconnected the cable from the lifting eye and signaled Gwen to lift the hook. Once free of the boat, Gwen shut off the crane and climbed to the dock. Ten minutes. Roger was already descending the ladder to the deck of the boat. Sam followed with Gwen close behind.

The deck hand was untieing the lines holding the craft to the dock. The three new passengers made their way to the wheelhouse where, away for the noise, it was possible to talk in normal tones. The skipper was backing away from the dock.

"Where to?"

"Bligh Reef. Wide open all the way," Roger said. "We have 1 hour and 31 minutes to unload it on the reef and get at least 5 miles away and into a sheltered area. If we fail, we're dead. Any questions?"

"How much does this doomsday machine weigh?" skipper Davis Williams asked.

He was no stranger to exploding cargo. He had been a Lieutenant in charge of a river boat on the Mekong River in Viet Nam. He had hoped his years of dodging bullets, mortars, and bombs were behind him.

"Sixty-six-hundred-pounds," Gwen volunteered.

Williams keyed a button of the radio panel and spoke; the sound came from a loud speaker on the front of the wheelhouse.

"Donny, wheelhouse please."

The deck hand opened the door and entered the cabin. "Yes sir?"

"Tie 50 feet of cable to that thing on the skids. Get some chain ready. When we get to Bligh Reef, lower the front and I'll put you up to the light. Hook a chain on the light and fasten the cable to it. We're going to anchor that thing to the light and back out from under it. Double check all the ends; we don't have time for mistakes. Do you understand?"

"Gotcha," Donny said as he turned and left to attend his task.

"I'll go help him," Gwen said.

"I'll give a hand too," Sam said as he quickly followed Gwen from the wheelhouse.

The sea was calm allowing the Captain to get top speed from his craft. "We're getting 38 knots now, but we'll have to slow a lot once we reach the narrows where the water is much rougher. If we can get to the reef before the tide changes, we should have smooth water there. After we dump this thing, we'll cross the narrows and hide behind the point. That should give us a safe place."

Roger looked at his watch and began to tell the Captain the story.

Back at the Pig Receiving Station, Captain Deitz became frustrated with lack of information he was getting. The trooper was gathering information and evidence. No one had seen anything, or heard anything. Judging from the wounds, the two officers had been shot with a fairly powerful handgun—possibly a 9mm. The trooper had retrieved two spent cases and were now in the process of getting fingerprints from the forklift, door handles, and other areas. He was not sharing his findings.

Mike Deitz was known for his impatience. He had done all he could at the scene and was driving to the gate. George had given him full authority. He agreed, the option of placing the explosion on Bligh Reef was a good move. Once at the gatehouse, Deitz poured a cup of coffee and rubbed his eyes. He was exhausted; stress was the only thing keeping him going. He asked the officer standing near the check-in window, "Have you checked the computer and the security pass list for any strangers unaccounted for?"

"Yes sir, and George and I think we may have a possibility.

George is writing the report now." George Densow and Pat Morrison were the two officers on duty at the gate tonight.

Deitz was encouraged for the first time tonight. "Good."

"We had a brand new TAPS badge check in tonight. His name is Warren Bystock."

Had he known the shape of events in Valdez, Dan Webster would not be sleeping so soundly as he and Beth neared Seattle in the Alaska Airlines, Boeing jet.

Chapter 13

Morning light filled the sky as the Alaskan Star made its way through the narrows on a direct route to Bligh Reef. Scattered clouds, warm air, slack tide, and calm seas allowed the captain to maintain a good speed. Bligh Reef's blinking light was a temporary buoy held in place by an enormous chain cemented into a huge concrete and steel anchor.

The reef itself was a geological anomaly. The overlapping plates of the earth's surface are not stable in this area and move with surprising frequency. A land mass broke off and shifted out to sea, and when discovered was called Bligh Reef. The phenomenon was extremely apparent during the great earthquake of 1964.

Valdez was totally destroyed in 1964. The land sank: a tidal wave swept into the shallow harbor through a narrow neck and carried railroad cars and fishing boats into the hills. To the north, Anchorage shifted and twisted. Turnagain, along the shore scuttled off the mainland and rode it's slippery clay into Cook Inlet. Home owners watched in horror as the ground, which once belonged to them, fell into the sea along with their homes and belongings. The earth's plates were shifting and Alaska's face was changing.

Latouche Island, once the headquarters for a thriving mining and timber industry, began to sink on the north end. The south end of the island raised 50 feet in just under 7 minutes. The face of the earth is constantly changing, especially in this area of the globe. Here at the apex of the world's great land masses, the continental shift and the movement of the great Continental and Pacific Plates make geological rearrangement a daily occurrence.

There is debate about the formation of Bligh Reef. Did it push up from the bottom? Did it break off the surrounding mountains, during some great earthquake, and fall into the sea? Was it a mountain that has sunk into the bottom of the sea? Whatever its origin, it has been a natural stumbling block in the path of supertankers. The obstacle, like a hidden snare awaiting its prey, snatches at the careless. In 1989, the super tanker Exxon Valdez strayed from the designated highway in the sea. The inexperienced helmsman turned south too quickly and struck the reef thus creating the largest oil spill in United States history. And the reef remains—waiting.

The skipper reduced the power of the twin Detroit Diesel engines. Roger looked at his watch. Forty-four minutes remaining. As the small craft approached the lighted buoy, Donny the deckhand, began to lower the square front end of the boat. The boat was barely moving now, less than a hundred yards from the light. Donny lowered the front until the waves splashed over the ramp.

Sam stood near the bow, pulled his collar up around his ears and grasped a length of chain. Gwen stood near the front of the ultrasonic pig with the end of the cable in one hand and a large steel clevis and pin in the other. The Alaskan Star began to rock from side to side in the wave action against the reef. Donny took one end of the chain from Sam and moved out onto the ramp.

There is nothing in the open sea to give size reference. The buoy had seemed to be a small object as Roger viewed it from the wheelhouse. As they got closer to the light, it towered like a monster bobbing in the sea. It was plain this would be a dangerous task. The buoy rocked back and forth with its bell clanking and the Star seemed to rock in just the opposite direction. Donny stood on the jutting platform giving hand signals to the Captain as the boat inched closer.

No words were spoken as Captain Williams maneuvered the boat. Hand signals directed him. Donny's closing fist signaled "Stop." The giant buoy tilted and rolled close to the front of the boat. Roger thought it would hit the platform at any second and he felt helpless. It was up to them now. Thirty-nine minutes.

A thick steel ring on the front of the buoy had been used to tow the light into place. Donny deftly threaded the end of the chain through the steel eye. He pulled the chain through and snapped the hook around the chain, then pulled the slack from the chain. "This'll hold," he thought to himself.

Sam held the other end of the chain with a large steel ring affixed. He held the ring as Gwen assembled the clevis, and attached the cable. Donny watched, assuring himself the pin was securely in the clevis.

"Get back. Now. Behind the load. With the boat rolling like this, it's very dangerous." Donny yelled over the sound of the engines.

Sam and Gwen stepped back; Donny climbed onto a steel rack welded to the side of the cargo deck. He gave the okay hand signal to the wheelhouse. Everything was ready.

"Here we go!" the skipper said in a quiet voice.

Roger grasped the hand rail mounted below the windshield. The captain slowly pushed the throttles. The big diesel engines puffed black smoke and delivered maximum horsepower to the propellers mounted far back and close to the bottom. A good boat for working along the beaches and shoals.

The Alaskan Star picked up speed as it backed away from the light. When the cable became taut, the buoy swung slightly toward the boat, causing enough resistance to offset the weight of the ultrasonic pig. The boat backed out from under the titanium monster. The deck sloshed with water washing over the lowered ramp. The pig ground slowly toward the front of the ramp. The front of the boat pitched down from the 6,600-pound load. The nose of the pig was out over the water.

Suddenly there was a lurch and the boat stopped. Engines screamed and the propellers cavitated, splashing idly along the surface of the water. The craft listed slightly, and the load shifted to the right side of the loading ramp.

Donny jumped from his perch. "Hold it! Hold it. A big flange is hung up on one of the cleats on the loading ramp. The props are out of the water from the weight; we can't pull back any more," Donny yelled at Sam. "I need that snatch block from the front of the wheelhouse."

Sam found the pulley and Donny fastened it to the cleat on the left rail. "I'll run some cable out from the davit. Pull the cable out and run it through the snatch block. Then hook the end to the rear of the load. It'll swing and fall off. We don't want a tight hook to the load from the davit line."

As Donny reversed the davit winch, Sam pulled the cable and attached it. Donny knew the davit did not have the power to lift the heavy load, but it might have enough to swing it around. With the propellers out of the water, there would be little help from the boat.

Sam signaled and Donny began taking up slack on the davit line. He continued to add power to the line watching the mast for it's breaking point. Sam saw a steel pry bar on the deck near the engine compartment door. He retrieved the bar and began to pry on the rear of the pig. It moved. Then it began to roll. The cable went slack and the pig rolled crosswise on the ramp—then stopped. Icy water, 2 feet deep was rolling over the ramp and onto the cargo deck. The davit cable slacked, so Donny left the winch controls and found another pry bar and helped Sam. Gwen found some small blocks to place under the pry bars to increase leverage.

Each man drove his steel bar under the pig. Gwen knelt down in the cold, cold water and placed a block under Sam's bar. She completely submerged to reach the right spot. She repeated the process on Donny's side of the pig. She stood, shook sea water from her face and hair.

"Okay!" she yelled.

The two men pried down with all their weight. Gwen waded to Sam's bar and added her weight to his. The effort was enough. The pig began to roll slightly; then, the energy from the weight of the pig took over and the pig slipped over the end of the ramp. The other end of the boat dropped and the loading ramp surfaced. The action scooped up a wave, propelled it to the rear of the cargo deck and hit the wheelhouse. Then it rushed in the opposite direction to the opening in the front of the boat.

Donny was hanging on to the right side of the opening. He dropped the pry bar and clung precariously. Sam had lost his balance and fell back against the side of the boat. The rush of water knocked Gwen off her feet and she was washed back into the cargo deck and out again. She was bobbing around like a rag doll.

"Help!" She screamed.

Sam made a grab for her; he missed and quickly grabbed again. He grasped the steel hook on the end of the davit line and waded into the center of the opening and caught Gwen just as she was being carried through the opening. This time he caught hold of her jacket. He pulled her close and wrapped his legs around her until the water drained out of the deck and the two could stand again.

The two moved back while Donny raised the loading ramp. She coughed and brushed the wet hair from her face.

"Sam, you just saved my life."

"All in a day's work," Sam smiled.

The skipper backed the boat away from the reef.

Roger was amazed at the efficiency of the three people, on the deck below. When the pig hung up on the welded cleat of the loading ramp, they had improvised and jettisoned the load. He had watched, in helplessness, as Gwen was tossed around on the deck below, and realized this was a very dangerous enterprise.

Eighteen minutes.

The crew quarters and galley were under the wheelhouse. The three, wet and very cold, made their way to the galley. Donny gave each towels and disappeared into the crew quarters to change clothes.

Gwen was shaking violently. Sam poured hot coffee.

"There's dry clothes in there for you two. They probably won't fit too good, but it's the best I can do," Donny said as he picked up one of the hot cups.

"Go ahead, Gwen," Sam said. "I'll wait until you are done. Coffee's warming me up."

Gwen looked at Sam and then began to cry. He put his cup down, held her close, and rubbed her back. "It's okay, kid. It's okay"

"Oh, Sam, I could almost see my own death. I'm okay now. I'll be back in a minute."

From the intercom; "Roger says we have 9 minutes. We should just make it around the rocks, and, I hope, behind the point before it goes off. The Coast Guard has cleared the area. They've been broadcasting an emergency message on the marine band for an hour. Everyone should be clear. Donny I'm going to need you to drop the hook. I want to anchor from both ends."

"You got it, Skipper," Donny spoke into the intercom. "We'll be up in a couple of minutes."

Captain Williams had the throttles pushed hard against the firewall. He hated abusing boat engines but this was different. He swung behind the rocks and got as close as he dared. "Gotta hide." he told himself.

Gwen was composed and dressed in men's pants and a naval sweater with sleeves too long for her arms. The cuffs hung down passed her fingers and she grinned sheepishly at Sam.

"You feeling better?" he asked over the rim of his cup.

"Yeah. Thanks. Comin' topside?"

Roger smiled as Gwen stepped along side him. "You scared the hell out of me, lady."

"If we live through this, I'm going to make you put Band-Aids on all my scrapes." She joked.

"Best offer yet." and Roger took a second look at this lady.

The skipper spoke to Donny, "I don't want to beach the boat because I don't know how big a wave the explosion is going to generate. We'll anchor off that rocky beach ahead. Get ready to drop the anchor."

"You won't have time to get back here before detonation. Stay behind the shadow of the rail and don't look at the flash."

"Gotcha," Donny replied as he hurried to the deck below.

Sam came into the wheelhouse as the skipper slowed the boat and then reversed the propellers to stop the forward motion. Donny released the forward anchor and ran to the rear of the craft and dropped the other small one that required being thrown over manually. He tied off the rope; he took a few steps to a place he could crouch between the rail and the wheelhouse bulkhead and got as comfortable as he could.

"Better open the doors to keep concussion from breaking out the windows," Gwen offered.

The Captain looked at Gwen. "Good Idea. It's all safety glass but better to be safe." He shut down the engines and turned off all electrical power. "Open that tarp; we can put it over us for some protection." They had just settled against each other when the bright, ultra-white flash reflected off itself. The heat at the reef instantly vaporized the shallow water above it, turning it to a caldron of geysers of steam. The intensity turned the surface of the reef to molten lava.

Seven miles away, around the point, in the small vessel, the occupants huddled. When the flash occurred, a wave of electrical energy charged the air and shocked their bodies and raised their hair. Two waves of energy like two puffs of air, touched them. The sound came last. A rumbling; quickly building to a roar, and then a crack. The sound filled their chests first then their ears. They couldn't get their hands close enough to their ears to help. Then there was silence. The sound was so intense it was beyond the range of human hearing. Sam later said it was like standing behind a jet engine, where sound waves were so extreme, there is no sound.

The sound came again, deadening the senses with its volume. Then total quiet. The gentle breeze became a gale, a shock wave. The opposite side of the rocky point from the boat was afire. Birds, squirrels, sea otters, seals, trees, every living thing was dead and burning. The wave generated by the nuclear blast was over 20 feet high, but once it escaped the narrow passage and moved into wider, more open, water, it lost its power and was reduced to a rolling 2 foot wave.

The familiar, mushroom shape cloud appeared over the hill, and the world returned to a dimension human senses could identify. The four people under the tarp began to move. Sam looked out from under the tarp. All seemed to be clear.

"Damn!" Roger exclaimed.

"You're right Roger. My ears sure hurt." Sam replied. "I'll get my testing meters and check the air quality."

He stepped out of the wheelhouse and descended the ladder to the deck level. The others began to survey damage. Two cracked wind-shields, but otherwise the little craft seemed to be intact.

Suddenly Sam called out, "You had better get down here, captain."

"Let's get him inside, on a bunk." The Captain ordered. Blood oozed from Donny's left ear as he lay inert.

They carried the young man inside. Gwen began to examine him. No broken bones or internal injuries. She found a flashlight and checked his pupils; they weren't reacting equally. "He probably has a concussion and a broken ear drum. He needs medical attention as soon as possible."

The Captain turned to Roger. "Grab those cable cutters near the door and cut the rear anchor line. I'll start the engines. I'll need you back here to run the windlass to the bow anchor."

"You start the engines, and I'll run the windlass," Gwen said as she stood up straight and stretched her aching muscles.

Sam remained with Donny. Roger used the sharp cutters to cut through the 5/8 inch nylon rope. He saw a small, bright red, rubber buoy hanging from the rail. He tied a loop in the loose end of the rope and attached the spring clip on the buoy to the loop before tossing the end from the boat. The skipper could pick up his anchor and rope later.

The skipper turned on the electrical power and turned the starter switch on the left engine. It caught and ran. He did the same with the right, and it too seemed to run perfectly. He switched on the radios. As each came to life, they were filled with static. He tried to call to Gwen through the wheelhouse speaker. That wasn't working either. He poked his head out and shouted to her,

"Take it up."

She began to wind the rope on the windlass. It wound up a few turns then stopped; the anchor was hung on the rocky bottom. The Skipper engaged the power to move the boat ahead. When the direction of pull on the anchor was reversed, the hinged steel anchor released its grip on the rocks below. Gwen wound the anchor up from the bottom, and the boat began to move from the protection of the rocky shore.

Roger went to the bridge and Gwen returned to the injured man. Roger looked out the window wondering what he would see when the Alaskan Star moved into the channel. As the boat moved past the rocks at the end of the point, he could see nothing where the lighted buoy had been. A huge gray cloud drifted over the spot; upward and dissipating as the wind pushed it out to sea. They would be bucking an outgoing tide as they motored back to the Marine Terminal. It would be a slower and less anxious trip. The radios were out of commission which made it impossible to report their survival. It would also be impossible to get an ambulance to the dock to meet them.

They had been running toward shore for about 15 minutes when Roger spotted something in the sky. It was the red Bolkow helicopter. The pilot had seen them first and was on a direct line to intercept them. As he passed over, Roger saw the observer trying to call them on the radio. Roger stepped out of the Wheelhouse and was finally able to convey, by hand signal, that he wanted a portable radio. The observer tied one to a small nylon cord, and, as the aircraft hovered, lowered the radio to the boat. Roger retrieved the radio and turned it on.

"Good to see you, is everything all right at the Terminal?"

"Everything is fine. There was no damage in town or at the terminal. Captain Deitz was worried about you and sent us to check. Is everyone okay with you?"

"Almost everything" Roger replied. "We're going to need an ambulance at the dock. The deckhand is hurt, possibly a concussion and a broken eardrum. Everyone else is okay, but we'd better get checked out. Sam is monitoring our radiation levels. We should be there in about a half hour."

"We'll report all this for you and get an ambulance on the dock. If you stay out on the deck, you should be able to contact OCC. The radios went down there, but most are up and running now. The repeater is out so the Captain will have to talk with you from the main radio in the OCC. We'll deliver these messages and come back to escort you. Good luck, you saved a lot of lives, and one of them was mine; thank you."

It was still early in the morning, a little before 7 AM, when Captain Williams maneuvered the Alaskan Star into position at the onshore dock. He had an injured crew member, cracked windows, and all his radios were out. He ached, he was tired, he was hungry. He had a headache, and he didn't know who to be mad at. Still, in all, he considered it a successful night's work.

The ropes were secured to the dock and Medics climbed down the ladder to the deck of the boat. They quickly examined Donny and took vital signs. Three Medics loaded him onto a stretcher and carried him out onto the deck and up to the waiting ambulance.

Roger stopped the skipper on the open deck, "Captain Williams, I owe you a cup of coffee."

Chapter 14

TAPS' Marine Terminal Manager, Elwin Shaw, was in the Operations Control Center building when the group arrived. Mike Deitz met them in the conference room. "Bad night, huh?" Deitz asked. "Is everyone all right?"

Sam was closest; "Yeah, we're fine. A few bumps and bruises, but other than that, we're okay. Donny, was hurt though. He probably has a concussion and a broken ear drum. He was still unconscious when we got here. Captain Williams, here, did a great job for us. We're going to owe him for some damage to his boat though."

Elwin looked at the Captain of the Alaskan Star; "Good job. Thanks for responding so quickly." They clasped hands. "Sorry to hear about your deckhand. I'm sure you want to go to the hospital and check on him."

"Yes, I'd like to see Donny. Can someone give me a ride into town?"

"Take my truck." Deitz interjected. "It's the first one at the bottom of the stairs, out that door. Leave it in the Westward Hotel parking lot. I'll pick it up there. When you get rested, I'll need a written report on your participation tonight. Thanks again."

Everyone was tired and happy to take a seat at the conference table. Shaw stood and spoke in a sincere but very weak voice. "Before we get on with the mandatory agenda, I want to take this opportunity to personally thank each of you. You not only saved this facility but the lives of the people working here. You are heroes. There is no reward great enough to compensate you for what you did tonight. You will, no doubt, be called to court, harassed, and second guessed for months to come. I can't change that, but I can, and will, stand by you as long as you want my support. That also goes for the Company; TAPS will support you 100%. For myself and for the people whose lives were saved tonight, thank you and we ask God's blessings on you for being there."

"Kind words, Mr. Shaw." Roger said. "I'm sure I speak for us all when I say we don't feel like heroes. We did what had to be done. Now we must get on with finding the people responsible for this act of treachery. And we can do a good job with your support. Thank you."

Sam brought the discussion back to business. “There are some things you can do, Mr. Shaw.”

“Just name it.”

“I tested the radiation out there and it was very low. It was also dissipating. My equipment isn’t adequate to accurately test the air and water. There is a ~~NOAA~~ (National Oceanographic and Atmospheric Administration) research vessel docked at Seward. They’ve been doing bottom surveys in Cook Inlet and Prince William Sound. They have equipment to do a damage survey. They can also see how much of the reef we’ve changed.”

“Is there anything else?” Shaw asked.

“Yes. Contact the U.S. Fish and Wildlife Service and have them check out the loss to wildlife. We are not going to be able to hide a nuclear event. The media is going to be here in force before long, and you’d better be prepared. It won’t matter to them that none of this was within your control. The number of lives saved won’t sell papers or shock people on the Nightly News. The emphasis will be on how TAPS Company damaged the environment. Get the jump on them; contact these agencies and start a damage assessment. It’ll be up to you to show the world you care about what happened.”

“Any word on the individual responsible for killing your men?” Roger asked Mike.

“One possibility.” Mike shook his head. “Only one new TAPS badge issued this week and he was here this evening, left the facility about the time we figure the men were killed. I have a short preliminary report for you.”

“Good. Fax a copy of the badge and picture to my office with my name on it. Tell them I want a rundown on this guy as soon as possible,” Roger said. “Tell my office to forward a copy of the information to Dan Webster in Arizona. They’ll know where he is. My secretary is Miss Dill; she’ll take care of all that. I think we’ve enjoyed all this we can stand for one day. If someone will give us a ride to the hotel, we can get some sleep. We’ll be ready to go again about 1300 hours.”

“I can drive you to town,” Deitz said. “I’ll have breakfast with you and pick up my truck.”

The drive to town seemed like a million miles. Everyone was tired, hungry, dirty, and emotionally spent. The adrenaline that sustained them throughout the night was now gone, leaving their bodies drained of will and strength.

Gwen was rubbing her sore shoulder. “I hope Donny’s all right.”

Roger turned around to look at her. "We'll check on him after we've rested" He paused. "Gwen, I'd like to have your company assign you to my office until we have this situation cleared up. We have the Japanese technicians, but we don't know, at this point, who else is involved. I don't think you should go back to your job until we get some answers. Does that sound all right to you?"

"I hadn't thought much about it. You're the expert. I'm too tired to think." Gwen hoped she could work with Roger for a while. She was beginning to like him more all the time.

Mike parked the Suburban next to his own pickup. "I'll leave this rig for you and I'll take my own. Come on, I'll buy breakfast."

"Don't you ever sleep?" Sam asked.

Deitz grinned, "Sure I do. In the winter."

John Sutter was waiting when Dan and Beth arrived in Phoenix. They caught up on the affairs of the Sutter family while he led them to the baggage carrousel and while waiting for their luggage. John looked good. He was slim and tan. He looked like man with his life under control.

While driving to the motel, John asked, "Have you heard the news this morning?"

"No. I haven't had a chance to see the news for over a week. The last I heard was someone had kidnaped the Saudi and Kuwaiti royal families. I've been too busy to read."

"On the news this morning," John filled them in, "There was a bulletin about a nuclear explosion near Valdez, Alaska. It was somewhere offshore. No one was hurt. But, there weren't many details."

"Damn!" Dan said in shock. "That's Roger and his bunch. Let's get to the office and call. I want to know if they're all right."

"Do you mean to tell me that you and Roger have been sitting on an atomic bomb? What are we dealing with here?"

Dan spent the rest of the drive explaining how he and Gwen had become involved and how they had contacted Roger. He explained DeGrosso's involvement. He explained they had gone to Valdez to arrest the technicians and to confiscate the device while he had come to Phoenix to pursue Nels Bergstrom.

"I have a brief case full of papers and information. We can discuss this in more detail when we get to your office," Dan commented.

"We can get you checked in at the motel and I'll call Sonja to come pick you up," John said to Beth. "She'll be anxious to see you."

"That will be nice, since you so seldom bring your wife to see us," Beth teased.

The Desert Sands Motor Lodge was on the west edge of town. It was away from the traffic but close to shopping centers. The room reserved for Dan and Beth was more like an apartment than a motel room. Dan and John carried the luggage to their suite. Beth wasn't accustomed to the Arizona heat so the air conditioning was welcomed. The shimmer of a swimming pool glittered into the living room through French doors, like lights from a dance hall rotating ball.

John picked up the telephone.

"Hi honey. I've got them all checked in. Dan and I are going to the office. When will you be meeting Beth? Just a minute, I'll let you talk to her." He turned and handed the telephone to Beth.

Dan retrieved his briefcase from the bedroom and returned to the living room. He opened it and checked to be sure the proper files were inside.

"I guess we can go." He said as he leaned over to kiss Beth.

"Please be careful," and she grabbed his collar and kissed him.

John's secretary stopped them as they entered the office. "Mr. Sutter, you have a lot of messages."

"Miss Edwards, this is Dan Webster. He'll be working out of my office for a few days. Give him the same considerations you give me, will you? Dan, this is Judith Edwards. She's a great secretary, but more like the boss," John said, laughing.

"Pleased to meet you Mr. Webster. The FBI just delivered an envelope for you. It's marked, urgent."

"Mr. Sutter, there are two men from the FBI waiting to see you."

"Okay Miss Edwards, show them into my office. I have been expecting them. If there's a call from Roger Dorfmann, put it through to my office immediately. Otherwise, hold all calls"

John had a rather large office, as federal offices go. A desk with a high back chair behind it dominated the room. Two straight back upholstered chairs sat at attention. Book shelves lined the walls. There was a small conference table at the left end of the room. Dan followed John to the conference table and seated himself.

Dan was opening his brief case when the door opened and the secretary entered followed by two men in slacks and sport coats. She had a large manila envelope in her hand which she delivered to Dan. "Will there be anything else, Mr. Sutter?"

"Not now, but some iced tea later would be nice. Thank you."

The two newcomers watched as the secretary left the room.

"I'm Dave Vrobec. This is Larry Felson, with the CIA, but temporarily assigned to DEA. We are here to coordinate our investigation."

"Sit down. I'm John Sutter and this is Dan Webster. The reason for coordinating through this office is that we've had an ongoing investigation of Nels Bergstrom. I think the first thing on the agenda should be to combine our information; then, with a plan, we can catch as many rats as possible and with luck, catch King Rat."

Dan had opened the manila envelope and was reading the information it contained. "Listen to this." He had everyone's attention. "First, let me give you some background. I'm with Pipeline Security Company. One of the technicians, on the north slope found, what she suspected was an atomic bomb inside a corrosion detection pig, a large bullet shaped machine that travels inside the pipe. She and I flew to Fairbanks to report it to Roger Dorfmann, with FBI, Anchorage. He enlisted the help of a nuclear expert and CIA man, Sam DeGrosso. The three of them followed the pig to Valdez and I came here." He continued, "According to this information, they were able to arrest the Japanese technicians handling the pig. At that time, they couldn't find the arming device. Night before last, someone killed two guards and installed an arming device. Sam couldn't disarm it, so they took it out to sea and dumped it on a reef."

He looked around, paused and then said, quietly, "Then, the damned thing exploded." He shook his head. "There were no casualties and no property damage except on the reef. That is being surveyed now. One crew member suffered a concussion but he'll be okay. I have a picture of the suspect in the shooting of the guards. Do you recognize this guy?" Dan asked as he passed the picture of the TAPS badge to the FBI man.

"You're saying all this has to do with the nuclear explosion we've heard about?" Larry asked.

"Yes," Dan answered. "Sam told us the CIA had information of a connection between Bergstrom and a Japanese tycoon named Yamamata. Sam thinks Yamamata is responsible for building the pig containing the bomb."

"This is incredible." Larry opened a file folder he had been carrying. "Gentlemen, what you are about to hear is a matter of national security and not to leave this room. I was authorized to offer this information only if it was initiated by one of you. Since Dan has opened the door, I'll give you what I have."

National security, my left hind foot, John Sutter thought to himself. When will the government learn that one agency hiding information from another only complicates our war on drugs, the war on crime, and the war on everything else.

Larry continued, "I'll leave a copy of this report here for your file, John; you can get flight numbers and dates from there. For now, I'd like to just hit the high spots. If you have any questions, when I finish, I'll be happy to answer them here. Don't call me and try to ask questions over the phone. I won't know what you're talking about."

"What do you have, Larry?" John asked, the irritation showing in his voice.

"When the Soviet Union began to break up," Larry began, "a Soviet general by the name of Lianid Kisishkin arranged a meeting with Bergstrom and Yamamata. We don't know exactly what took place, but we suspect they were attempting to turn the demise of the Soviet government into profit.

"We have information that Kisishkin has under his control an army and a considerable amount of military goods somewhere in southern Kazakhstan or Uzbekhstan Our information says, when he inventoried his nuclear weapons, one warhead came up missing. The Russian government, officially, says the missing warhead is just a bookkeeping error. We think it was smuggled out of their country. It now appears it went to Japan where one company, belonging to our friend Mr. Yamamata, built it into the Corrosion Detection Pig sent to Alaska.

"You've heard the news about the kidnapping of the Saudi and Kuwaiti royal families? Well, we believe General Kisishkin is responsible. He has the men and equipment and is in the geographical location to accomplish it. The President has the information I have given you. He is passing it to the U.N.. The United Nations is meeting today to discuss these kidnappings.

"The Japanese government is investigating Mr. Yamamata. We are cooperating with them in an effort to couple him to the kidnappings. This morning they told me we are trying to tie him to the terroristic acts on the pipeline in Alaska.

"What we don't have is a motive. Why would men as rich and influential as these, want to commit acts of simple terrorism? The answer could concern their oil holdings. In recent years, the price of oil has dropped dramatically. We think these three men have conspired to gain control of the world oil market. They have bought off the people in Venezuela and Mexico. We think they kidnaped the two royal families in an effort to influence the OPEC council. The nuclear

The nuclear device sent to the Alaska Pipeline may have been an effort to cripple Alaska oil production.

"Mr. Yamamata has huge holdings in the tanker industry. He builds supertankers and owns tanker companies transporting oil throughout the world. General Kisishkin has control of the Soviet Pipeline. He and his troops control the transport of virtually all the oil produced in the old Soviet Union countries. Our friend Nels Bergstrom has controlling interest in almost every small independent oil company in the United States. He's also a large shareholder in large oil companies. He made his money in the drug trade, but has put those dollars into legitimate business, mostly oil. He's one of the richest men in the world.

"Bergstrom is the key and the toughest to get. He is surrounded by politicians, lawyers, and a lot of friends. He knows how to use his money. His one big mistake was to accept an invitation from Kisishkin to meet him and Yamamata in Paris. If we can prove that Kisishkin and Yamamata are involved in kidnaping and international terrorism, I think we can link Bergstrom to them. We'll have to destroy his protection. If we can prove he has been involved in drug trade and other illegal activity, political figures in this country will desert him to protect themselves. When that happens, maybe, just maybe, we can get some of his associates to come forward and testify."

Dan had listened carefully and taken a lot of notes.

"All this sounds really good and you can try to convict him of immoral political conduct if you want, but I plan to get the fat scumbag for conspiracy to murder in the killing of the two PSA guards. I want this guy to get the death penalty." Maintaining control of his emotions was tougher than he thought.

"Easy, Dan; we'll get him," Sutter said, through clinched teeth.

Dave Vrobec spoke up, "John, I can get surveillance teams started at both Bergstrom's offices and his desert ranch. What do you say, we take some time to evaluate the information we have and meet again this afternoon to formulate a plan?"

"Good idea, Dave. Can you two be back here at 1500 hours?"

They agreed to return at 3 PM and were just leaving the office when Miss Edwards entered with a pitcher of iced tea and several glasses. She placed the tray on the conference table and asked, "Will there be anything else?"

"That will be all, Judy. Hold all my calls and see that Dan and I are not disturbed, thank you."

Chapter 15

Salt River, 35 miles east of Phoenix, on 25,000 acres was "The Home Place" of Nels Bergstrom. Downstream was Theodore Roosevelt Dam and just west, Tonto National Monument. Situated in high desert foothills, there was good surface water available for animal grazing. The main house, 11,000 square feet, more like a large resort than a home, stood on a small ridge overlooking Salt River Valley. Constructed of native rock and landscaped with native cactus and plants, it was a low single story ranch house. Bergstrom prided himself on authentic southwest decor furnishings; a large amount bought from people dealing in artifacts stolen from Indian burial grounds. The dignitaries, presidents, senators, congressmen, and business men, he entertained there were very impressed.

Bergstrom had constructed a 5,000 foot, lighted and paved, private airstrip. There were two nearby hangars. One housed his Cessna Citation II. The other protected his Bell Jet Longranger helicopter. The latter was used extensively to maintain ranch security, chores like herding sheep and cattle and patrolling fence lines. Bergstrom used it as personal transportation to and from the ranch. Although he had a large, 12 story, office building in downtown Phoenix, he preferred to manage his huge empire from the ranch. No one could blame him. Country around Apache Lake is what inspired the stories of Louis L'Amour.

At 7 AM, the story was on CNN News. Bergstrom was on the patio eating his breakfast. He'd expected the news, but was startled to hear the nuclear device exploded offshore and not at the Valdez Marine Terminal.

"Talbert, get out here," Bergstrom slammed his coffee cup into its saucers, spilling coffee on the linen tablecloth.

Russ Talbert was a small man, with accountant-type, round, gold rimmed glasses; and loyal to the core. He'd been Bergstrom's aide for over 15 years. Bergstrom yelled at him constantly, but both men knew it was Talbert's ability to maintain an orderly business schedule that made him valuable. Before Russ Talbert came into the Bergstrom enterprise, Nels' life was constant chaos.

"Yes sir?"

"Have you seen the news this morning? The news about Alaska?" Nels took a large bite of toast spread thick with Marmalade. He stared into the open space of the desert while he chewed noisily, paused a moment, then took a swallow of orange juice.

"No sir, I haven't."

"Damn it all to hell! They failed. The SOBs failed! The whole thing is up in smoke." He flung his chair and began pacing. "Yamamata's team failed. Even my back up failed." Then he began to think aloud. "They never destroyed the control center for the pipeline. A worldwide plan in operation and people don't do their job." He threw his napkin down. "Have you heard from Al Bates this morning?"

"No sir." Talbert let him have his tantrum

"He was my back up, Talbert. I want to know as soon as he calls. I want to know what went wrong. "We must press on with our plan although we didn't shut down the pipeline. We set off a nuclear device there and that may be intimidation enough to accomplish our goal. Get Kisishkin on the secure line."

"Right away sir," Talbert said as he returned to the house.

Talbert returned with a telephone attached to a large brief case, identical ones had been supplied to each of the three conspirators by Mr. Yamamata. Talbert placed the case on the table and opened it. He dialed the long overseas number and the access codes for the security scrambler. A device identical to this one was now ringing in Dushanbe, Tajikhstan, a military base never on the regular Soviet military inventory, and built and maintained with equipment and funds skimmed from the regular military budget. The soviet government had unknowingly established a private military force under the authority of General Lianid Kisishkin. Now, with the demise of the Soviet government, the General was using the private army for personal gain, to control the flow of oil from the Russian and OPEC sources.

Talbert handed the receiver to his boss. "The General is on, sir."

Bergstrom took the phone and waited.

"General. Nels Bergstrom. Have you heard the news this morning?"

"Yes. It is not good. You know what happened?" Kisishkin asked in broken English.

"Won't know 'til later this morning. I'll give you a report as soon as possible. Meanwhile, I think we should move ahead as planned. We haven't destroyed the ability of the pipeline, but we've set off a nuclear device close enough to the Marine Terminal to cause a panic in the government. We've demonstrated we have the capability to do great damage. We should move to step three of Operation Cinch Knot as scheduled. Your opinion, please"

The General was silent for a moment,

"You are right. Ve must go on as planned, quickly, not to lose advantage. Ve cannot sit on the OPEC officials and their families forever. Yah, step three' good. You, spoken with Yamamata?"

"No. I wanted your opinion first. I'll call him immediately. If he agrees, I'll notify you and we'll begin the next phase. I'll call you back."

Bergstrom handed the receiver to Talbert. "Get me Yamamata." He straightened the chair and buttered more toast. He always ate heavily when under great pressure.

Yamamata's aide answered the phone.

"Mr. Yamamata, please. Mr. Bergstrom calling," Talbert announced—then handed the phone to Bergstrom.

Yamamata, educated at UCLA, spoke perfect English. He was a brilliant man, ambitious and resourceful, but ruthless and greedy. He had financial holdings in electronics, manufacturing, construction, ship building, oil tanker transportation, and other companies. He had connections with Japanese politics as well as with mobsters in the Yakuza.

"Mr. Bergstrom, it is a pleasure to hear from you. I was expecting your call. You have heard that my men were arrested?"

"No. Will they talk? Will they jeopardize our plan?"

"Relax Mr. Bergstrom. My men will not talk. I have lawyers on the way to Anchorage from Los Angeles. They will confer and decide what to do with them. They have been instructed in what to say if they were caught. The important thing is that our mission is not yet finished. I see there was an explosion, but out at sea?" Yamamata inquired

"The reason for this call. I talked with the General, and we agree that we should go ahead as planned. If you agree with us, I will call my friends in Mexico and South America to initiate plan three. If American oil companies do not capitulate as planned, then we have an alternate plan to eliminate production from the Alaska north slope."

"I am in agreement," Yamamata said. "No plan is 100 percent perfect. We must step over our errors and take new advantages. I will notify each of my tanker companies to proceed with their loading schedule in all ports. They will load and sail for their destination but will anchor offshore when they arrive. They will be instructed to wait at anchor until further notification from me. Is there anything else you need from me at this time?"

"I don't think so. I'll get back to Kisishkin, and we will initiate our parts of the plan. I'll call if there are any changes. Good Bye." Bergstrom hung up the phone.

"Get the other phone." Nels instructed Talbert. "I want to talk to Edwardo Martinez. He'll be in Merida, Yucatan, and Donald Piersol in Caracas. They'll probably be sleeping but I don't care. Get them up."

Talbert returned with the other telephone and a red file folder. He found the directory in the file and dialed the number. "Mr. Martinez, please, Mr. Bergstrom calling."

The fat man took the phone, "Edwardo. I don't care if I did take you away from a very important lady. We have to talk!"

"Ah, Nels. Edwardo hissed sarcastically. "You sound, ah, very well today. The news is not too bad?"

"Everything is fine, Edwardo. Are you ready to launch Operation Cinch Knot from there?"

"Yes, I can begin the shutdown immediately. When do you want to start?"

"It's 8 AM here now; it must be 9 there. You have 7 hours. We'll have the plan in full effect by 3 this afternoon, our time. Satisfactory?"

"Yes. I will instruct my people to begin at once. Friends in the government will be contacted. We will proceed as planned, and I expect their cooperation."

Nels handed the phone to his aide. "Get me Piersol."

"Already done, sir."

"Hello, Donald. How are things in Caracas?"

"Fine, Nels. I have been watching CNN; problem in Alaska, huh?"

Nels wadded up his napkin. "Everything is under control. We are initiating the plan. Are you ready."

"I am ready. In fact I had a meeting this morning with the President and the oil company officials. They are ready. Say when."

"Mexico will be down by 3 PM, Arizona time, just under 7 hours, can you be down by that time?"

"Communication to one or two of the four sites will be slow, and there will be four sites that will have to be notified in person. We can have all but those four sites down by your deadline. Those four will take a few hours longer. But, they will all be down by 6 PM your time, I assure you. We will shut down all the north coast, Guyana, Brazil, Colombia, and Venezuela. Will that be satisfactory, does that meet your needs?" Piersol was Regional Director of Operations for Bergstrom Enterprises in South America.

"Sounds good, Donald. You have handled this well. Keep me posted. I don't want any surprises. Let's get started." Nels hung up the phone and waited as Talbert dialed the secure phone again.

"It's ringing, sir," Talbert said.

The General answered the phone personally. "Kisishkin here. Nels, Vhat did you learn."

"Everything's a go. There'll be total shutdown by this afternoon. Yamamata will keep loading tankers as long as possible. There will be no deliveries made after this time. What about you?"

"I vill give orders as soon as I am off the phone. I vill check again with you in the morning. If all is vell, I vill contact the OPEC principal and the oil companies to call them to meet in Brussels on Saturday. Ve should review plan and confirm ve have met all crises. If you feel confident about the plan in the morning, ve will proceed to part four. I look forward to seeing you in Brussels." Kisishkin was more than confident, he was cocky and arrogant.

"By morning," Bergstrom warned, "the world will be aware there is something wrong. The U.N. will still be hunting the two royal families. We have to keep the upper hand until after Saturday, a very long time. Make ready that airborne delivery to Alaska. If we are ignored in this country, we must be ready to strike. I have a lot of influence bought and paid for in Washington, but we need to be ready in case something goes wrong,"

"You are right my friend. I vill be ready. I vill talk mit you tomorrow," and he was gone.

Bergstrom went inside and was snacking on a bowl of fruit when Al Bates called. Bergstrom's hit man had just arrived in Phoenix. He had booked through several airports in Canada. He had changed airlines and his name twice during the trip.

"Hello Al. Good to hear from you. Nice to have you back in town. Take a cab to the office. I'll have the helicopter pick you up. We'll talk soon." Bergstrom was anxious to hear what had taken place in Alaska.

He was just finishing lunch when Bates arrived at the Apache Lake Ranch. He had spent the night memorizing faces of passengers on the several flights to be sure he was not followed from Anchorage.

Talbert showed Bates into the office. "Al! Good to see you; how about lunch?" Nels greeted him.

"I just want to give you my report and get some sleep." Al shook his head. "It was a long night."

"Talbert, bring Al some iced tea."

As soon as the door closed, Bergstrom turned to Bates. "What the hell happened up there, Al? I put almost seven million bucks in a bomb that wasn't delivered to the target. I can't afford those kind of mistakes."

"I don't know what happened. I used those credentials you gave me to get an identification badge from TAPS and got inside Pump Station Ten. Everything was okay there. There was no indication that anyone was aware of the plan. The technicians handled their job as instructed. Everything was perfect. So, I went to Valdez and waited. About the time the pig was scheduled to arrive at the Marine Terminal, there was a leak. The FBI was at the pig receiving station. They arrested the technicians that drove the truck. Then they waited and arrested the technicians when they came in on the helicopter."

"It's a good thing I hand carried the arming device," Bates continued. "The FBI searched everything on the truck and in the pig. They knew what they were looking for. They questioned the Japanese technicians, but I don't think they got anything from them.

"After they took the technicians away and everyone left, I went back to the pig receiving station. Two guards were on the door. I had to kill both to get inside. I loaded the pig on the truck and installed the arming device. Then I took it over to the OCC building and parked it. I figured if they found it and figured out what was inside, they would just try to disconnect the arming device and our objective would be met. Then I got the hell out of Dodge. I rented a private plane and flew it to Anchorage. I don't know how they knew the bomb was in the pig, and I don't know how they knew not to disconnect the arming device."

Bergstrom rang for Talbert who returned with a pitcher of iced tea and crystal glasses. "I don't know how they found out. Maybe we should've had more people involved with the pig. I thought it best to have as few as possible. We'll look into it later. Right now, we've done all we can. Get some rest and we'll discuss it again later. I believe we have demonstrated we are serious. If they don't take this as a warning and submit to our demands, we try the secondary plan. Show Mr. Bates to one of the guest rooms and get him whatever he needs."

Alone in his office, Bergstrom sipped the iced tea and thought about details. Everything seemed to be in place. He could find no flaw. He looked to the TV monitor which displayed the stock market report continually all day long. He noted the price of Texas crude was now $14.57 per barrel. On Monday, next week, after the weekend meetings in Brussels, the price of oil would be any price Bergstrom wished it to be. Monday it would be $50 per barrel, worldwide.

Chapter 16

Hours passed as John Sutter and Dan Webster studied reports and documents piled on the conference table. They worked through lunch and into the late afternoon. The intercom buzzed and John answered.

"Yes, Judy?"

"Mr. Vrobec and Mr. Felson are here to see you, sir."

"Show them in."

Dave Vrobec waited for the door to close behind him.

"I think we got lucky, Dan. You know that photo you gave me—the one from the TAPS ID badge?"

"Yes," Dan lifted a sheet of paper from the table, "This one?"

"That's the one. Our surveillance turned up something. A couple of hours ago a guy matching this description went to the Bergstrom Enterprises building. The company helicopter landed on the roof, and picked this guy up. Then it flew to the ranch. My man says he is Al Bates, a hit man for Bergstrom."

Larry clapped his hands.

"Oh man! If we could tie Bergstrom to Bates and place Bates at the scene of the killings in Valdez, we'd have enough to arrest them both. Call Roger in Anchorage and tell him about this guy, and see if there's any hard evidence Bates is the murderer. Dan said the troopers took fingerprints from a forklift. Roger can check them out."

Dan turned to Larry, "Do you think they'll make another try at disabling the pipeline?"

"A possibility for sure. If their plan is to demonstrate their power to destroy the pipeline, then the answer is no. They've made that point. But, if they really want the pipeline out of commission, then, yes, they'll try again."

"I know Bergstrom, Dan worried. "He always has a back up plan. His motivation has always been money and power. Let's assume you're right about him, the Russians, and the Japanese. What do all three have in common, besides their investments in oil?"

"All three are heavy into production and transportation."

"Right. Larry and I figure the plan is worldwide, and will cost millions of dollars to complete. That brings up the next question; if they invest a billion dollars and a year in planning, how'll they profit?"

"Good question, Dan, have you got any ideas?" Dave asked.

"Maybe. If I owned oil tankers and storage tanks all over the world, and I controlled the major pipelines of the world, and I filled my tankers and storage tanks with oil costing $15.00 a barrel and then shut down all my oil pipelines and tankers, what would happen?" Dan posed.

"I see what you're getting at. If they could hold, say, a billion barrels of oil, from getting to market, and the price went up to say, $50.00 a barrel, they'd realize an instant profit of $35 billion dollars. You may have just hit the jackpot. Let me run this scenario past my office. Good work Dan." Larry was impressed.

"Okay, you two work on that and I'll take Dan to see the ranch," Dave said. "Tomorrow is Wednesday and if Dan is right, by the first of the week the world economy is going to take a terrible blow."

The two men departed, and Larry said to Dan, "If we don't take our wives to dinner, we won't live until tomorrow. Let's call it a day. In the morning, I'll have one of the DEA pilots fly us out to the ranch for a look see."

It was 5 PM when the two men called it a day and left the office. They took a detour and circled the Bergstrom building down town. It was a bronzed glass and steel structure with immaculately manicured grounds. A large parking lot sat at the west side and a circle drive curved in front. Security was tight.

Along with Sonja and Beth, John gave Dan the guided tour of "El Rancho Sutter" before going inside. Sonja had cold beer waiting inside a spacious living room done in stucco and Indian artifacts.

John left to change clothes while the women gave Dan a running account of the afternoon of visiting and shopping.

The two couples caught up on the years of separation letters couldn't fill; stories of the kids; Webster boys were now flying and working at Lake Clark; Sutters were happy about the Governor's award to their daughter; the new house, and how Sonja's family loved John for not moving her away from them. John and Sonja Maria Costa-Ruiz met shortly after he moved to Phoenix. She worked in a jewelry store near his office and they met one day during lunch. She was second generation American. Her father worked for the highway department and struggled to earn a living for his wife and eight children. Sonja quit high school and went to work to help support the family. She studied nights and finished high school. Her dark complexion and black, shining eyes drew every man's attention, John was no exception. Their's was a proper and traditional courtship with a beautiful wedding, and John promised to never to take her far away from her family. He kept his promise. John spent a great deal of time with troubled kids from his children's school. John and Sonja liked their life. It was an evening of old friends watching the setting sun turn the sky a Navajo red and turning the blue sky to a black sea of twinkling stars. A soft breeze filled the night with the cooing doves and the gossip of crickets.

John stretched, "Okay ladies, we have an early start in the morning. I think we should pack it in. Back to the motel, a good night's sleep and I'll be there to pick you up bright and early." It's been a very pleasant evening.

Dan hated to leave Beth's warm soft body, but he eased himself out knowing later she would meet Sonja again. He was outside, looking at the cactus garden, when John arrived. It was still cool for an Arizona morning in July. Only 89 degrees. John described the area surrounding Bergstrom's ranch as they drove to Sky Harbor Airport. John stopped the car at a large hangar with a sign near the office door which simply stated, U.S. Government.

Their pilot, Art Smokey Stover, met them in the office. "John. Where you been hiding?"

"Hello Smokey. Good to see you again. Staying out of trouble?"

"You know me, John. Low profile all the way."

John laughed. "Dan Webster, meet Smokey Stover. Contrary to what you might think, he didn't get his nickname from the cartoon character. In an operation out in the desert, one time, the suspects were holed up in an old cabin and there wasn't any way to get them into the open. Every time we tried to get close enough to get a tear gas grenade into the cabin, they sprayed the area with bullets. Smokey here, got some smoke grenades and flew them, in a Piper Super Cub, right to the cabin. A couple got through the window. The bad guys came rolling out of that cabin just a bawling. The airplane looked like Swiss cheese. So, now we call him Smokey."

The men laughed and shook hands,

"Hope you like flying; it's going to be one hell of a beautiful trip this morning. That area along the Salt River is really pretty. Bergstrom's ranch takes in the prettiest of it all."

"Dan is a pilot, too," John said.

"Oh yeah? What do you fly?" Always the first question from one pilot to another.

"I own a Piper PA-14."

"Good reputation." Smokey replied.

"Piper only made 237 of them back in 1948 and 49. There are only about 40 of them left flying. It's a 100 mile an hour plane, too slow for cross country, but for flying the bush in Alaska, it can't be beat."

"If you two are done hangar flying, we should go," John prodded.

The elevation at Sky Harbor airport is only 1,132 feet but the heat made the air thin. The Cessna 185 seemed to roll forever before gaining enough speed to lift the tail. Once in the air, the pilot made an easy climb out. The heat caused thermal turbulence close to the ground, so Smokey climbed to 5,000 feet and headed to Apache Lake. On the way to the ranch, John pointed out roads, trails and general points of interest.

Closer to the ranch, Smokey descended to 2,000 feet and circled the ranch. He then maintained about 700 feet above the ground. Dan could see that the river and Apache Lake provided water for the ranch. The foothills to the north were a low but formidable barrier. The house sat on a small ridge and commanded a view of the river valley. It would be almost impossible to approach from the ground without being seen.

Smokey circled again and made a pass over the private airstrip. A Cessna Citation II was parked outside the hangar; a crewman in a white shirt was walking around the plane—doing a takeoff, pre flight Dan thought.

They flew north and left the ranch along the low hills. Small canyons, or washes, appeared dry and hot. Heavy rains washed sand and dirt out of the canyons to form large flat sandbars at the mouth of several canyons. Some of these were close to a 1,000 feet long and flat. "Good place to land a cub," Dan thought.

Back on the ground at Sky Harbor, Dan thanked Smokey for the ride. He looked at his watch, 0755 hours. "Com'on, Smokey; John's buying breakfast."

"Thanks but I'll have to pass. I've another flight in a few minutes."

Back in the office, John read the morning reports and signed a pile of reports and requests for Judy, who would forward them to the home office. She brought the two men fresh coffee and the morning papers.

"Will there be anything else, Mr. Sutter?"

"No, thank you, Judy. Let me know if Dave or Larry call."

Dan was deep in thought as Judy left the office. He sipped his coffee while John worked. Then suddenly he remembered.

"John, remember seeing the Cessna jet on the runway at the ranch?"

"Yes, why?"

"The guy in the white shirt was the pilot, I'll bet. He was making a preflight check. I wonder if he's taking Bergstrom somewhere?"

"Check with the FAA to see if he filed a flight plan," John said, still going through papers on his desk. "He throws some wild parties out at the ranch and sometimes brings his guest in by jet".

John looked in his Roladex for the telephone number of the Phoenix Flight Service Station. He found the number and dialed and handed the phone to Dan.

"Phoenix Flight Service, your aircraft number please."

"This is the DEA." Dan winked. "There's a Cessna Citation departing from the private strip at Apache Lake. Can you read his flight plan to me?"

"I'll check with my supervisor." Dan was put on hold.

"This is Ben Riley; I'm the supervisor here. What is it you need?"

Dan handed John the receiver and just shook his head.

"This is agent Sutter with the DEA." John stood and stretched. "I need the flight plan of the Citation at Apache Lake read to me. Is there a problem with that, Mr. Riley?"

"No problem. Always willing to cooperate with another agency. The flight plan's right here. It reads as follows.

Filing VFR/IFR flight plan. Aircraft number, N111NB. Cessna Citation II/U. Beige with brown trim. TAS(True Air Speed) 350 Kts. Departing Apache Lake at 0230 Zulu.

Flight level 330, Direct, DCA (Washington National Airport, Washington, D.C.). ETE, Five hours. Six hours fuel on board. Alternate field, Dulles International. Pilot, Rigby, copilot, Wells. Two souls on board.

If you're not a pilot, then what all this means is he is flying to Washington, D.C. and will be leaving Apache Lake at 8:30 this morning. He will be 5 hours getting there and the pilot and copilot are the only ones on board the aircraft. Is that all, sir?"

"Yes sir, Mr. Riley. Exactly what we need to know. I'd appreciate it if our inquiry was kept private. Thanks."

John turned to Dan. "It looks like Mister Bergstrom is calling a meeting and has sent his jet to Washington to pick up some of his friends. We'll pass this on to Dave when he calls and maybe his

We'll pass this on to Dave when he calls. and maybe his surveillance team can tell us who comes in on the plane tonight."

"There doesn't seem to be much we can do until we get some return on the information we have coming in. I don't like all this waiting, but I can't think of anything else to do right now. Let's call Roger and see if he has anything new." Dan knew it was too early for evidence to be arriving, but he wanted to make something happen.

"Good idea, He probably won't be in his office for another hour." John could see Dan's anxiety. "Take it easy. We can't force it. We'll have to take things as they come. We don't want to blow this case because we got in a hurry."

Dan picked up the newspaper and began to scan the front page. The entire page consisted of two stories. The U.N. had not yet determined who was responsible for the abduction of the two Arab families. And the nuclear detonation in the Gulf of Alaska. No casualties and no one was claiming responsibility. Environmental factions were lobbying Washington to investigate the damage to the ecosystem. The paper also noted the Trans Alaska Pipeline Service Company had contacted the National Oceanographic and Atmospheric Administration, requesting a study of Bligh Reef and surrounding waters. Six suspects had been arrested, the paper bragged, in connection with the bombing but gave few details.

The phone rang, John answered, "Just a second, Larry, let me put this on the speaker phone."

"Dan, Larry has something. Go ahead, Larry."

"My office received some interesting information this morning. First, there's been a flurry of activity among the OPEC ministers. They're making plans to go to Brussels this weekend. We also have word that Yamamata is traveling. And, word is Bergstrom has just bought tickets to Brussels for tomorrow evening."

"Something is in the wind. "John whispered to Dan.

Larry again. "It looks like Dan was right. A conspiracy to manipulate the price of crude oil, is in the works. Mexico and most of South America have stopped shipping oil. Yamamata's tankers are loading crude today but none have entered any port to unload. Europe has been notified that the Russian pipeline will be out of service for several days. They can't last more than three or four days without fresh supplies. Importers into the U.S. are slowed. Alaska oil is still being shipped without interruption. The DOT (Department of Transportation) has approved shipments as long as there's no danger from radiation in the Gulf of Alaska. It's been a busy morning, boys."

"Have you given this information to Dave?" John asked.

"He's in my office now. We're on speaker phone, too."

"Good morning, interesting morning, isn't it?" Dave said.

"Yes it is. In fact, let me add to it. Bergstrom is sending his jet to Washington. We think he is now in a meeting at the ranch with some of his political contacts. Can you check who gets on that plane?"

"I'll see what I can do," Dave replied. "What about Bergstrom? Should we detain him."

"We don't have enough evidence to arrest him yet. Since we know where he's going; why don't we let him go? Larry, does your office have the personnel to follow him once he's in Brussels?"

"The top brass is interested in the case now, so we'll get what we need. I'll get back to you this afternoon."

John hung up the receiver, thought for a moment and then picked it up again and dialed Anchorage to Roger Dorfmann's office. Miss Dill transferred the call.

"John, good to hear from you. How are you and the new agent getting along?"

"We're doing fine. We've been worried about you; are you okay?"

"Yes, we're fine. We had a few anxious hours, but we came out of the deal without any personal damage. You heard, of course, that we disposed of the device on Bligh Reef?"

"Yeah. I understand you and your crew escaped without a scratch. Didn't your mother ever tell you not to play with atomic bombs?" John said, laughing.

"That's not exactly true, John. Our deckhand got knocked off his feet during the shock wave and hit his head. One of his ear drums ruptured in the blast and he fractured his skull in the fall. He's recovering. The kid's a real hero."

"I'm glad he's all right," Dan said into the speaker phone. "Are Gwen and DeGrosso okay."

"Dan, How's Arizona? Yes, they're fine. Gwen's staying in town for a few days until we find out who's involved in this thing. I have her working in the office here. By the way, we checked with the troopers, and they found none of Bates prints. Can't link him to the murders. But the two guards, at the gate positively identified him. Do you know where he is now?" Roger asked.

John spoke. "He's out at Bergstrom's ranch. It would be a real chore to arrest him there. One more thing, Roger. Bergstrom is going ahead with his plan. I don't think he knows we're on to him. He knows

He knows something went wrong, but I don't think he knows what it was. You can bet he has TAPS people on his payroll. You have managed to keep this quiet until now, but, with the arrest of the Japanese technicians, it's going to go public. I don't suppose those technicians have talked."

"Naw. Not a word, and their lawyers are swarming all over. High priced ones from Los Angeles, I suspect. It looks like a long weekend of waiting. I'll issue an arrest warrant for Bates. It'll be Monday before we can move on it though."

"Bergstrom is going to Brussels tomorrow, Roger. We've decided to let him go. There appears to be a meeting of OPEC and other big-time oil producers there this weekend. We probably won't have anything before Monday either. We'll put all we have together and send you a coded copy. Call you Monday, sooner, if we have anything new." John hung up the phone.

It was 11:25 AM when the two left to office, met their wives for lunch and spent the afternoon sightseeing and shopping. It would, without a doubt, be a long, slow, weekend.

Chapter 17

It was 8:30 PM when the Cessna Citation circled to land at Apache Lake. The 6-hour flight from Washington had been uneventful and the four passengers had wiled away the time sipping champagne. Senators Tillman, Wayman, and Frost were accompanied on the flight by Undersecretary of Commerce, Belafont. Each of the men had been entertained at the ranch in the past and enjoyed being there. This time it would be to explain what happened in Alaska. Each of the four knew explaining to Bergstrom would not be a pleasant experience. He had his way and did not like it when his plans went awry.

The helicopter ferried guests to the ranch all evening. The party became boisterous before the jet landed. There was food of every description. A bar was set up on the west side of the patio, near the pool. There were drugs available: cocaine and marijuana. Bergstrom knew how to entertain his friends. Girls in bikinis served drinks and food. A small dance band, set up on the east end of the patio, kept up a rhumba beat. Watchful eyes took careful note of which guest indulged in self gratification outside an accepted social norm.

The four new arrivals were greeted by Bergstrom. In Bergstrom's office, they each took a seat while Bergstrom sat in the large leather chair behind the desk. A pitcher of iced tea and a plate of sliced pineapple and sugar cookies were on the desk.

"Good evening, gentlemen," Bergstrom began. "I hope you had a pleasant flight. I have called this meeting to verify information in the oil industry. It's very distressing to hear someone may have actually attempted to destroy the south terminal of the Alaska pipeline. Secretary Belafont, any ideas?"

"I will give you what I have, Mr. Bergstrom, but it isn't very much, I'm afraid. Somehow the ultrasonic corrosion detection pig, which had been shipped from Japan to Alaska by TMC, was substituted with another. The TMC technicians have disappeared and they were replaced by six others. The plot was discovered by a TAPS technician and a security guard. They followed the substitute pig to Valdez where the

FBI and state troopers arrested the Japanese. The warhead inside the pig was armed before anyone could find the arming device. An FBI agent, the TAPS technician, and a technician from Elmendorf Air Force base took the pig out to Bligh Reef and dumped it. It exploded there.

"NOAA reported the preliminary soundings indicate Bligh Reef has changed considerably. The full report is not in yet, but it appears the reef may no longer be a threat to normal navigation. In other words, the explosion blew the hell out of the reef. The tide is still moving debris, but new soundings indicate a minimum depth of 8 fathoms over the reef. There is 51 feet of water over a reef that used to be exposed at extreme low tide. No damage or injury is reported at the Valdez terminal. It'll take several weeks to assess the total damage and to file the report."

Belafont felt confident he had covered everything.

"Your report is full of holes," Bergstrom sat forward. "Two people were killed at the Valdez terminal. Who was the TAPS technician? Who was the technician from Elmendorf? How was the bomb detected? I want answers, Belafont, a full report when I return from Brussels."

At that moment, Russ Talbert entered the office. He had a note pad in his hand. He stepped behind the desk and whispered to Bergstrom. He laid the pad on the desk and stepped back. Bergstrom was stunned.

"Are you sure?"

"That's what the informant in Anchorage said. I don't know if it's the same Dan Webster and Roger Dorfmann, but it seems too remote a possibility to be a coincidence."

Nels Bergstrom turned ashen. "Get Bates. I want to see him when I'm finished here."

His thoughts and attention came back to those present.

"Gentlemen, I'll be as brief as possible. The flow of crude oil has been reduced worldwide by more than 70%. I'm leaving for Brussels to attend a conference with Arab and other oil interests. We will discuss the price of oil and its distribution. I want you to stop any governmental intervention until after the conference. You go back to Washington and tell our friends to keep this issue confused as long as possible. Do you understand?"

Each squirmed in their chairs and nodded. There were unanswered questions but each knew they did not dare ask. Bergstrom was not a tolerant man and none of the men wanted to tempt his wrath.

"Belafont, I want a complete report as soon as possible, and keep the Department of Transportation out of it. I don't want anyone from the government meddling in this business." Nels said, biting into a sugar cookie.

"Yes, Mr. Bergstrom. Will there be anything else this evening?" Belafont said facetiously.

"That'll be all gentlemen. Go and enjoy the party. I've brought some lovely ladies from town to keep you company. You should each find what you want."

The men were silent as they left the room. Each was listing options in their heads. It was political suicide to publicly endorse Bergstrom, but it was personal suicide to cross him. Each man knew he was trapped by one of the world's most powerful, and ruthless men. The four stepped onto the patio and joined the party. It was a welcome diversion.

Talbert made certain Mr. Bergstrom was alone before escorting Bates into the office.

"Al. Did you rest?" Nels asked.

"Yes, I did. You have a job for me?"

"Umm humm." He said from the rim of a glass. "Two old enemies have resurfaced. One is an FBI man by the name of Roger Dorfmann. I'm not too worried about him because his position with the FBI will keep him restrained. The other is an ex-deputy sheriff from Northern California by the name of Dan Webster. I want him taken care of. He was the security guard that followed the pig from Prudhoe Bay to Valdez. I nearly killed him once and he may try for revenge. He's a tenacious SOB and more dangerous. Check it out.

"I'll be leaving tomorrow afternoon, for a few days. The pursuit is in your hands. Our plan must move forward as scheduled or we'll lose a great deal of money. We can't be distracted by some security guard."

"I'll take care of it, Mr. Bergstrom," Bates said and he left to join the party.

Talbert had remained in the office with Bergstrom. "I've everything packed and all the papers ready for tomorrow. I believe I have everything ready to go. My assistant will be here to forward any new information to us in Brussels. Will there be anything else tonight, sir?"

"No. I think we've covered everything. Take the night off. Just have the cook send me some dinner. I think I'll eat and go to bed. I'm tired of worrying about Webster. I don't like surprises."

In the DEA supervisors office Monday morning, stacks of files and papers smothered the desk; reports on passengers aboard the Citation on Friday evening; reports on guests attending the party at the

Apache Lake Ranch; interviews with the Japanese technicians in Anchorage; no new information; a list of probable people expected in Brussels. The list of names was interesting. It included the OPEC ministers, the Mexican and South American oil interests, representatives from the major oil companies of the United States and Europe. The list also included General Kisishkin, Mr. Yamamata, and Nels Bergstrom. The CIA would keep an eye on the proceedings in Brussels.

An interesting situation occurred Sunday morning. The surveillance team had seen Al Bates board the helicopter, presumably for a ride to town. A hurried trap was set at the Bergstrom Enterprises building, downtown. The FBI had agents at the front door and at the garage entrance. The helicopter never showed. Instead of making its regular landing at the office building, it went directly to the airport where Bates caught a flight to San Francisco. He left the airport by the time agents from the San Francisco office of the FBI could respond.

Although the FBI had no way of knowing, Bates had not left the airport through the front door. He had changed his name and boarded a commuter plane bound for Santa Rosa. He rented a car there and drove the hundred miles to the small northern California town where Dan Webster had once been a deputy sheriff.

Bates had been trained for his profession by the United States Army. He was a Captain in the special forces during the Viet Nam conflict. The army had taught him well and he knew how to gather and correlate information. He also knew how to formulate and carry out an attack strategy. In the years since the war, he had become an efficient, intelligent killer, and an important member of Bergstrom's staff.

Bates spent Monday at the courthouse gathering information about Webster. He was surprised to find that many people still regarded him as an outstanding law man. Many remembered when Dan married Beth. A trip to visit Beth's folks provided more insight into the private life of Dan Webster. Dan's father had been killed in a logging accident when Dan was in high school. Dan's mother died shortly after he returned from his army tour. The Webster family didn't come back from Alaska often.

Monday evening Bates chartered a small plane and flew to Eugene Oregon where he again changed his name and boarded a plane to Seattle. He changed his name again and flew to Anchorage. There he assumed the identity of a government agent checking the background of Dan Webster through the Trans Alaska Pipeline Service Company, Personnel Department. A secretary at Pipeline Security Corporation was doing individual timekeeping on Webster. Using his phony government ID, he was able to obtain a copy of time cards, travel and per diem vouchers. Dan was in Phoenix with John Sutter. On the return flight he changed his name in Seattle, Houston, and Denver—always the careful man.

Thursday morning, the news from the World Oil Summit was shocking. The oil producing nations had agreed on a world crude oil price of $65.00 per barrel. Oil production would be reduced by 40%. The Arab countries had agreed, only, after assurances that the gross income to their countries would be greater than at present. They had an added incentive of assurances that the two royal families of the two largest oil producing nations would be released unharmed. Attempts by the press to interview delegates to the conference were waved off, and the participants departed from Brussels as quickly as possible.

The United States called an emergency meeting of the United Nations Security Council to protest the manipulation of oil prices on the grounds it would destroy the world's most industrialized country's economic structure.

By noon Thursday, a furor exploded unequaled in Congress since the bombing of Pearl Harbor. Senator Tillman called for economic sanctions against OPEC. Such a sanction made as much sense as shooting yourself in the foot, but it created confusion and divided the voting blocks into debating teams.

Senator Frost called for a congressional investigation of the major oil companies in the United States. He demanded to know who authorized the American oil companies to go along with the agreed new price of crude. "The entire economic and monetary structure of the United States is under attack," he said. "If allowed to continue, the most mobile nation in the world will grind to a stop. The most stable currency in the world will be shaken from its base and become as worthless and the postwar German Mark. I demand this nation take a stand against this assault on our economy. And I ask the other consumer nations of the world join us in our fight to return stability to oil pricing."

It was late Thursday afternoon when John Sutter called Roger Dorfmann at his office in Anchorage. Roger was very busy in recent days, preparing his case for the Federal Grand Jury. It was no easy task. No one, with current FBI experience, could remember the last time a foreign national had been indicted for acts of terrorism in the United States. He didn't want to leave anything to chance. Two security officers were dead because of this crime. Terrorism, as well

Terrorism, as well as
as murder, carries a death penalty. Since Roger asked the Federal District Attorney to file for the death penalty, it was important every fact be documented and verified. Gwen worked very closely with him. She had also been a great comfort and had taken the edge off his tensions.

Miss Dill was on the intercom when Roger lifted the receiver.

"Mr. Sutter and Mr. Webster are on line one for you, sir."

"Thanks, Judy. Send Gwen to my office; I want her here for this call." Roger pushed the button transferring the call to line one. "Hello John. Are you there, Dan?"

"Yes, I'm here. How are you Roger? Anything new?"

The door to Roger's office opened and Gwen entered. Roger motioned for her to pick up line one on the other phone in his office. "Nothing new on this end. I have Gwen on the line now. How are things going down there?"

"Hi, Dan," Gwen interrupted.

"Hello. How is that old man treating you?"

"He hasn't made me ride three hours in an airplane with no flight attendant or bathroom, like you did." She laughed.

"Then things are looking up for you."

Things are really heating up in the oil market, aren't they?" Roger commented. "Is there any information that hasn't made the papers?"

John answered his question. "I might have something for your office. Friday night there was a big party, including hookers, out at Bergstrom's ranch. I have an officer under cover, working the midtown business bars. She was with another girl who was invited to work the party. She asked my officer if she would like to go to the ranch and attend the party; pay was good drugs would flow freely. My officer, Debbie, said when she got there, it was unbelievable. I have a copy of the guest list; all prominent Arizona and California businessmen. Then the jet came in from Washington, D.C. with three senators and an Undersecretary of Commerce. Debbie positioned herself near the bathhouse where the drugs were distributed to see who came to the bait.

"The list of drug users she compiled at the party is extensive. I'll fax you a copy. The interesting thing is, it included Senator Frost and Senator Wayman. It also includes Undersecretary of Commerce Belafont. Senator Tillman attended the party but was too busy chasing bikinis and drinking expensive scotch to get involved in drugs.

"Debbie said when the four first arrived they had some kind of meeting with Bergstrom. She didn't know what the meeting was about, the four left very unhappy."

"The FBI has been investigating influence peddling for a long time," Roger said, "If you've got accurate documentation from Debbie, we can nail those four to the wall. It may be the break we need to get inside the group. I'll go to Washington myself and check it out. That way I can find out what they know about the pipeline bombing. When I go, I'll take Gwen. I'm not leaving her alone until this mess is cleared up."

"Sorry I didn't get this to you sooner, but I didn't get to read the report until this morning. Let me know what you find out in Washington. If you can get just one piece of evidence against Bergstrom, we'll haul him in." John was excited at the prospect.

"I'm getting tired of sitting around while Bergstrom keeps on manipulating people and making the world a mess. There must be a way to make him nervous or force his hand," Dan said, his frustration showing through.

"Patience, patience," Roger said, "We'll get him. It's coming together. He's too big a fish to fry in one pan. We have to divide and conquer. I know how you feel, Dan, but if we go after him head on, we'll lose."

Friday morning, 7 AM, Al Bates sat at the table on the patio with Nels. "You were right about Webster. He's very dangerous. He's intelligent and resourceful and is after you for revenge, to even the score; it's personal with him. We'll have to take him out to stop him."

"Do you have a plan?" Nels asked.

"Yes, but it may be expensive."

"Do it."

Talbert came to the patio, walked to the small television set and turned it to CNN news. The President of the United States was speaking. "...my fellow Americans. In the past we have been able to reason with these people resulting in a fairly stable oil price and the continued stability of world economy. This new oil price increase has not been discussed with diplomats from this country nor from any other industrial nation. Attempts to meet with the ministers of the OPEC countries and with the executives of South American oil companies have met with failure. They refuse to communicate. One week ago, the price of a barrel of crude oil was $14.58 and today, it is $65. The transport of crude oil has virtually stopped in every nation. We cannot, and will not, stand by while American business and Commerce is threatened, or blackmailed, by irresponsible coalitions.

Therefore, I have proposed the following temporary measures, effective immediately.

"First. Effective at midnight tonight there will be rationing of all petroleum products. The Department Commerce will open offices in government buildings across America. Booklets of ration stamps will be issued on a Use Priority Basis.

"Second. I am meeting with U.S. oil producers and asking them to increase the flow of domestic oil. This will put a heavy burden on Texas, California, and particularly Alaska oil producers. The Department of Commerce will attempt to soften the price of petroleum products to consumers by keeping the prices for domestic oil at a $20 level. I know this places an unfair burden on domestic producers, but it is necessary for the economic salvation of this country. I will not nationalize oil production in the United States as long as the oil companies comply with your government's request.

"Third. The Ambassador to the United Nations will take a plea for responsible negotiation to the Security Council. As your President, I am doing everything within my power to return this situation to normal. I am asking for your cooperation during this time of crisis. I will release a statement to the press as soon as there are any developments in this situation. Thank you, good day, and God bless us all."

Talbert turned the television off and turned to Bergstrom.

"Sir?"

"Al, take care of the problem we talked about." Then turning to Talbert he said, "Get me Kisishkin on the secure phone."

Chapter 18

Lianid Kisishkin had been an extremely busy man in the past few days. The capture and kidnaping of the Arabs had taxed his resources. He easily controlled the Russian pipeline, but the men he controlled would soon demand payment and Lianid did not have the money. He was well hidden and communications among the new nations, which once were the U.S.S.R., were inadequate. Kisishkin spoke into the secure telephone,

"Nels, it is good to hear you. Is everything progressing?"

"Going well. A few minor complications but none to worry over. I have a problem though; it has to do with the Alaska pipeline. The U.S. government is trying to supplement imported oil with Alaska crude, thus negating the OPEC oil price by controlling domestic production. They are successful because we failed to disable the pipeline. The oil flowing in the Alaska pipeline will fuel a political debate and prolong submission to our cause," Bergstrom explained. "In the end we will prevail, but much time will be lost."

"Vhat can I do?" Lianid asked.

"We are going to the alternate plan for disabling the Alaska pipeline. Are your stratagems in place?"

"Yes. Vhat iss timetable?"

"Will 24 hours be enough time for you?" Bergstrom asked.

"The target vill be destroyed in exactly 24 hours. Shall I proceed with the repatriation of the two Arab royal families?"

"Yes. We must follow through with the releases to maintain our credibility with OPEC. We must keep as many friends as possible along the way."

"It vill be done," Kisishkin hung up.

So far, everything had gone according to plan. Governments of the newly formed confederacy had more to worry about than the antics of a renegade General. The rumors of his army were, after all, only rumors. If he did own an army, he was not using it to interfere with the politics of the new confederacy.

"Politicians, Bah! This plan vould not have been possible had the

Politicians Bah!

This plan would not have been possible had the
politicians spent more time seeking solutions and less time defining the problems," Kisishkin thought. Soon he would be rich and he could afford to ignore politicians. He lifted the receiver of his military hot line. "Colonel Novonyi, this is General Kisishkin. Proceed with plan Alpha Echo Two."

"I confirm. Proceed with Alpha Echo Two. Vhat is target time, sir?" Novonyi asked.

"Twenty-four hours. Any trouble with that Colonel?"

"No, sir. Everything is ready. The 'Training Mission' will commence as planned and on your schedule. I will keep you informed."

Al Bates was operating on his own timetable. He "acquired" a large motor home with legitimate license plates. At 8 AM he and his henchman parked the Sportscoach in front of the Desert Sands Motel. Dan and John were already gone. Beth was alone in the motel room.

Bates waited in the motorhome until two more trusted employees arrived. Bates walked to the door of the ground floor room and knocked. He heard rustling noises inside and the door opened.

Bates put his foot against the bottom of the door, preventing it's closure. He lifted the tail of his loose fitting shirt to expose the butt of an automatic handgun. "Don't make any noise Mrs. Webster. I don't want to hurt you, so come quietly."

"I'm not going with you! What's this all about?" Beth began shaking, but at the same time she was looking for a way out.

"You're coming with me awake or unconscious. It's up to you." Bates snarled.

Beth slammed the door against his foot, then turned and ran toward the patio door. Bates was right behind her. A man appeared on the other side of the glass door. She panicked and turned back only to face Bates. He grabbed her by the left arm and twisted. She yelped and fell heavily to the floor. The carpet fabric was rough and scraped a large patch of hide from her chin. Her shoulder and chest hurt from the brutal treatment. The pain in her left arm was unbearable. Bates wrenched her arm even higher behind her back; then a knee hit her elbow and stabbed her in the middle of her back, again knocking the wind from her lungs.

The second man had opened the patio door and entered the room, bent down and twisted her right arm behind her back. She was gasping for breath as the two men lifted her from the floor by her twisted arms. She felt herself get woozy. She thought her arms were being pulled from her shoulder sockets. The two men half carried, half-dragged her to the front door of the motel room.

Greg Monday, in the Sportcoach, saw the door of the motel open and opened the door of the motorhome. Monday and Bates lifted Beth into the motorhome and closed the door. Monday climbed into the driver's seat while Bates forced the frightened woman to the back of the vehicle. There he forced her to the bed, face down, and handcuffed her hands behind her back and taped her mouth.

Monday maintained a legal speed as the motorhome, and the car that followed, went west on highway 10. A few miles west of Phoenix they turned off the main highway and followed secondary roads through Goodyear and Buckeye. They turned south near Palo Verde, through Arlington, then about 5 miles south to a dirt road that circled west, then south through the Gila Bend Mountains.

They had gone about 25 miles along dusty dirt roads when Bates picked up the cellular telephone and dialed the DEA office. The secretary transferred the call to Dan Webster in John's office.

"Dan Webster speaking."

"Hello, Dan. You don't know me, but we are about to become better acquainted. I have something you want very much. I want you to meet me out in the desert on the road to Sundad. Come alone. Rent a red Jeep; we'll stop you when you get here," Bates instructed. Dan motioned for John to pick up the other phone and listen.

"I don't think I want to do that. What do you have that I want?"

"We have your wife. She stays alive as long as you do what I say. I'll expect to see you by noon." The line went dead.

Dan's face went white. He held himself up with the edge of the table, and dialed the motel; there was no answer in the room. John was already holding the door by the time Dan got his wits back on line, then they bolted from the office. Going out the door, John turned to his secretary and yelled, "Get an investigative team to Dan's motel! Now!"

Evidence of a struggle in the room was plain. Dan recognized the signs, the scuff marks in the nap of the rug, the smudges on the patio door, and the black shoe marks on the base of the front door. Neither the maid nor desk clerk had seen anyone. They had seen a large motorhome parked in front for a few minutes this morning. It was white, big, with green trim. They hadn't seen anything strange, and they hadn't seen Mrs. Webster.

"I don't know the country, John; is there anything we can do?" Dan paced the floor. He really needed a drink!

John thought a moment. "I'll get you a jeep with a radio in it, from the agency motorpool. I'll see if Smokey Stover is available to fly over the area and try to spot them. I have to be honest with you, Dan; there's an awful lot of desert out there. There isn't any cover for sneaking. Even if we find them, the only concealment is the contour of the land. I'll mark a road map for you. It's going to be hot, but I want you to wear a vest. I'll get you a boot gun for a backup."

While a jeep was outfitted, John called Smokey. He agreed to try to spot the Sportscoach. Dan was fit with a bullet proof vest, John marked the road map and gave Dan a .38 Special, Smith and Wesson Airweight to carry in the holster on his ankle. Dan was as prepared as he could be on such short notice. He left the agency garage and headed for the desert.

Smokey cruised at 125 knots, 1000 feet above the desert floor. He'd stay low, over the open desert, and if he spotted the suspect vehicle, he would only fly by it and not circle. As bad as he wanted to be with Dan, John returned to the office and stood by the radio.

Meanwhile, in Washington, D.C., Roger and Gwen were entering the office of Undersecretary Belafont. The office was appointed nicely, better than the average governmental office. A large mahogany desk centered the room. There was a large, high back, leather swivel chair behind the desk. Several straight back, leather seat chairs were scattered about the office. There was also a large brown couch on one wall. The government warehouse had provided large paintings for the walls. Upon entering the office, one got the feeling he had just been transported back to 1946.

The undersecretary motioned for the two to have a seat in front of the large desk. "How do you do? I am Jason Belafont."

"Pleased to meet you, Mr. Belafont. I'm Roger Dorfmann and this is my assistant, Ms. Stevens. We represent the FBI and would like to ask you some questions regarding your affiliation with Nels Bergstrom. Do you mind?"

"I don't mind answering your questions, but I have no 'affiliation' with Mr. Bergstrom. I barely know the man."

Gwen and Roger had rehearsed their response to this lie. Gwen said. "Mister Secretary. We know about your trip to Arizona Friday. We know about your expensive taste for 'nose candy.' We have enough on you right now to arrest you for influence peddling and drug possession. Before we're through, we could add terrorism and treason. Do we have your attention now Mr. Belafont?"

He looked as though he'd been stabbed. His shoulders pushed ahead—then began to droop. His lips parted as though he wanted to speak but no sound came. His face became a pale, ghostly white. He began to slump in the leather chair until he was barely visible behind the huge Mahogany desk.

"Did you hear what she said?" Roger asked.

"Yes, I heard," Belafont squeaked.

"I don't have a lot of time to debate issues with you," Roger began. "I want your cooperation and I want your help in convincing the others they have no alternative but to cooperate. I need to know everything you know about Bergstrom. I want to know what part you're playing. I want to know his involvement in the bombing of the pipeline in Alaska. I want to know what his plans are now."

Belafont gave a big sigh.

"All right. All right, I'll cooperate with you," he said as he poured a glass of water and took a large drink. "I never wanted to be involved with Bergstrom in the first place. It was my...habit."

He pushed the button on his intercom. "Miss Boucher, will you come in here a moment?"

His secretary entered with a pad in her hand. "Yes, sir?"

"Miss Boucher, call Senators Tillman, Wayman, and Frost. Tell them there is to be a meeting in my office in one half hour."

When she closed the door behind her, he began to tell his story.

Belafont related his tale of drug use to the two FBI agents. He told them how he had been introduced to "recreational use" of cocaine at a party for government officials and representatives of the natural gas industry. A few of the younger people there were tooting some cocaine and invited Belafont to join them. He had been drinking and his judgment was less than perfect. With some encouragement from one of the female guests, he tried the white powder. It was wonderful. He had never experienced such a sensation. He was instantly hooked. For almost two years now, he had never experienced the original sensation again. Now he needed the stuff to maintain his daily routine. He could not work without it.

Bergstrom supplied the cocaine for that first party and had been supplying it for him since. His habit had not cost him anything. He admitted that he was suffering some tinges of paranoia but had discharged his governmental duties faithfully. This was the first time Bergstrom had made any demands on him in return for the drugs he had supplied. Belafont was crying now. He had not wanted to make

He had not wanted to make
concessions to Bergstrom, but it was either that or lose his job. The promise of the availability of more drugs was not a bribe but a benefit derived from his association with Bergstrom.

Bergstrom had personally given Belafont packets of cocaine on several occasions and supplied the drug for parties on others. Belafont said he would get help for his addiction and that he would testify against Bergstrom in court, for drug trafficking. Belafont was sorry and now wanted to help if he could.

The three senators took seats on the couch after the introductions. Tillman and Wayman were very nervous. All three men had hidden secrets that would interest the FBI, but had no idea for which transgression they were now being investigated.

Gwen was the one to break the news to the Senators. "Gentlemen, we represent the combined investigations of the FBI, the DEA, and the CIA. I will not go into individual charges, but I will say we have enough on each of you to get you convicted of several felony charges. We don't have a lot of time to spend here and are asking for your cooperation. You know we can't make any deals with you, but we can make recommendations for leniency, and we can tell the judges that you willingly cooperated in the investigation."

Senator Frost looked at the others; then he spoke, "I don't have the slightest idea what you are talking about."

"Senator!" Roger raised his voice as he stood up and faced the men. "I don't have time for your political posturing. We have a situation in which many people may die. There has already been an attempt to destroy the Alaska pipeline terminal with a nuclear weapon. Had that been successful, hundreds of people would have died. Each of you was elected to an office responsible for protecting the citizens of the United States of America. You have each forsaken the duties of your office to form allegiance with a lunatic. He would destroy the political system of this country by corrupting its elected leaders. He would destroy the strong monetary base of the country and in turn, the world. He would destroy the lives of the citizens you have each been elected to protect.

"I'm sworn to protect the citizens of the United States, too. I'm offering you a way out of your situation and giving you an opportunity to redeem yourselves by doing what you were elected you to do. Don't waste my time, gentlemen. I need your help and in return can, possibly, give you a way to save some self respect. Are you going to cooperate?"

"Can you give us a minute to discuss it?" Tillman asked.

"Yes, but only a minute." Roger said. He motioned to Gwen and the two left the office. He asked the secretary in the outer office for a cup of coffee.

Gwen was just finishing a diet 7-UP when the secretary came to the small break room and told them the senators wanted them to return. Gwen held up her right hand with her fingers crossed and winked at Roger.

Back in the office the senators looked solemn. "What do you want us to do?" Tillman asked.

"The four of you know, better then we do, what you've done to ensure Bergstrom's power. Each of you knows what strings you pulled to allow him to manipulate the price of oil. It will be up to you to sabotage that power base. Time is short. The economy of the country will be ruined in only a few days if we cannot restore stability to the previously agreed oil prices." Gwen commented, "Think of what the present situation will do to the U.S. Dollar. Think of the people who have died in Bergstrom's quest for power. You must go to congress today and do what the people of this country elected you to do: protect them from Nels Bergstrom."

Roger added to her statement, "You must go to the Congress and reverse the stand you have taken. You have to use your influence to convince your colleagues regulations are needed to control prices and return the flow of oil to normal. You have to destroy Bergstrom's power. The President has protested the actions of the oil producing countries. You will have to put teeth in his decisions. Let me warn you one more time. This is the only chance you have to come out of this with any self respect. You must begin the campaign today."

Senator Frost spoke meekly, "We know what we have to do. It will take a few hours to formulate a plan and to align enough power factions to accomplish what you ask. You must know that Nels will not allow this to happen without a fight, we are in jeopardy once this thing gets rolling."

"I didn't say there weren't risks. We have people working in Arizona. We'll assign people to protect you. If you hear from Bergstrom, contact my office here in Washington. Are there any questions?" Roger asked.

"No questions. We should have something going by morning," Tillman said. "And, please, don't judge us too harshly. We didn't get to be this way overnight. We have been drawn in a little at a time until it was too late to turn back."

"We're not here to make judgments," Gwen said. "You can do your explaining to the American public. Right now we are in a race against time to stop Bergstrom and his associates from destroying the economic, political, and industrial strengths of the world."

Smokey called the DEA office from the hangar when he landed back at Sky Harbor. "John. I just landed at Sky Harbor. I found the motorhome about five miles north of Sundad"

"Dave Vrobec and Larry Felson are here. Dave had four agents follow Dan. They have contact with him on the radio. They are about 15 minutes behind him. Anything in our favor?"

"I think so. How do you feel about flying out there with me? I think I can land within half a mile without being seen. I have the location marked on a map that we can drop to those agents. I saw another car with two guys standing by it about a mile away from the motor home. I think I can land the Husky on a sand blow, in a canyon not far from them. We might use the low sides of the wash to sneak up on the two in the car. Then if Dan can keep the men in the motorhome distracted long enough, we might just use the car to drive right to the motorhome."

"Get the plane ready. I'll be there in less than 20 minutes."

John had given the whole story to Dave and Larry on the way to the airport. Dan was informed by radio, and the four agents following him would be watching for the small airplane.

DEA owned a large number of the small two seat Christen Husky aircraft, manufactured by a company now owned by Aviat. They are an extremely efficient aircraft for short field, low altitude, slow speed surveillance. The 180 horsepower Lycoming engine and constant speed propeller gave it amazing performance characteristics. It is small though, with two seats arranged in tandem, putting the passenger seat directly behind the pilot.

With John Sutter strapped into the back seat, Smokey taxied to the nearest runway, pointed the nose into the slight breeze and was off the ground in less than 800 feet. Smokey took a direct route to the desert, cruising above the low hills at 120 miles per hour. It was not long before he intersected the dirt road to Sundad and turned south. Almost immediately they spotted the car carrying the four FBI agents. Smokey passed low over the car, slowed the aircraft, and settled onto the road ahead of it.

One of the agents stepped out of the car and jogged to the left side of the plane. He stepped under the left wing as Smokey slid the window open. Smokey held the brakes to keep the plane from moving. He held the folded map up for the agent to see. He pointed to a spot marked on the map and explained that this was the side road where he had seen the motorhome.

As the agent stepped out from under the wing, Smokey moved the throttle ahead and released the brakes. The plane rolled a short distance and was airborne again. It was now only about 5 minutes to the spot Smokey had picked for a landing site.

"Better tighten your seat belt and shoulder harness," Smokey said. "This landing'll be a little rough."

He was flying low to keep the hills between the airplane and the guards. He throttled back and flew directly at a low ridge of sandstone. John watched as they approached the ridge; he was certain the wheels were going to hit. As soon as they cleared, Smokey made a sharp right bank, cut the power and shoved the nose into a small canyon just wide enough for the wings of the little fabric covered airplane. As they settled deeper into the wash, the pilot leveled the nose and slowed the aircraft. There was a small turn in the canyon, and once around it John saw a flat area of sand that looked too small for a landing. Smokey pulled on the final notch of flaps, let the plane settle to the ground, and stopped after one gentle bounce in less than 150 feet of soft sand.

They crawled out of the plane and stretched. Each man checked his weapon to be certain there was a live round under the hammer. Then they walked toward the road. The small canyon emptied into the open where the two guards had parked the car. The two officers were within 20 yards of the car and could see the two men inside laughing and talking. They bent low to the ground and made it to the rear bumper of the car without being detected.

John was on the driver side and whispered to Smokey, "Go, Now."

The parked car's engine was left running to keep the air conditioning working to fend off the desert heat. Noise from the engine hiding their approach, John and Smokey stood upright and stepped to the side windows on each side of the car, their weapons pointed through the glass at the occupants. The two guards stared out their respective windows in total surprise.

"Step out of the car," John said. "We're Federal officers. You're under arrest."

The two men opened the doors of the car and stood. "What are you arresting us for? We were just sitting here enjoying the sunshine. You can't arrest a man for that," The driver said.

"We'll call it kidnaping unless we can come up with something else," John told him.

"I have some handcuffs." Smokey said. Just then they heard the noise of the Jeep coming down the road. When the handcuffs were on the two guards, Smokey left to retrieve some rope.

John stepped into the open and waved to Dan. The Jeep came to a stop in a cloud of dust.

"We got the two guards, Dan."

"Did Smokey see my wife when he flew over?"

"No. He said he couldn't see anyone at the motorhome. He doesn't know how many there are either. Drive the jeep there and Smokey and I will drive the guard's car to cover you."

"They're messing with my family. I have to get Beth out of this. It's getting difficult for me to keep my eye on the big picture. I hate these guys for what they've done to me and my family." Dan's frustration was showing through again.

"You're going to have to get a grip on your feelings, Dan. If we blow this thing, Beth is going to get hurt. Save the hate for later. Right now we have a job to do," John counseled.

"You're right, John, and I'm trying. But it isn't easy," Dan said.

The two guards were secured to a large sandstone boulder, shaded by greasewood. Dan returned to the Jeep. John and Smokey were in the Dodge, previously owned by the guards. The Jeep bumped slowly down the dusty road with the dark sedan following. It took only 3 or 4 minutes to reach big white and green Sportscoach.

"Here they come," Monday called to Bates as the Jeep approached.

Bates walked to the rear of the motorhome and dragged Beth to her feet. Her face was stained with tears. Perspiration had soaked the front of her torn blouse. Her hair was a mess and she ached all over. "Come on lady, it's show time," Bates said, as he ripped the tape from her mouth. Her tender skin oozed blood.

Monday opened the side door of the motorhome as the Jeep stopped near the front of the vehicle. He stepped to the ground with a broad smile on his face. Dan scowled as he stepped from the Jeep. He was in no mood for levity or small talk.

"Where is my wife?" he said through clinched teeth.

"Right here," Monday said, turning to watch Bates push her ahead of him, out of the coach.

The doors of the dark sedan were open, but the two men inside had not exited the car.

Monday had focused his attention on Dan. He walked to where Dan stood and patted him down. He found the Smith and Wesson automatic under his shirt and took it from him. Dan raised his hands and spoke to Bates as he walked slowly toward him.

"Okay. You have me. Let my wife go. Let her take the Jeep and leave. You have no need for her now," Dan pleaded.

"Sorry, I can't do that," Bates said. "Monday, take him over there and finish him. I'll take care of his wife."

Beth was crying as Monday motioned for Dan to move to the edge of a small ditch.

"Dan!" she screamed.

Monday's attention was diverted for an instant and Dan hit him with an elbow. Beth forced her shoulder into Bates and knocked him off balance and he fell. The two agents in the car stepped out and aimed weapons at the two suspects.

"Drop your weapons. You're under arrest," John yelled.

Monday looked surprised to see the strangers in the car but was able to swing the gun in his hand in the direction of the men. John fired, hitting Monday in the left shoulder. The force from the bullet slammed Monday to the ground. The army had taught John marksmanship. He spent a great deal of time on the pistol range and would ride his horse into the desert, find a quiet place, and practice shooting. Had it been his intent, Monday would have been dead. Monday dropped the gun. Dan retrieved his gun and ran toward his wife.

Bates saw Monday fall and fired two shots toward the car. He hit only the car. Lead was now flying in his direction. To escape, he rolled under the motorhome. Dan lifted Beth from the ground and ran in the direction of the Jeep. He was almost to the red CJ-5 when he felt a hot, searing pain in his left lower leg. He stumbled but regained his balance and continued to carry Beth to the safety of the Jeep. He loaded her into the car and started the engine. He backed up, spinning the tires and causing a huge cloud of dust. The distraction was enough to allow Bates to roll to the protected side of the motorhome.

Once on the hidden side of the motorhome, Bates stood and hurried to the driver door. He opened the door and slid into the seat, started the engine and slipped it into gear. He raised his head above the dashboard of the coach and mashed the throttle to the floor. He caught the Jeep as it backed to safety behind the sedan. John and Smokey were firing at the Motorhome, but it gained speed and hit the front of the Jeep, rolling it on its side, spilling Dan and Beth to the sand.

Bates pointed the coach toward the exit road just as the four agents in the backup car arrived. They saw the motorhome coming at them and kept their car straight on. Bates turned hard to the right, making a 180 degree turn. He sped back toward the overturned Jeep. Smokey and John were running toward the unconscious pair on the ground. They reached them in time to drag them from the path of the big motorhome. Bates had his foot on the floor when the motorhome hit the rear of the Jeep. The gas tank on the Jeep exploded, sending flames into the air and engulfing the smashed front end of the motorhome and its driver.

The impact drove Bates' knee into the steering column, numbing his right leg. He hobbled to the side door, away from the flames leaping up in the front of the wrecked recreational vehicle. His leg would not support him when he stepped out of the burning coach. He fell to the ground but pointed his weapon in the direction of the agents helping John. Bates fired two more shots before being hit by bullets from Smokey's gun.

Two of the agents who had just arrived ran to Bates and dragged him away from the burning vehicles. He was still alive but hit hard with two bullets in the upper chest.

John unlocked the handcuffs from Beth's bruised arms, as she began to regain her senses. She opened her eyes and recognized John.

"Oh, John! I was so frightened," She sobbed. "Is Dan okay?"

"Yes, he's starting to come around now. He got nicked in the ankle, but he'll be all right."

Smokey and John helped Beth to where Dan was lying on the ground. He was trying to shake the stars from his vision when she spoke to him.

"Are you all right, Dearest?" she asked.

"I think so. I'm getting too old for full contact police work."

"Call for an ambulance," John said. "We'll meet it with the wounded prisoners. Beth you can ride with the officers in the other car. Smokey'll want to fly his plane back."

"Yes, I'll take the plane back. I can fly down here and pick Dan up and take him back with me for medical attention. If Beth wants to crowd into the back seat with him, she can ride to town too."

"Good idea," John said. "I'll meet you in town."

"Thanks for what you did," Dan said, giving Beth a hug. "Beth and I owe you our lives."

"What are friends for," John smiled as he winked at Beth.

"One of you officers will drive Smokey back to his plane and pick up the other two prisoners. We'll follow with the wounded and head out to meet the ambulance," John spoke, then turned to Beth and Dan. "Smokey will come back here and pick you up to fly you into town where you can get that leg looked at, Dan."

Bates didn't make it back to town. He died in the ambulance on the way to the hospital. Monday, however, was rushed to surgery and lived. The damage to his artery would cause him circulation problems, and he would lose the full rotation of his left arm. It would be a couple of days before Dave and John could question him.

Dan walked with a limp for a few days but no serious damage was done to his leg. Somehow the shooting had made Beth understand that a cop accepts the dangers of his job, and, though he reduces the risks with skill and training, he must still put his own safety on the line to protect others. She would never again suffer the uncontrolled fears of the past. She knew Dan was able to make instant judgments and react instinctively to protect himself while saving others. She finally understood why he felt so strongly about his profession.

Chapter 19

Alaska has 19 remote radar sites picketing the shoreline of the huge state. Each is tied into a central control room at Elmendorf Air Force Base. This, Regional Operations Control Center, (ROCC) is the eyes of the far north. From here operators can detect activity in the sky at 200 miles. In the late 1980s, the Soviet Union tested the radar capabilities about once a week. These days, however, since the breakup of the Soviet Union, there are about six intrusions a year. Even those are routine and many are Russian "Coots," a slow, propeller driven observation craft, checking the ice pack off the Russian coast. The urgency of foreign threat is gone, but the watchful eyes continue to look across dark seas, often bored but ever vigilant.

The radar operator was half asleep when the small dots of light appeared on his screen. On duty for an hour, he was on his second cup of coffee. Three small dots of light were traveling to the northeast out of Russia. It was the usual cat and mouse game played by the northern air commands: U.S. and Russian. They send aircraft to test our radar limits and intercept capability. The U.S. did the same thing by intruding into Russian air space.

The Airman 1st class picked up the phone and notified the Weapons Acquisition Officer, the WAO. "Sir, I have three unidentified aircraft moving northeast in Russian airspace. On their present course, they will be flying the north coast in 12 minutes. Estimate they will reach our airspace in 8 minutes."

"Can you tell what type of aircraft they are?"

"No sir, Captain Winston. The speed and size of the larger aircraft suggest a Bear. The other two look too large to be fighters."

"I'm going to have them suit up at Galena. Keep me informed on the location of the intruders. Do we have an AWACs in the area?"

"No sir. The only one on duty is too far south to do us any good. I can see them as far as the Canadian border, and there the Canadians will pick them up at Inuvik. It looks like they are going to follow the northern coast. That's an unusual course for them, though." The airman was giving the captain as much information as possible and his best guess scenario from the short radar track.

"Thank you Airman, prepare intercept coordinates for the F15s. I'll call the ANRDO for permission to launch the fighters."

Eighty miles north of the Chukotskiy Peninsula, just crossing the 70° parallel were five, not three, ex-soviet aircraft. The largest, was a converted transport, an Ilyushin Il-38, designated the May by the U.S. government; an airliner turned antisubmarine patrol plane. It had been converted to a refueling aircraft for the fighters of General Kisishkin. The turboprop transport had a cruise range of 3,900 miles and a cruise speed of 400 miles per hour. It was an ideal aircraft for the job at hand.

Flying formation with the May were two MIG-25, Foxbats. Directly under the fighters were two more. On each side of the May, tucked under the top two and flying so tightly to the bellies of the top aircraft that the radar was only painting the profile of a single fighter, were two additional Foxbats. It was a tactic discussed frequently in officers clubs but not considered a valid military maneuver. The formation was at 25,000 feet, at the extreme range of the U.S. radar. A final refueling would be difficult because of the formation. The lower fighters, designated Attack One and Attack Two, would take on full fuel while the top two fighters, Cover one and Cover two, would take on only enough fuel to reach the separation point and to fly outside the U.S. territorial limits.

Major Gregorie Iniskin, mission commander, was flying Attack One. As the formation passed to the north of Barrow, Alaska, they started a descent to 500 feet above the surface of the Arctic Ocean. At 1,200 feet they would be too low to be detected by the American radar. They would be below the radar for only 1 minute. During that minute the four fighters would separate and the May, with the two MIG 25s, Cover one and Cover two, would return to 25,000 feet. They would return to Russian airspace and would continue to the Chukotskiy Peninsula for landing and refueling. The May would circle in a holding pattern and wait for Attack One and Attack Two. After refueling the second pair of fighters, it too would return to Russian soil.

Major Iniskin would fly his "training mission" to the oil fields of Prudhoe Bay, drop his "training bombs" on Pump station One and return to Russian airspace to refuel from the Il-38 tanker. This would be a true test of the response time for the F-15s from Galena. With luck the Major would encounter one of the F-15s and indulge in some playful dogfighting. The plan was simple and Iniskin was proud he

had been selected to participate in this, the first international training missions between the United States and the new Republic of Russia.

Lieutenant Sergei Popov looked out the left side of the MIG canopy. "Iniskin comes from a long line of military men. He is, no doubt, thinking that he may be the first of his family to become a General."

Sergei never set long term goals for himself. His only ambitions were to drink as much beer as possible and to bed as many women as possible. The handsome Lieutenant had many ladies to help him meet his goals. He was a lighthearted young man with exceptional athletic abilities. Everyone in the command thought him to be the best combat pilot in the Russian Air Command.

Having passed over the permanent ice pack, the Russian airmen relaxed as they flew over open water, just 500 feet above the waves, enjoying the summer sun. If the ploy worked as planned, the two men would drop their mock bombs and return to Russian airspace to refuel and go home without encountering American fighters.

Captain Winston gave the order to scramble two F-15s from Galena. Each aircraft was carrying three external fuel tanks supplying enough fuel to last until a refueling tanker could be dispatched to the area. Each aircraft also carried two radar controlled missiles and two heat seeking missiles and a full load of ammunition for each of the guns on board. The flight would be designated "Eagle One" and "Eagle Two." It seemed to be the usual except for the course the intruders had chosen. Winston looked at the huge map in the center of the room and asked the operator, "Who's this you have marked north of the Brooks Range?"

The airman checked his clip board against the numbers on the master map. "Two F-16s and a tanker from Eielson Air Force Base, Sir. On routine training maneuvers."

The Captain thought a few seconds, then told the airman, "Let's call Eielson Air Force Base and find out if these two have any ordinance on board. If so, see if we can divert those two to the Colville River area. I'm just not comfortable with the unknown blips on the radar and the unusual course they are using for approach."

The flight leader was Major Donald, "Dragonfly," Pierce. His wingman was Captain Al, "Slapshot," Spencer. The two were just completing a midair refueling when the message was received.

"Proceed North to the mouth of the Colville River, then West along the coast to intercept and identify unknown aircraft in U.S. airspace west of Barrow. Use flight level 250, expedite."

In just minutes the two had piloted their aircraft to the delta of the Colville River. There was a large fog bank to the north, above the ice pack, but the air was clear and the sun was nearly straight overhead as they cruised at 25,000 feet over open water.

The two targets were on the screen as the search radar was initiated. A voice channel was opened directly to the Regional Operations Control Center.

"Top Rock, I have two unidentified aircraft moving low at high speed. They appear to be headed for Prudhoe Bay," Dragonfly reported.

"Intercept and identify. Turn them around and send them packing." Simple orders.

"What are the coordinates for intercept?"

"Intercept will be 15 miles north of the Colville River Delta," Dragonfly recited into the mike.

On the squadron frequency Slapshot was speaking. "Dragonfly, we're going to have to get within gun range if we are going to engage these two. We don't have any real hardware to throw at them."

"Yeah, I know. Let's go over the top and come in from the east about 100 feet above. When we get within gun range, we can hit them with the gunsight radar. They should turn around when we do that. If they don't, we will dive past their nose and give them some wake turbulence to think about. Just stay on my wing and have some fun."

Major Iniskin was alerted to the approaching jets by the whine of the search radar. He had visual contact now and saw the two F-16s pass overhead and begin their descent. When they got within gun range, he would surprise them by attacking. He would drop his mock bombs on the target at any cost. Anyway, some simulated combat would be good training for him and his wingman. If he and his wingman could show victories over the two American jets, it would look good on the mission report. After all, he had everything to gain and nothing to lose; it was only a game.

"When I give the signal, we'll turn into them and press an attack. The instant we are within gun range, we'll lock on targets and record the sight picture. Move out to combat formation."

"I'm ready on your signal, Major," Lieutenant Popov replied.

The two Americans were now approaching from the east and about 100 feet above the MIGs. Iniskin judged the distance and shouted into the radio, "NOW."

The Russian fighters snapped into a hard 60° left bank and rolled out on a direct course on the noses of the F-16s. The Russians snapped on the gunsight radar the instant the wings were level. Iniskin only had a second to wait until the oncoming jet was in the square of his gunsight. He pressed the red trigger button on the stick of the Foxbat to record the sight picture as evidence of the kill. He felt the sudden recoil of the canons as tracer bullets and smoke of live canon fire erupted. He lifted his finger from the trigger as quickly as his reflexes would allow. Without thinking he slammed the throttle forward and pulled back on the stick to achieve a 70° climb angle. At 5,000 feet he leveled and began a slow circle as Popov again moved in tight on his right wing.

There were only three hits on the F-16, but they were enough. One was a tracer that sent burn marks down the left side of the fighter. The second went through the skin behind the canopy and severed a stainless steel hydraulic line. The third struck the top of the canopy with enough angle to shatter the lexan at the entry and exit points. The canopy was still intact, but dangerously close to tearing apart.

"Top Rock, Top Rock, Mayday, Mayday." Dragonfly called. "Tell Command I have taken hits from live fire. Attempting an emergency landing at Deadhorse. Do you copy? We have encountered live fire."

"Affirmative, Dragonfly. We copy. Are you okay?" Top Rock inquired with concern.

"I'm okay but my wingman is on his own. We are going to need help as soon as possible."

Slapshot slowed his Fighting Falcon to under 200 knots in order to stay on his flight leader's wing. White smoke streamed from the rear of the fuselage. "You're smoking. Looks like hydraulic fluid. If your controls are okay, get your gear down and locked before you lose all hydraulic pressure."

A thumbs up signal signaled affirmative. Slapshot dropped below the other aircraft and watched as the landing gear extended and locked into place. He then slid under and up on the opposite wing. "It looks okay. Are you all right?"

"Yeah, I'm okay. I can make it to Deadhorse. I'm showing three green. You had better keep an eye on those two. Don't let them get near dry land."

"I'll buy you a beer later," he said; then changed frequency to talk with the control tower at Deadhorse.

"Top Rock, this is Slapshot. Do we have orders from Command?"

"They do not have any notification of Russian aircraft in that vicinity. Do not engage them again unless they try to approach land. Repeat. Do not engage unless they try to approach land. Orbit there until they can get you some help."

"Roger, Top Rock."

Major Iniskin was still trying to comprehend what had taken place. Finally he looked through the canopy at his wingman and ordered, "I don't know what happened. I did not select canon operate—only target acquisition. Test your targeting switch."

Popov nodded to acknowledge; then set his switches to target acquisition. When he pressed the trigger, to record the radar picture of a centered target, the chatter and vibration of firing canons were felt through his craft and the fiery tails of tracer bullets could be seen dancing toward the surface of the Arctic Ocean. He immediately released the trigger and shut down the arming system.

"Mother of Stalin! What caused such a serious malfunction in both aircraft?"

"I do not know. We have a mission to complete. Let us finish our job and return for fuel. We will search for answers when we are on the ground in our own country."

"Are you certain we should continue with the mission? Under the circumstances it seems prudent to return home now."

Iniskin was adamant.

"We did not come this far to be this close and yet return home while we still have the capability of completing our mission. Assume combat formation; we are making a run at our target."

The Eagle flight from Galena had gone directly to the circling tanker to head off the two fighters sighted on the radar. It had taken almost a half hour to intercept the Russians. As the F-15s approached, the two Foxbats disengaged from the tanker and turned west toward their homeland. The two Eagles followed the fighters while the "May" turned to the north and further into international airspace. The Russian fighters were just entering their own airspace when the call came to break the pursuit and return to help the F-16s east of Barrow. "Contact the tanker for fuel," Top Rock ordered.

Slapshot was orbiting over the shoreline at 6,000 feet. He had visual contact with the two Foxbats. He was on the radio to Top Rock the instant the invaders changed course for the shoreline.

"Top Rock, the hostile are descending and increasing velocity. On their present course they're headed for Pump Station number 1. They've crossed the shoreline. I'm engaging, repeat, I'm engaging."

The F-16 responded to full military power as the pilot pointed the nose down to intercept the lead intruder. "You are cleared to engage. Be aware of civilian personnel and property in your path." The voice was that of the Colonel responsible for assembling all the approvals needed to engage an enemy, the ANRDO.

Iniskin had turned on his bomb targeting systems and was now lined up on the pump station. Popov was 50 yards to his right and was still unsure about the wisdom of the attack. He was distracted by his thoughts when he heard the high pitch generated by gunsight radar of an attacking F-16. Iniskin would not be swayed from his mission, but continued on a track that would put his payload on its target. This was, after all, in spite of the incident with the guns, only a training exercise.

Slapshot waited until the MIG-25s were over open tundra, and then he squeezed the trigger. He saw the stitches of destruction sewing up the back of the MIG. There was immediate smoke and flame. The stricken aircraft suddenly snapped to the left and nosed almost vertical toward the ground. The American pilot pulled the nose up and added throttle, making a hard left bank in an attempt to gain position on the other fighter. It was too late; the Russian turned inside him and passed under and slightly behind the Falcon. Then, instead of attacking, he throttled behind the right wing of Slapshot's fighter as though flying in close formation.

Captain, "Slapshot," Spencer was amazed to look out the right side of his canopy and see the Russian raising his hands above his helmet in a gesture of surrender. He pointed a finger toward the Deadhorse airport, showing he wanted the Russian to land there.

"Top Rock, this is Slapshot. One MIG destroyed and the other wants to surrender. I am escorting him to Deadhorse. Better have someone there to arrest this guy."

"Roger, Slapshot. Oh, yeah! Dragonfly reported on the ground and is okay."

"Thanks, Top Rock. Switching to Deadhorse frequency."

Eagle One and Eagle Two arrived just in time to see the smoking MIG spin into the tundra and were speeding to aid Slapshot when they saw Popov maneuver into position on his wing. Eagle Two dropped back for weapon separation while Eagle One edged into position on the right side of the Foxbat. Flanked by the two Americans, the Russian flew a direct route and approach to the Deadhorse airport. Slapshot was the first to land with the Russian only seconds behind. The two Eagles from Galena circled above the scene until the canopy of the MIG opened and its occupant climbed down to surrender to the waiting uniformed Borough police officers.

"Eagle flight," Top Rock relayed the orders. "Refuel and return to Galena. All other intruders are off the screen."

"Roger, Top Rock," the two fighters banked to the south.

Chapter 20

The events of the past few days had an exhausting effect on Roger and Gwen. The heat and humidity of Washington were not making it any easier. The last 24 hours had gone from hectic to frantic. Both had worked through the night compiling information gathered in interrogations, from statements of suspects in Arizona, Alaska, and in Washington D.C.. They had just finished briefing the newly formed investigative team at FBI headquarters.

As they were leaving the office together, Gwen's hair brushed against Roger's cheek. He could smell the perfume he had become familiar with the last few days. He enjoyed working with Gwen and found her company a pleasant and exciting experience. The touch of her hair and fragrance of her presence triggered Roger to voice what he had been thinking. His words caught in his throat and wouldn't come out as he stammered, "I...uh...I don't know how to say this...any better, but Gwen, I like being with you...as they say in the movies, I'm attracted to you."

Gwen slipped her arm through Roger's. She gave it a little squeeze and laid her head momentarily on his shoulder. "I feel the same way."

"Good. Let's spend some quiet time together. After we change and rest, we could spend the afternoon swimming and relaxing."

"Sounds wonderful. Where can we swim without having to fight a crowd?"

"As a matter of fact, a friend of mine owns a house on the Virginia side. It has a pool. He said I could use it any time. This weekend he's out of town on assignment." They stopped at the car door, standing only inches apart.

"I'd like that very much." She paused while Roger opened the car door—then turned to face him. "I like you, too." she said and kissed him lightly on the cheek.

It was late afternoon when Roger called Gwen. "Did I get you up?"

"No, I just finished my shower and was thinking about coffee. Is the swim still on?"

"Definitely. I have a pot of coffee here; why don't you come down and we'll enjoy a cup. I'll call John and Dan from here. After I fill them in, we can go for a ride in the country."

"I'll be right there."

As she combed out her wet hair she thought to herself, "the feelings I have for Roger have been dead since...I like it, it's nice to feel them again."

Roger answered the door, smiled and handed her a cup of coffee.

"Ummmm, just what I need," she said.

"Mr. Sutter, Roger Dorfmann's on line two." It had only been a couple of days since they had spoken, it seemed much longer.

"Roger. How are things in the big city?"

"Good afternoon, John. Well, our four party goers said they'd like to cooperate. They were reluctant at first but, with a little persuasion, saw it our way. Hopefully, they'll have influence in Congress. Copies of all reports will be forwarded to you for review. How are things going there?"

"A few problems have surfaced, but I think we have the upper hand, at least for the moment. You heard about Dan being shot again, didn't you?"

"No, what the hell happened? Is he all right?"

"Yes, he's okay. Some of Bergstrom's men kidnapped Dan's wife. They took her out into the desert and planned to kill Dan and her when he came to get her. There was a gunfight and Dan got hit in the leg. It's just a flesh wound, but he's more determined now than ever to get Bergstrom."

"How is Mrs. Webster?" Gwen asked.

"Oh, Hi, Gwen. Didn't know you were on the line. Beth is okay. She has some bruises and scrapes from the ordeal, but she's all right. She's a neat lady; Dan's lucky to have her."

"That's what I understand. I haven't had the chance to meet her. I'm looking forward to it, though."

"I see the kidnaped Arabs have been returned home. Anything else I should know about?" Roger asked.

John was silent a moment—thinking. "I can't think of anything. I hope to have enough hard evidence to get a warrant for Bergstrom by tomorrow. I'll let you know when we're going to serve it, so you can be here, if you want."

"Thanks John. Gwen and I are taking the rest of the day off. We deserve it. Talk with you tomorrow."

"Bye, John. Give Dan our best."

"See you soon," Gwen added.

There was little conversation in the car on the way to Virginia. The drive wore on and each began to relax and enjoy the scenery. As they neared their destination, Gwen began to ask questions about the area and the types of trees she saw. She marveled at the small farms and old buildings. Roger did his best to be an adequate tour guide and teased her about not being able to identify a maple tree.

Upon arrival at the country home, the two made a short trip around the grounds to a see the beautiful old farm. When they finally came back to the house, Roger made iced tea while Gwen changed into a swim suit and robe. She was lounging on the patio, beside the pool, when Roger joined her. He poured two glasses of tea—then began to chuckle.

"What's so funny?" Gwen asked. "Are you laughing at me?"

"No. I'm laughing at us." He chuckled again. "Our skins are so white we look like we came from another planet. I guess Alaskans don't get much time to sit in the sun and get a tan."

"You're right," Gwen was laughing now. "It's a good thing you mentioned it. We had better be careful of the sun. If we stay in it very long, we'll look like lobsters."

They swam, lounged, talked, and drank iced tea. Gwen was quite surprised at how easy it was to tell Roger about her life. Roger seldom talked about himself, but enjoyed telling Gwen about his career and how he had met Dan. It was a pleasant, albeit too short an afternoon. As they packed the car to leave, Gwen turned to face her friend. He looked into her eyes for a long moment, then pulled her close and kissed her.

"You are becoming very special in my life," he said.

"And you in mine," she replied.

There was a message waiting at the desk when they returned to the hotel. "Call the office immediately. Urgent."

Roger used the lobby telephone to contact his office. "Something has happened. We have to go to the office."

Lou Zimmer, the head of the newly formed task force, met them at the door.

"Where have you been? We've been trying to contact you for over 2 hours. There has been an air strike in Alaska. We've been holding up the briefing until you got here."

The key members of the task force were all present and took seats at a large conference table. Roger and Gwen found seats next to

Zimmer, near the head of the table. The room became quiet as Zimmer's aide got the nod. "Go ahead with your report."

"What I have here is a preliminary report from NORAD and the Air Force. I can't read the entire report, but I can give you a condensed version. Then, if you have questions, I'll do my best to fill in any blanks.

"At 1309 hours, Washington, D.C. time, today, three aircraft were detected by our radar. Their course indicated they were from Russia, and were skirting the north coast of Alaska. Later, it was learned there were five, and not three, aircraft in the flight. The largest of the aircraft was a Russian Il-38, May. The other four were MIG-25, Foxbats. The insignia painted on the aircraft was that of the Soviet Union, not Russian—Soviet. The aircraft, in very tight formation, entered U.S. airspace and descended below the radar coverage. After exactly 1 minute, two of the aircraft climbed back into radar range and flew back into international airspace to refuel from the May.

"Two F-15 Eagles were scrambled from Galena to intercept and identify the intruders, at the refueling point. When they got there, the May headed north and the MIGs headed west, toward Russian territory.

"Two F-16 Falcons were training close to Barrow, so they were sent to back up the F-15s. As it turned out, the Falcons intercepted the undetected MIGs just north of the Colville River on the Arctic Ocean. The U.S. fighters had been on a training mission and had no missiles, but did have live ammunition in their guns. The MIGs were on a course for the Prudhoe Bay oil fields. They did not answer the international hailing frequencies. As the Falcons closed in to turn them back, the MIGs turned in the direction of the F-16s and fired. One F-16 was damaged but was able to land at the Deadhorse airport. The pilot is okay.

"When it was determined that the other two MIGs were returning to Russia, the F-15s were sent to help the Falcons get the two Foxbats out of U.S. airspace. It is curious though, after hitting one of the F-16s, the Soviet planes climbed up and circled for several minutes. We don't know why they didn't immediately press the attack. The remaining F-16 positioned himself above the MIGs to keep them away from the shoreline.

"The two MIGs resumed a course that would put them in line with Pump Station Number One of the Trans Alaska Pipeline. The F-16 pilot did his job and took out the lead MIG. Then another strange thing occurred. The second MIG surrendered. He was escorted by the F-16 and the Eagles to the Deadhorse airport and forced to land. The Soviet pilot is in custody and being taken to Fairbanks for interrogation.

"The only damage to U.S. aircraft is minor and repairable. The Soviet MIG was a total loss and the pilot was killed. Are there any questions?" There were none.

Zimmer spoke. "The State Department and the President wants a report as soon as possible to decide what action, if any, to take in response to this attack. Roger, you've been in on this from the beginning and probably have the best handle on it." Roger scowled, and stared at the table. He pushed his chair back and stood, placing a gentle hand on the shoulder of Gwen, giving reassurance and confidence to both.

"Gentlemen," he began. "We are dealing with the worst economic disaster in this country since the great depression. The entire industrialized world has been dancing to a tune played by a coalition of unscrupulous, powerful men. We have little control over General Kisishkin whom, we believe, is responsible for the abduction of the royal Arab families. He is holding the trans Russian pipeline hostage and dictating the price of petroleum in Europe. We have little control over Mr. Yamamata in Japan. His companies control the majority of the tankers and petroleum shipping in the Pacific. He also owns the company we believe is responsible for building the magnetic pig containing the nuclear device used in the attempt to destroy the pipeline terminal in Valdez, Alaska. Each of these men must be dealt with by their respective governments. But we have in this country, possibly the most dangerous member of the coalition. We must deal with him.

"Nels Bergstrom is a powerful, ruthless man. He's made billions of dollars in the drug trade and we've not been able to stop him. He has converted much of that drug money into legitimate business, mostly oil. He's corrupted politicians and businessmen. He's paid off policemen. He's ordered the execution of, we don't know how many. And we have never been able to assemble enough hard evidence against him.

"We are sure he's the mastermind. He devised the plan to use a nuclear bomb in the pipeline. He's a cautious, resourceful man, and, as my friend Dan Webster likes to say, he never does anything without a backup plan. In my opinion, the attack on the pump station by the Soviet MIGs was at least part of Bergstrom's backup plan.

"It is time to stop Nels Bergstrom. I have statements from some senators, an undersecretary of commerce and some undercover DEA agents, stating Bergstrom provided drugs to participants at a party at his ranch in Arizona. It isn't a murder charge, but it's enough to get a warrant and have him arrested. If we can prove he's a major player in the drug trafficking business, maybe we can have him held without bail until we can get evidence against him of murder and terrorism.

"We have already begun to destroy his power structure. One of his hitmen has been killed and some others arrested. We may be able to get them to incriminate their boss in a conspiracy to murder charge. His political allies are beginning to turn on him. I think, if we wait too long, he'll disappear and resurface again in a jurisdiction where we have no legal authority. We must move now." Roger thumped the table with his knuckles.

"Sorry. I didn't mean to get on a soapbox. But, I've been trying to put this guy away for a long time, and I don't intend to lose him again." He sat down and looked around the room.

Gwen reached for his hand under the table and squeezed it gently. She understood his frustration.

Lou Zimmer opened the table for discussion. It took just under 2 hours to finalize a plan and to draft a recommendation to the President.

"It's up to you now, Roger. I have a feeling that tomorrow will be one of your longest days. There's a flight to Phoenix at 0600. I'll meet you at the airport with your tickets. I'll bring the warrants. I want you in Arizona to head the arrest and cross all the "T"s and dot all the "I"s. Good luck to both of you. See you in the morning."

It was after midnight when Zimmer got the call from Fairbanks. The initial interrogation was completed, and the pilot confirmed his unit was under the command of General Kisishkin. He swore live ammunition wasn't part of their plan and that Major Iniskin was just as surprised as he was when live bullets exploded from his guns. The pilots had been told in briefing that this was to be a training mission only. It should have been a routine flight, but something happened, something mechanical, Popov thought, that allowed the MIGs' guns to fire. There was no intention of aggression and that is why Lieutenant Popov neither pursued the Falcon, which shot down his flight leader, nor attempted an escape back to Russian airspace.

At 0200 hours Lou Zimmer presented a short verbal report to the National Security Advisor. The advisor awoke the President, excused and thanked Lou for his quick attention to this situation, then dismissed him.

Lou left the White House immediately and drove through the hot

Washington night to the home of Federal Judge Rudolph Carstairs. The federal prosecutor assigned to Lou's office had prepared a warrant for the judge's signature. The judge was sipping a cup of hot chocolate when Lou rang the bell at three AM. "C'mon in Lou. At this hour everything is important."

There is an 8-hour time differential between Washington, D.C. and Moscow, Russia. Direct telephone satellite link between the White House and the office of the Russian President came alive at 1024 hours Moscow time. There had been many calls on this line during the current economic crisis. The Russian President was doing everything within his power to aid the United States and the European powers in stabilization.

"Mr. President, what can I do for you this morning?"

"Mr. President, we have a new problem. Four of your MIG-25 Foxbats flew into U.S. airspace in Alaska and two of them attacked the Trans Alaska Pipeline. One of your fighters was destroyed and another has surrendered to our Air Force. Can you tell me about this new situation?"

"Mr. President! Please accept the apologies of my country and of myself. I have no knowledge of this attack."

"Other than the loss of your plane and pilot, we suffered no damage. The pilot's remains will be returned as soon as possible. There was slight damage to one of our F-16s when the Foxbat fired on him, but the pilot is unhurt and the plane suffered only minor damage. They were intercepted before they could do any damage to the pipeline or other ground facilities."

"This sounds like the work of General Lianid Kisishkin. We have been trying to locate and arrest him. He has commandeered a great deal of military equipment and forces, and maintained their loyalty by telling them he is sanctioned by the Russian government, which, I assure you, he is not. We think he is in Tarjikhstan. I promise we will give this our highest priority. I will inform you of our progress by 1600 hours Moscow time."

"Thank you. I will be expecting to hear from you this afternoon," The President hung up the phone.

"I'm going to try to get a couple of hours more sleep. Wake me if there are any changes. I think this is going to be a very long day." The President left the room and headed toward his bedroom.

Roger and Gwen were sipping coffee and munching whole wheat toast when Lou Zimmer arrived at the airport. He dropped his tired body into a nearby chair and let out a weary sigh. He placed a large plastic folder on the table and opened it to withdraw a typewritten list. "I'm getting too old for these all nighters," he commented.

"Did you get all the warrants?" Roger asked.

"Yup, they're all in here. Search Warrants, Arrest Warrants, both for Bergstrom and his key people. There are Search Warrants for the ranch and for the offices downtown. Here's a list of everything in the packet. If you need anything else, give me a call; the White House has given us a green light. Use whatever assets you need. We have authorization to use drug war funds for this one." Lou asked the waitress to bring him a Danish roll and coffee.

"Can it really be true?" Gwen asked. "Will we actually stop Bergstrom and his cutthroats today?"

"I hope so," Roger said. "John, Dan, and I have been trying to stop this guy for almost 20 years. Bergstrom has been a personal nemeses for the three of us. I, for one, will be happy when he's put away."

"It's almost plane time, so I'll say goodbye and good luck to both of you. Gwen, it has been a real pleasure meeting you. Roger is a damned fool if he lets you get away." Lou shook hands.

"Well, thank you. I hope to see you again some day."

It seemed like hours to Roger before they called for boarding. He'd passed the time by checking the contents of the folder to ascertain everything was there. It was almost impossible for him to imagine an end to Nels Bergstrom.

Chapter 21

Tokyo is a giant city of ancient but modern; a city taking pride in its thousands of years of visible history. Ancient temples and palaces, with gates of wood and hinges of bronze, nestle among modern high rise office buildings with doors of glass and brass. Super highways, eight lanes wide, cut through and over neighborhoods to speed business traffic from the airport to the inner city and business area. Under the super streets are narrow streets and homes.

Farmers come into Tokyo to peddle produce at restaurants in which they cannot afford to eat. The farmers dress in traditional garb and wear sandals. The people who eat at the restaurants are usually seen dressed in Hart-Shaftner and Marx suits and Italian shoes.

The United States is made up of peoples from all over the world. Immigrants, fleeing oppression in their own countries, enter the United States for its freedoms. Once here, they attempt to preserve the culture from which they escaped. This multi-cultural system derives its strength from its pool of blended knowledge.

Unlike the U.S., Japan has few foreign born citizens. Its cultural strengths come from centuries of practiced tradition. The same values and traditions practiced behind the giant wood and bronze gates are practiced in the glass, brass and plastic world of the high rise office. Japanese people have built one of the greatest modern, industrial and financially strongest nations of the world using techniques taught by an ancient traditional culture. The ancient culture has survived by adapting to this modern world.

Inspectors Oni Mastana and Ito Hisony had been investigating the business world of the great Mr. Yamamata for over 2 years. Powerful and wealthy, he insulated himself from the daily workings of the criminal nature of his business. One of his companies, Norita Nuclear Kinetics or NNK, is involved in a conspiracy of international terrorism. Oni and his partner were convinced that Yamamata was using his tankers to transport drugs and other contraband. Customs never found anything on his ships, but conceded the impossibility of searching every hiding place on a supertanker.

The two detectives received the statement of one of the technicians arrested in Valdez, Alaska. In his statement he related how he was working late one night at the NNK office complex, on the grounds of the company research facility. He stated he had overheard two of the company executives talking about how the regular technicians would be replaced by the ones selected from NNK personnel. He learned that the six regular TMC technicians would be murdered and their bodies put into the hold of a supertanker now in dry-dock for engine overhaul. Once at sea, the body bags would be retrieved, wrapped in chain for weight and dumped into the Pacific Ocean.

It had taken the two detectives several days and late nights, working with computer lists, to locate the Athenian Pride. It had simply disappeared from the waterways. It was in a dry-dock for repairs and out of normal governmental channels. Yesterday, however, it was floated again and was due to leave port for engine trials.

It was 6 AM in Tokyo when Ito picked up his partner from his home on the west side of town. They stopped for breakfast and then drive the 35 kilometers to the Yokohama harbor. Traffic was slow, and it took more than an hour to reach their destination. It was nearly 9 AM when they stopped in front of the Harbor Master office.

Inside, the two men were directed to a desk in the front part of the large office. Inspector Mastana presented his identification and asked the elderly clerk if he knew the whereabouts of a supertanker carrying the name the Athenian Pride.

"The Athenian Pride, is 265,000 deadweight tons, double hull, built in Yokohama but registered in Panama, is owned by the Maruma Corporation, a division of Yamamata Enterprises Limited. It is a fine ship. It has just been refitted with new engines and has returned to sea."

"What do you mean, 'returned to sea?'" Hisony asked, urgently.

The small, elderly clerk was intimidated by the authority of the two detectives and appeared shaken when confronted by Ito Hisony's brusque attitude. "The Athenian Pride was escorted from port this morning at 5 AM. It will be at sea for engine trials for the next 3 days. It will then return to pick up the regular crew and drop off the testing crew. It will be in port for only 24 hours at that time."

"Someone here must have a chart of the proposed course for the engine trials. Would you be kind enough to get these for us? And, may we use a private telephone to call our office?" Mastana asked. "You have been a great help. We didn't intend to upset you, but we must reach that ship as quickly as possible."

The small man relaxed a little. "The Harbor Master, there, in that office, has a boat. But it is, also, possible that the Harbor Master can obtain the use of the Port Authority helicopter. Come, I will introduce you."

The clerk led the two detectives to the office of the Harbor Master, introduced them—then departed. Commander Ichiba was 46 years old, rather tall for a Japanese, nearly 6 feet, and had been at this job for over 10 years. He bowed in polite traditional greeting—then sat. "It is unusual for Tokyo police to come this far out of their jurisdiction; it must be important. What can I do to help?"

"We are here under authority of the Ministry of Justice, Commander. This means our jurisdiction extends anywhere in Japan and this includes offshore Japanese waters. We would like to have your cooperation. If all goes well, we should be out of your hair by noon. We can go to the Maritime Commission for assistance. I'm sure they will be interested to know how you contributed to our investigation." Hisony didn't know exactly how much weight he carried with the Maritime Commission, but he did know the ship was getting farther away each second, and he didn't have time for posturing; it was time to bluff. It worked.

The Commander only paused a moment—then picked up a pencil and asked, "All right, what is it you need?"

Oni explained. "We believe a ship, the Athenian Pride, is carrying evidence of a heinous crime. We need to get to that ship without announcement and to inspect it for evidence. Can you help us do that?"

Ichiba had written a couple of notes—then picked up the phone. He spoke only briefly and hung up. He made a couple of entries on his note pad before looking up at the two officers.

"I have arranged for you to use my helicopter. The pilot will meet you at the heliport. I will also send my motor launch to follow the ship in case you need it. The tanker is only a few miles from the entrance of the port so it will take only a few minutes to get to her. Is there anything else you need?"

"Not right now, thank you," Ito said as he stood to leave.

"My secretary will give you a printed map of the port which will tell you how to get to the heliport."

It was only a short drive to where the helicopter was parked. The pilot completed his preflight check in preparation for departure when the detectives arrived. He motioned for them to get in the aircraft. He provided each man with a headset and flipped the switch to intercom.

"Can you hear me?" he asked.

"Yes," Oni said into the mike. "Did the Commander explain where we need to go?"

"Yes, he did. I understand you don't want me to contact the tanker until we are ready to land, is that correct?"

"That's correct. We are here to gather some evidence, and we don't want to give them an opportunity to dispose of it."

Ito used the cellular phone in the rear of the helicopter to report to his office. He wanted someone to know where they were in case anything went wrong. The pilot was pointing out the Athenian Pride when he hung up the phone. Ito saw a postage stamp size area on the rear deck of the ship with a large red "H" painted on it. This was the landing pad. "I don't think I like this," he thought.

The pilot gently dropped the shiny red and white helicopter onto the small landing pad. Two men, one in uniform and the other in dungarees, stepped onto the platform as the rotors slowed to a stop. It was warm and surprisingly quiet as the two policemen hopped from the helicopter.

They were met immediately by the uniformed officer.

"Who are you and what is your business? You are trespassing on this ship." Each detective presented his identification to the officer.

"We are here under authority of the Ministry of Justice. We have information there is evidence of a crime stored on this ship, and we want your cooperation in locating it. Can we count on you for your cooperation?"

"Is this a serious crime?"

"Yes, sir. A very serious crime," Hisony commented.

"I will have my crew cooperate with you then. I must report this intrusion to my home office in Tokyo though," the Captain said.

"We'd appreciate it if you'd not do that just yet, sir. We believe people in your office may be involved. We have a specific location we'd like to investigate. If there is nothing there, then we'll leave and you are free to do as you wish. I would like your assistance in locating the right area. Would you accompany us?" Mastana asked with the hint of authority in his order.

The Captain turned to a sailor, "Come with us seaman, we may need you."

"Thank you, Captain. Here is the location we wish to inspect." The Captain read the piece of paper and ordered the seaman: "Open Hold number three, compartment one."

"Aye, Sir," the seaman said nervously. Two other men in dungarees came into view, leaning on the steel pipe rail of the deck above. The seaman looked at the two sailors with fearful eyes and shrugged his shoulders as he made his way toward the manway hatch on Hold number three.

Compartment one was a small room containing tools and fire fighting equipment. There wasn't much room to enter and the light was dim, but the black vinyl body bags were visible behind the turnout gear and boots. Mastana pushed the coats aside, so he could reach the zipper of an available bag. He looked at his partner with anxious eyes, took a deep breath, then lowered the zipper about 16 inches to allow a look inside.

A bloated face appeared in the opening, followed by the stench of putrefied flesh. Mastana zipped the zipper shut as quickly as possible, but the smell had sent the captain and the sailor scrambling back to the open deck and fresh air. Hisony followed them, but Oni stopped to count the bags, to confirm their number was six, before making his way to daylight and fresh air. All four men had their faces pointed into the wind for a long while before Ito Hisony finally turned to the Captain and spoke.

"Captain, we would like to use your radiotelephone to contact our office. Of course, we must ask you to return to port. If there is no berth available at the pier, you'll make a boat available for us to get our forensics team here to recover the bodies and begin an inspection. We will need the hold secured until our crime team complete their work. We'd like to interview your crew one at a time on the way back into port if that is possible. Will you arrange this for us?"

"Of course. I will take you to the galley. There is a telephone there. I will have the Mate bring you a copy of the crew manifest and assign an officer to help you in locating the men. If there is anything else I can do, please feel free to ask." The Captain was shaken. "How soon may I contact my Maruma corporate headquarters? My superiors must be advised as soon as possible."

"How many of these radiotelephones are available to the crew of the ship?" Ito asked the Captain.

"There are several on each deck and in the engine room. We do not restrict the use of these telephones while we are close to port. It is good for morale to have the men in contact with their families and friends while in port."

"That being the case, I would guess word has already been sent to the people responsible for this crime. You may as well contact your

~~company and explain what has happened.~~ We want you to know that this act has far reaching ramifications, and we don't want word of our discovery spread ~~about.~~" any farther.

"Of course. Now if you will come with me, I'll show you where you can interview the crew. I have many things to attend to in order to take my ship back to Yokohama."

In the galley, the first officer was introduced and assigned to help the policemen. The Captain returned to the bridge to take command and turn the ship. The list of crew was placed on the table and Oni Mastana began the interviews while Ito called his Tokyo headquarters to arrange for a crime investigation team and officers to guard the scene on the ship. It was very late at night when the two officers left the ship and returned to Tokyo. After midnight, the two men finished and left the office for the day.

The secure phone rang in Nels Bergstrom's office late in the afternoon. The rotund man had just finished a sandwich and chocolate cake and was tipping a large glass of milk when the call came. "Hello. Hello."

"Lianid. How did it go today. I have been waiting for word."

"Not vell, my friend. Ve were intercepted, and one of my planes was destroyed before ve could disable the pump station. Sorry, but ve failed our mission."

"You told me you could get this job done. I thought you were a man I could count on. I may have misjudged your abilities, Kisishkin."

"How vital do you think this is to our overall plan? Do you think we can apply enough pressure on the world markets without disabling the Alaska pipeline?"

"We must disable the Alaska pipeline in order for our plan to succeed. Our project is in jeopardy as long as congress knows Alaska oil is available to supplement the reserves. They have begun rationing, which will not set well with the public, but the public usually bands together when a crisis arises."

"I think you are letting your anger cloud your thinking. Remember that in every var battles are lost. The trick is to know the difference between losing a battle and losing the var. I can send another sortie to attack the pump station. They vill, no doubt, be more cautious. Ve will have to engage their fighters in order to get through to the target."

"Lianid. You're right. I am impatient and some facets of our plan haven't gone according to the timetable. Hold your fighters in place for now. I'll try to find an employee at the pump station willing to accept a bribe for sabotaging the pumps or valves. This, in fact, may be less costly in the long run."

Bergstrom hung up the phone and poured another glass of milk from the pitcher on his desk. He sipped the milk then called Talbert.

"Have the cook cut me another piece of that chocolate cake and you bring it in here."

Talbert was soon in the stylish office. "Yes, sir. What can I do?"

"I am beginning to have a bad feeling about this plan of ours. Too many break downs. Those bastards in Washington are beginning to act as if they have nothing to lose. I wish Al hadn't got himself killed. I'd send him to Washington to correct that problem. I got word this afternoon that Monday will live. I don't know how long he is going to keep quiet. Too many things are unraveling, Talbert. We must think of the future." He wiped the chocolate from his face.

"Go to town with three or four men and pick up all the files that could be incriminating. Destroy all but the essential ones. Try to get the mess down to three or four boxes. We may have to make a move, and I don't want to leave anything for the Feds to find."

"I'll get on it right away, Sir. Is there anything else?"

"Yeah. Have the jet prepared for a long flight...Just in case."

The police force in Japan is structured quite differently from that of the police in the United States; more like a National Guard than the police. Large personnel vans with water canons on the roof are stationed at strategic locations around the city. Inside each is a contingent of riot police, waiting, in case of trouble. The Tokyo police department has access to huge amounts of manpower at any time.

Hisony and Mastana had instructed the captain in charge of the 100 man contingent to secure the building and especially the underground parking and the helipad on the roof of the Yamamata Business Plaza. Yamamata lived in an apartment occupying the entire top floor. They didn't want the business tycoon to leave before they could arrest him. The man was rich and intelligent and owned resources not available to most criminals. This was not going to be one of those "Walk in and cuff him" arrests.

As the contingent of security police took their positions, Ito and Oni double checked the building directory for the office of Mr. Yamamata. It was the same as the information they had in the notes; on the 16th floor. The two officers went directly to the security desk and spoke with the officer on duty.

"We are here on official business. Access the executive elevator, please." Oni said, showing the officer his credentials.

"Of course, Sir. What floor do you want? It must be accessed with a key."

"The 16th floor. Don't announce us; we want this to be a surprise," Ito said, motioning to one of his officers to guard the desk.

Nothing was said on the way up in the elevator until reaching the 14th floor. Here, Oni spoke into his radio. "Is everyone in place?"

Each assigned position reported in quick succession. The elevator stopped smoothly on the 16th floor. Oni nodded to Ito as the doors began to open. This was it. After 2 long years.

The two men stepped from the elevator into a lobby with a desk and receptionist. She seemed surprised when the door opened and the two men stepped into the lobby.

"You must have the wrong floor," she announced. "How did you get here?"

"We're on the correct floor," Ito said. "We want to see Mr. Yamamata. Which of these offices is his?"

"Mr. Yamamata will not be in today. Do you have an appointment with him?"

"This is all the appointment we need," Ito said, presenting his police identification. "Where is he?"

"I cannot tell you where he is. He does not wish to be disturbed today. Now, please leave?"

"Oni, you look in those offices and have a couple of officers look in the offices on the rest of this floor."

The receptionist was still complaining when the officers set off to search the offices. The effort was futile. Yamamata was not to be found on this floor.

Oni returned. "He isn't on this floor, but I think we found his office. There is a large corner office back here with a stairway leading to the next floor. That should be Yamamata's apartment."

Ito again turned to the receptionist.

"Is your boss up in his apartment? I want an answer. We're here to arrest your boss, and if you don't start cooperating, you'll be going with him."

Tears began to well up in the receptionist's eyes.

"I don't want to be arrested. It is my job to keep people from bothering him."

"Okay, okay. Just tell us where he is."

"He is up in his home. The security officer will have a key to operate the elevator."

"Thank you," Oni said. Then turning to the officers. "One of you stay here and keep her off the phone. The other go to Yamamata's office and stop him if he comes down those stairs."

The two policemen and the security guard entered the elevator and made their way to the 17th floor. One of the servants met the group. He too, attempted to keep the men from his boss. After identifying themselves as police, the man led the two officers to a large living room. The entire west wall of the room was glass and presented a magnificent view of the moat, walls, and East Garden of the royal palace. The businessman continued staring at the view without acknowledging the presence of the strangers.

"Mr. Yamamata," Hisony said. "We have been commanded, by the Ministry of Justice, to take you into custody. You are being charged with accessory to murder in the deaths of six technicians from the TMC corporation. I must ask you to come with us, please."

Yamamata gave no indication he had heard the officer. After several seconds, Mastana stepped directly in front of the man and said, "Did you hear what my partner said, Mr. Yamamata?"

He looked up slowly—then spoke softly. "Yes, I heard. Will you allow me to call my office so I can appoint someone to take my place while I am absent?"

"Of course," Ito told him.

Going down the elevator, both officers thought how anticlimactic and disappointing this arrest had been. After 2 long and tiring years of investigation, for reasons neither man could understand, the arrest of a major criminal did not bring elation or satisfaction.

Chapter 22

Seven AM. John Sutter knocked on the door of the ground floor room at the Desert Sands Motel. "Probably be 105° today," he thought, looking up at the blue sky with its wisps of white clouds.

Dan answered the door. "Good morning John. Beth ordered breakfast. It should be here any minute."

"Morning, Dan. How's the leg this morning?"

"Good. Good. My ankle is sort of stiff, like someone hit me in the lower leg with a baseball bat. I'll be okay, though. I just won't be able to run quite as fast for a while. I'm ready to get back to work."

"Good. Roger will be here this morning with a fist-full of warrants, and I thought the three of us should serve Bergstrom personally."

The glass doors opened and Beth came in from the patio, an empty coffee cup in her hand. She smiled broadly when she saw John. "Good morning, John. Are you hungry? I ordered you some breakfast."

"Hi, Beth. Thanks, I can stand a little nourishment. You sure look good this morning. How do you manage to look as if you've spent the last few days at pool-side?"

"Easy, I just put on another coat of makeup," she laughed.

The three friends chatted over breakfast; then, during a second cup of coffee, John looked into Beth's blackened eyes and said, "My wife will be over here in a little while. I've asked her to stay with you today. I'm assigning an officer to the two of you. I don't think Bergstrom will try anything again, but I want to be certain. We're going to arrest him this afternoon and it should be over, finished for good."

"Thank you for your concern, John," Beth said. "But, well, I can't explain it, but since that ordeal the other day, I'm not afraid anymore. I don't know why, I'm just not. I used to get almost hysterical when Dan had to go out on a dangerous job. But since that incident in the desert, I guess I understand better. I'm still apprehensive, but the overwhelming fear is gone. Don't get me wrong, I'll still be glad when he is back checking badges at the gate of a pump station."

"You're a strong lady, Beth. Oh, did you hear me say Roger and

Gwen will be in this afternoon? She's looking forward to meeting you."

As the two men stood to leave, Beth said, "You guys be careful."

It was going to be a busy morning. Larry Felson and Dave Vrobec were called and came to John's office when they heard about serving warrants. The four men made lists of available resources and manpower. They divided the manpower and supervisory responsibilities as evenly as possible. One team, led by Vrobec, would enter Bergstrom's downtown offices and seize all files, records, and computers. Felson, would secure the airfield and all outbuildings on Bergstrom's ranch. John, Dan, and Roger would lead a team to the main house at the ranch and arrest Nels Bergstrom. It seemed too simple.

"Anything we have overlooked?" John asked the men.

"One thing, maybe."

"What," John asked.

"We thought we had Al Bates once, and he managed to slip away. I don't want the same thing to happen with Bergstrom. How about getting Smokey Stover to fly cover in case they decide to jump into the helicopter and run."

"Good idea. I'll give him a call and set it up."

The rest of the morning was spent briefing teams. Each team studied maps and charts. They looked at pictures of Bergstrom and his key personnel. They tried to make plans for every conceivable contingency.

It was almost noon when John and Dan got to the airport. Roger and Gwen had already picked up their luggage and were standing on the sidewalk in front of the terminal building. "You guys look great." Dan said as they all shook hands. John put their luggage in the trunk.

As the car merged into traffic, Roger asked, "Is everything set?"

"Yes," Dan answered, "We're going back to John's office to meet with Vrobec and Felson. We'll give Vrobec the warrants you brought for the downtown building. Felson gets the warrants to search the outbuildings and airfield at the ranch. The three of us get the pleasure of serving the warrants on the main house and arresting that fat toad. Everything is in place, so all we have to do synchronize our watches."

"Sounds like you have it under control. What about Gwen?"

"Gwen, would you run the communications center and keep track of the times on each of these team actions," John offered.

"That's good. I was concerned that she might..."

"Hey. I'm sitting right here. Talk to me, not about me. I can say yes or no, ya know."

"I think you should give her one of those blue FBI windbreakers anyway. She deserves it; she's part of the team," Dan squeezed her to him, laughing, thinking of his first windbreaker.

Back at the office, introductions were made and warrants were passed out to the team leaders. A timetable was discussed, and it was agreed that no time should be wasted. The more time they gave Bergstrom the more time he had planning an escape. Estimates of driving and set up times were made, and it was decided the operation would begin at precisely 1430 hours. Each team would get as close as possible but remain discreet until the appointed hour. All three teams would attack simultaneously. Each team leader spent the remaining minutes reading the warrant he was to serve. Too many cases had been lost because the officer did not adhere to the restrictions of a warrant, or they failed to notify the proper individual of the warrant. Search and seizure is probably the most complicated area of law enforcement. No one wanted to lose a case, as important as this one, because he failed to read the warrant he was serving.

Because of the lack of cover, the two teams assigned to the ranch were forced to stop over a mile from their destination. Five vans, six officers in each, were waiting and checking wristwatches. Three vans would move to take control of the airstrip and the buildings near it. The other two vans would drive directly to the front of the main house. Officers would move quickly to surround the main house.

At 1428 hours, John gunned the engine of the lead van, allowing 2 minutes to drive the mile to the farm house and give the other three vans time to reach their objectives by 1430. Dan looked in the rear view mirror just in time to see the Cessna 185 come around the low hills of the river valley; over the road and passing the vans in less than a minute.

As the motorcade reached a fork in the road, the first two vans turned left and stayed high on the low ridge, dust feathered high, as the vehicles raced toward the main gate. The other three vans turned right and descended to the valley floor and the airstrip. The doors on the side of the vans were open now, and officers were standing in the opening waiting to leap out and quickly take their assigned objective.

At exactly 1430 hours the first van stopped in front of two small buildings located a short distance from the main hangar. The second truck stopped at the hangar and men quickly ran inside. The third van had a short drive to a small building several hundred yards down the road. There, two officers jumped out and secured the building. The remaining four drove their van across the airstrip to a small house and two small buildings that looked like equipment sheds on the river bank.

When the two vans reached the paved circle drive of the main house, John and Dan saw the armed man on the porch disappear inside. Dan shouted into the radio, "Be careful, guys. We can see armed guards."

The van had not completely stopped when the officers began to exit. With military precision, the men surrounded the house and covered the rear patio and pool area. The men at the rear of the house were moving carefully toward the home, checking pool sheds and other small buildings as they went.

On the front porch, Roger stood with his back to the wall next to the front entry door. "Federal officers, we have a warrant to search these premises. Open up. Federal officers. Open up."

No answer. John took a position in front of the door, kneeling, gun poised to shoot, while Roger tried the knob to see if the door would open. It wouldn't. Roger backed up a step and gave a healthy kick to the door near the lock. The force shattered the door jam inside, and splintered the casing. The door flew open with such force it hit the wall behind it and swung partially closed again. John pushed the door open slowly and peered inside. Nothing. Roger and Dan stepped inside, guns ready. There were two doors in the hall—one on each side—both closed—as well as an open arch visible at the end of the hall on the left side. Glass doors to the pool were at the far end of the hall.

With Roger on one side of the door and Dan on the other, John entered and began a slow march down the hall. He stopped at the closed door on the right. Dan moved up the hall behind him to cover him while he opened the door. John swung the door open and stepped inside. It was a large office, probably Bergstrom's. A check was made of the rooms next to the office—nothing.

Back in the hall, Roger stepped across the hall to open the left door while Dan covered him. John moved down the hall toward the archway. Roger opened the door to find another office, smaller than the first, but nice indeed. The two men carefully opened each door in the office. Again nothing.

Turning to leave the room, they heard automatic weapon fire. Two short bursts. Roger quickly poked his head out of the office. Someone was lying, face down, at the end of the hall. One of his officers slowly opening the glass door. He reached inside and gently dragged the fallen man through the open door to the outside of the house.

Roger turned to Dan, "John's been hit." He dashed into the hall with Dan on his heels, stopping before reaching the open arch. Roger again took a quick look around the corner and surveyed the room as thoroughly as possible in the instant he had to look. He had glimpsed a large leather couch toward the center of the room, just to the left of the entry.

"There's cover to the left. Move fast. There's a door on the other side of the room, to a kitchen, maybe; I think the shooter's in there," Roger whispered to Dan.

"I'm with you," he replied in a low voice.

The two men crouched low, one behind the other, they made a dive for the floor behind the couch. Two shots were heard from the kitchen. Dan jumped up and ran to the open door leading to the next room. He motioned for Roger to follow.

Dan bent low and looked into the room. He could see a glass exit door on the far side. An officer in a blue jacket was outside, trying to get a shot to the inside. A man was using the refrigerator door as a shield and holding what looked like an Uzi.

Dan peeked around the corner, putting his pistol into firing position. "Drop the gun," he shouted.

The man at the refrigerator instinctively turned to fire. He was too slow. Dan fired two shots, striking the man in the chest. He fell backward against the open refrigerator door, twisting as he fell, his grip on the Uzi squeezing the trigger, spraying the ceiling with random bullets.

The officer outside the door quickly entered and pulled the gun away from the man. He checked for a pulse; then looked at Dan and shook his head. Another officer in a blue jacket entered the kitchen. Roger pointed in the direction of the other two closed doors in the room, "Check them out."

Dan and Roger then returned to the hall where their friend was lying on the slate patio just outside the glass door. The left side of John's head was covered with blood and the clear liquid from inside his skull cavity was oozing out onto the slate. He had been struck twice in the chest, but his armored vest had absorbed the power of those shots. Two of the shots, both fatal strikes, one in the neck, and the other above the ear. The entry wound was not visible, but the exit wound on the left side of the head was a gruesome hole.

Dan knelt beside his fallen friend. Only moments ago they were attacking a common foe and now he lay here, lifeless.

Roger spoke softly to the officer standing near John's body. "Go inside and call an ambulance. Don't put this on the radio. I don't want any mention of this to get out until Dan and I can talk with John's wife."

The young officer nodded and moved into the house. Dan took a tablecloth from a table on the patio and covered their friend. He was fighting back tears when he finally spoke.

"I guess we had better finish what we came here to do."

"Yeah. Let's go. Be careful; I don't want to lose any more friends today." The lump in Roger's throat seemed the size of a basketball.

The search of the rest of the house turned up only two more guards, who gave up without a fight. There was a cook and a gardener. The cook said the other servants had been given the day off. She also said that Mr. Bergstrom and Mr. Talbert had left in the jet late last night.

Roger assigned several officers to get all the files and computer discs from the offices. A specialist would have to be summoned to open the three safes on the premises.

When the ambulance arrived, Dan and Roger stood silently on the front porch as John's body was taken away. Each remembered the good times with their friend. Years of friendship and association would be treasured memories. The task of breaking the news to Sonja and the children would be horrendous They were a close family and this was going to be exceptionally hard on them.

Roger contacted Felson on the radio. He asked the DEA man to meet them at the hangar. They also called Smokey Stover and asked him to land for a conference at the hangar.

The little Cessna landed and the engine came to a stop where the other three men were waiting. Felson suggested they talk inside the air-conditioned office. The temperature being more tolerable.

"John's dead," Roger hesitated. " He was shot by one of the guards in the house. Bergstrom skipped last night. His right-hand man went with him. We don't know where they went, but they took most of the records. We haven't had a chance to look at anything in detail, but I don't think there is very much left. The fat bastard beat us again." He turned away.

There was a long silence in the room. Dan was again feeling the heat in his eyes and the tears trying to escape. "Did you guys find anything?" he asked.

"We're still looking," Felson said softly. "We've arrested eight people so far. Two of them are harmless caretakers. We got four from the hangar here: they were destroying records and had the safe open. We found four Kilo bags of cocaine and a brick of marijuana and will tag the helicopter for seizure. The other two were armed guards but gave up without a fight. It's going to take some time to inventory all this."

"I don't like leaving all this work for you, Larry, but can you handle all the investigation here if Dan and I go into town? We'll check in with Dave to see if everything went okay on his end; then go to see Sonja Sutter. I don't want her to hear about this from a stranger. She is really going to take it hard." His voice cracked with emotion. He turned and stepped away from the group, in an attempt to regain his composure.

"Sure, I can handle it. I know you two were really close to John. I worked with him a few times in the past and liked him. I could count on him. Just one of those people you always like to have on your side. I'll wrap up here and see you tomorrow."

"If you don't need me here anymore, Larry, I can fly them back to town. I'll drive them from the airport back to the office," Smokey said, breaking his long silence.

"Good idea. See you all tomorrow."

The three men stopped at the Bergstrom Building on the way from the airport. They checked in with Dave Vrobec. Most of the real hard evidence they expected to find had been removed. The regular employees were unaware of most of Bergstrom's activity and no arrests were made in the offices. There was however, a mountain of data from files and computers which must be read and evaluated, a job that would take several days to complete. Roger told Dave about John's death and asked that he keep it quiet until they had a chance to talk with Sonja. After satisfying himself the job was being done properly and thoroughly, Roger returned to the office to break the news to Gwen.

Once inside the DEA office, Smokey went on his own way. Roger and Dan went immediately to the communications center to notify the head office in Washington of the death of one of their officers. It would be a sad afternoon in Phoenix and in Washington, D.C.. John was a respected bureau chief. A DEA officer was asked to take over for Gwen at the radio and Roger took her into John's office and told her what happened. Gwen let the tears come. "Poor Sonja" she repeated again and again. She held tightly to Roger and sobbed into his chest. He held her gently. They held each other for a long, long while.

Dan knocked softly on the office door and poked his head into the room. "I think we should go now," he said.

Roger helped Gwen to the waiting car and drove across town to the

Desert Sands Motel. Each wondering what to say, how to soften the news. There was no easy way. They were still pondering the question when they stopped in front of the motel. As they approached the door, the agent on duty stepped out.

"Stick around; we may need you," Roger instructed.

Dan opened the door with his key and the trio stepped inside. Beth and Sonja were on the patio, drinking iced tea. They stood when they heard Dan call. Beth slid the patio door open and stepped inside. Sonja was only a couple of steps behind. The two women were smiling and greeted the three newcomers. First Beth "Hi, are you through already?"

Then Sonja, "Well, that didn't take long."

"This must be Gwen," Beth said stepping further into the room. That's when she saw their grim faces. The realization hit her suddenly.

"Where is John? Oh, Dan! Has something happened to John?"

Sonja pushed her way past Beth to look Dan and Roger in the eyes.

"Where is John? Is he okay?" She saw the pain on the faces of the officers. She knew something terrible had happened but didn't want to admit it. Nothing could happen to her John.

"Sonja, John is...John is...gone."

"Gone? Gone?...You mean dead? That can't be. Is he in the hospital? Where is he, Dan?"

"I'm sorry, Sonja." Roger didn't know what to say but felt compelled to explain. "He was shot when we went into Bergstrom's house. He never had a chance; he just didn't know what hit him."

For an instant she stood transfixed. then hysteria set in. "Take me to see him. Where is he? Is he alone? " She screamed through her tears.

Roger held her tight. "Sonja." He continued to hold her while she cried. No one spoke for a long time.

Beth, too, was crying. She walked into the kitchenette with Dan close behind. In the kitchenette, she put her arms around Dan and sobbed.

"Oh Dan. Let's go home. I can't take it any more. I don't want to be involved anymore. Please, Dan."

"Okay Beth. It's over. Bergstrom got away. Right now we have to take care of Sonja and the kids. Come on, dry your face. Sonja needs a strong friend right now." Dan was trying to be strong, but it was all he could do to choke back tears of his own.

They stepped out of the kitchenette, Beth put an arm around Sonja's shoulders, and the two women sat on the couch. Gwen had been silent all this time. She stepped into the small kitchen, looked into the refrigerator and found a pitcher of iced tea. She found glasses in the cupboard. She poured a glass of tea for each of the sad group and stepped back into the living room, handing the first glass to Roger.

Roger gave her a weak smile. “I’m sorry. You ladies haven’t met Gwen. Sonja, Beth, this is Gwen Stevens.”

“Hello. I’m sorry we have to meet under these circumstances. Please let me know if there is any way I can help.”

“Maybe there is. Beth asked. “Could you and Roger get Sonja’s children and bring them here? They’ll want to be with their mother right now,”

Later, when the children were there, and more tears flowed, Dan felt a need for solitude. He stepped out into the heat, found a chair on the patio and collapsed. He felt sad, angry, weary, and most of all frustrated. What had gone wrong. It was supposed to be simple. He pounded on the arm of the chair, “Dammit, dammit, dammit.” Tears coursed down his burning cheeks.

Chapter 23

The previous day had been a long and busy one for Nels Bergstrom and his associate, Russ Talbert. After his talk with General Kisishkin, Bergstrom attempted to contact several elected officials on his payroll. Senators Frost, Tillman, and Wayman were "not available" or were out of town and would get back with him. Senator Frost was on an armed services junket. Undersecretary of Commerce, Jason Belafont, was in a meeting and couldn't be disturbed. "Couldn't be disturbed...Couldn't be disturbed!" Nels Bergstrom bellowed. "He'll be disturbed when I get through with him."

Nels Bergstrom was not a person to be double-crossed. When he was in the fourth grade, he organized a group of classmates to cause a disturbance in a coat room. When the teacher left the room to investigate the noise, another student copied the answers to the math test she was about to give. Bergstrom and his classmates all got As. When one student was accused of cheating because the teacher doubted he could get a perfect score, he said he had bought the answers from Nels. Bergstrom talked his way out of the accusation, but after school had two boys hold the snitch while Nels beat him severely.

Nels had also always been a good con man. He'd been heavy all his life, but his ability to obtain almost anything made him very popular with his fellow students, especially those needing his talents to pass a test in school.

Young Nels Bergstrom found it easy to manipulate people around him. He searched out their deepest desires and made a trade for whatever he needed from them. As he grew older and went off to college in his home state of Minnesota, he honed his skills even sharper.

By his second year in college he had accumulated a small amount of cash. He used the cash to finance a lucrative marijuana business. He ran the business, but never used the stuff. He was intelligent enough to never have any of the contraband on or near him. He saw to it that the supply was steady; and there were always people willing to distribute the product for a price.

By the time he graduated from college, he had a sizable nest-egg.

A good student, he graduated near the top of his class. His major was Political Science. He was hired, right out of college, as a legislative aide in Sacramento, California. There he attended school after work until earning his Masters Degree.

In California he earned that adults can be manipulated as easily as fourth graders and usually for the same stimulus as his college friends. At age 24, he had built a strong political base and entered California legislature. At the end of his second term, he met Dan Webster. The man's honesty and dedication to duty cost Nels a great deal of money and a profitable marijuana growing business. Bergstrom hated Webster, but admired and respected, more than he respected any other man, Dan's strong character.

Nels served one more term in the legislature, but found it increasingly difficult to satisfy questions about his involvement in the drug business. His business holdings gave him great wealth. He made the decision to quit politics in favor of pure financial gain. He surrounded himself with highly capable, loyal employees. The large man succumbed to few distractions. This, with his lack of standard moral values, had made him one of the wealthiest and most powerful men in America.

Nels was tired. His body ached. He slumped into the leather chair behind his desk, turned the TV to CNN News, and reached for a cookie.

"In the news at this hour, a report from Tokyo. Respected Japanese industrialist, Gaishi Yamamata, was arrested today by Tokyo police. The Japanese tycoon is charged with conspiracy to murder in connection with the deaths of six technicians working for TMC Corporation.

"CNN News has learned that Mr. Yamamata's Norita Nuclear Kinetics Corporation built the bomb that exploded just outside Valdez, Alaska. Details are sketchy at this time, but it appears the motive behind this terrorism was to control the world wide flow of oil.

"Mr. Yamamata also owns Maruma Transportation Corporation, whose main business is shipping oil, worldwide

"The U.S. Government has yet to make any statement in regard to this new development in the economic crisis.

"Our reporters are at the Ministry of Justice in Tokyo and will have more news as it develops. And now a word from our sponsor."

Nels turned the television off. It was very late and Russell Talbert was in bed when Bergstrom called. "Talbert, get down here."

Less than 10 minutes later, dressed and awake, he reported to his boss. He had become accustomed to these calls. The irregular hours were justified by the size of his salary.

"You look tired, Nels. Are you sure you're all right?"

"Yes, yes, I'm okay. My neck and shoulder ache something fierce. I must have slept on it wrong last night."

"What can I do for you, Sir?"

"Things are falling apart. Kisishkin failed to knock out the pump station. Those wimps in Washington are losing their backbone, and I just heard on the news that Yamamata was arrested in Tokyo. The Feds are putting the pressure on us here in Phoenix. This whole deal is falling apart. I think we'd better move our offices to a less hostile environment for a while. Did you recover everything from downtown?"

"Yes, Sir. I have four Banker Boxes full of files. The rest have been shredded. Fortunately, most of the files are on computer disc and don't take up much room."

"Good. Call Rigby and Wells and have them load the jet. We will headquarter in Venezuela for a while. I want to leave as soon as possible. Clean out the safe in your office and pack a bag. Have the cook prepare some food for the trip."

It was just 3 AM when the Citation lifted into the sky and turned south along the Mexican shoreline. Talbert noticed Bergstrom was massaging his left arm when he brought Nels' turkey sandwich and hot cocoa.

Bergstrom's size and weight, 395 pounds, demanded a specially constructed seat. The seat was double width and faced across the fuselage instead of ahead. This allowed the use of existing seat rails for strength and safety. The seat was placed over the wing for better balance of the craft's center of gravity.

Bergstrom asked Talbert for a pillow and blanket. Although the ache in his left shoulder and arm seemed worse, he slept all the way to Panama, where the Cessna landed for fuel.

In Panama City, Bergstrom was able to establish a telephone link from the airplane. He placed a call to Piersol in Venezuela to let him know of his arrival there, on the Caracas Oil Company air field, in about 3 1/2 hours.

The Citation had been airborne again about 1 hour when Bergstrom became nauseous. He told Talbert it must have been the turkey sandwich and tried to return to sleep. Sleep was intermittent, disturbed by the pain in his arm and now his upper chest. He dozed for a while—then awakened, nauseated again.

They were less than a half hour from landing when it happened. Bergstrom awakened with a cry of pain. He was clutching his chest and gasping for breath. When Talbert saw his bosses face contorted into an expression of terror, he rushed to the ailing man and loosened his shirt and tie. It was apparent something was seriously wrong. Talbert suspected a heart attack but couldn't be sure. He opened the cockpit door and shouted to Rigby the pilot, "I need help."

Wells, the copilot said, "I'll do it," and unstrapped his seat belt and harness. As he emerged from the cockpit into the cabin, he could see Bergstrom gasping for breath. He reached back into the cockpit, behind his seat, and extracted a small portable oxygen bottle. He brought it to Bergstrom's side and placed the small green plastic mask over the nose and mouth of the stricken man.

The oxygen seemed to ease his distress a little, but it was obvious they were going to need professional medical assistance. Wells returned to the cockpit and asked the pilot to radio ahead for an ambulance.

Talbert was still beside Bergstrom when Wells returned. They could feel the aircraft beginning its descent when Nels gave out a cry and bent forward as if hit in the stomach. He remained that way for several seconds, moaning, then leaned back in his seat and relaxed. He had stopped breathing. There was nothing the two men could do but watch as their boss, Nels Bergstrom, expired.

Russ Talbert was smiling to himself. He had known that, eventually, the overeating and stress would get the best of his obese mentor. This was the perfect time for him to take over as CEO of Bergstrom Enterprises. In fact it couldn't have been better had he planned it.

Talbert saw the bright blue flashing lights of the Brazilian built ambulance following alongside the Citation as it taxied to the paved parking ramp in front of the company hangar. He just sat there, looking at the lifeless mass strapped into the seat ahead of him, until the whine of the engines died away and someone outside the aircraft was attempting to open the door.

He loosened the buckle of his seatbelt and stepped to the front of the aircraft. He saw Piersol standing at the bottom of the steps, the ambulance crew directly behind him.

"What's wrong?" Piersol asked.

"It's Mr. Bergstrom. I think he had a heart attack. We did everything we could, but he didn't make it."

Talbert walked down the steps to allow the medical attendants inside. Piersol stepped up to the plane, alongside the stairs, and peered

inside.

inside. He saw the pasty pallor and slack jaw associated with death. The aura of life was gone, the fierceness, the intensity, all the things that had been Nels Bergstrom were gone.

One of the medical technicians stepped down from the plane. "We have checked, Sir. The man is dead. It is hard to tell, but it looks like a heart attack." Then turning to Piersol, "I know this was an important friend of yours, Mr. Piersol. We would not ordinarily transport a dead man, but in this case we would do this for you, if you wish."

"Yes, thank you. He is a very large man. You're going to need help removing him from the airplane. I'll have men from the hangar help you. There is a small fork lift in the hangar, you might put the stretcher on the forks and lift him down with that," Piersol offered.

The two pilots were now stepping out of the plane.

"Rigby, would you and Wells stay here and supervise the removal of Mr. Bergstrom? Then bring my bags and those four file boxes up to Mr. Piersol's," Talbert said; then turned to Piersol. "I'll find an office space to set up in just as soon as I can. Meanwhile, would you put me up for a short while?"

"Of course. It would be my pleasure. Come, I will have the men in the hangar come out to help; then we will drive out to my home. We can talk on the way."

In the car, on the dusty road to his home, Piersol spoke in a low voice. "I want you to know that I am very sad about the loss of my friend. He has done many favors for me over the years. I will miss him."

"Nels had a great deal of faith in you, too," Talbert began. "He respected you and trusted you. I am assuming the leadership of the company. I hope to enjoy a smooth transition. There are several problems that must be dealt with as soon as possible. I'm going to need an assistant I can trust, someone to do the job I have done all these years. I would like you to take over that position."

"This is very sudden and, frankly, almost overwhelming. I don't know what to say. I'm deeply flattered by the offer. And you are correct about some serious problems to be dealt with immediately. How much time will I have to think about this, Mr. Talbert?"

"You can call me Russ when we are in private. How much time do you need? Will tomorrow be too soon?"

"I'll have an answer for you by morning." There was silence in the car for several minutes before Piersol spoke again. "The house is just up this drive. We could use a drink. No?"

Talbert was sitting on the veranda, watching the rain, and sipping a scotch and water, at the instant the attack was initiated on the ranch. He, of course, knew nothing of the raid or the death of John Sutter. He sat on the porch planning his strategy. He knew the Feds were trying to get enough evidence to arrest Bergstrom. How could he come out of this with the company intact, remain the Chief Executive Officer, and not get arrested?

The first order of business was to establish a communications network. The Venezuelan government owned controlling interest in the telephone company; therefore, it should be relatively easy to bribe an official to get a satellite station with a direct link to the office in Phoenix and connect with their existing network.

Secondly, since he had control of the offshore bank accounts, he could continue to finance the drug running business. He must be careful though, not to connect himself directly with any drug cartels or members. He figured that, since he was in South America, there would be attempts to contact him in person. He could not allow it, for safety sake.

Third, and most important, he must shut down the attempt to control worldwide oil shipping and oil pricing. He must let the price of oil stabilize on its own. It would take some doing, but he must establish a good relationship with the very people Bergstrom had been manipulating and intimidating. This would be the difficult part, building trust.

When the communication center was in place, he could begin. Meanwhile, he would have Donald Piersol contact Edwardo Martinez. He would have the two men resume oil flow and production from their own companies and pipelines. It was almost certain Japan would take control of the Maruma Corporation and start the supertankers moving again. With Yamamata in jail, that portion of the plan was bankrupt. Oil flow in Europe and north Africa were still being controlled, but Kisishkin was becoming undependable. He attached too much importance to military logic and not enough on financial influence.

That was it then. He would start the oil flowing again and become the hero of this disaster. The Board of Directors would have to concede that Russell Talbert had saved the company from financial ruin and possible takeover by the government. The government would not arrest him because he had been able to end the present crisis. The price of oil would stabilize, but at a much higher price than before, increasing profits for everyone around the world. They would view him as a savior too, for helping to establish higher crude oil prices when no one else could accomplish that feat.

when no one else could accomplish that fete. Yes, the plan would work.

Talbert was tired. He had been up nearly all night. He had suffered an adrenaline rush during the moments of Bergstrom's attack. That, combined with the exhaustion and the Scotch he had just drunk, made him extremely weary. He decided he would take a short nap before going to dinner.

General Lianid Kisishkin didn't want to admit it to Bergstrom, but his political and military influence were rapidly eroding. The government was regaining control of the Trans Russian Pipeline. That pilot, Popov, landing in Alaska, could be traced back to his command. With the Russian government trying to cement relations with the U.S. and procure huge loans, it would be a disastrous blow to his authority, Boris would see to that, personally.

Bergstrom had provided a large amount of cash for him to use. This was deposited in several banks outside Russia. If he could get to the Switzerland banks before being apprehended, he stood a good chance of escaping to South America, where he could live handsomely for the rest of his life.

He had moved his headquarters regularly, every several days, during the past months. This made it difficult for anyone to find him. Now in Dushambe, He would take a car across the provincial border into Kirghiz, then to Pishpek where he would get a commercial airliner to Switzerland.

The Russian president, however, had different plans. He had put a bounty on the head of Kisishkin. He knew that, in these harsh economic times, cash was worth more than loyalty. His men had traced Kisishkin to Dushambe and were on their way to arrest him when word was received that the General, carrying one bag, had driven his own car off the military installation. A quick conference was called to discuss the possibility that he was running. The logical escape point was from another province where he'd catch a commercial airliner.

The nearest airport, with flights to Europe, was 300 kilometers east. It would take at least 4 hours to make the drive. The small, six man, contingent acquired an airplane from Kisishkin's base and flew to Pishpek. They waited more than 2 hours for the General's arrival. When he arrived, it was near time for a flight to Zurich to depart. As General Lianid Kisishkin entered the terminal, he was arrested by the six ex-KGB officers.

In Phoenix, Dan Webster, Roger Dorfmann, and Gwen Stevens were spending most of their time helping with funeral arrangements and comforting their fallen friend's family. The three had gone to the office for a few hours to write several reports, but the search of records and mundane tasks of investigation were now turned over to the officials from the task force. It would be several months before word of Bergstrom's death reached the trio.

After the funeral, Roger and Gwen returned to Alaska. Dan and his wife, Beth, flew to California to visit with her parents before returning to their life, their family, and their home in Alaska. That home and family life was even more precious to them now. Sonja Sutter and her children would become closer than before. It was going to take a long time to get over the sadness of their loss.

Roger and Dan were bitter because they had let Bergstrom slip through their grasp. Neither man could have prevented his leaving but each took it personally. Each felt responsible. They had again suffered the loss of a friend and the man responsible was free to continue his criminal activity. It was going to take Dan much longer to absolve himself of blame than it would Roger. Both men would, however, harbor bitterness for a long time to come.

Chapter 24

Gasoline rationing ended only days after the raid on the ranch in Arizona. The price of crude oil remained above $26 per barrel on the world market, nearly double the price of crude before the crisis. The Senate was talking about more oil industry regulations. For the most part, things were getting back to normal in America.

Three months passed since the death of John Sutter. Gwen returned to her position as technician at the pump station. She was moved to the top of the list for position of pump station supervisor. It had been a difficult 3 months, keeping her life her own. The news media, and in particular the pictorial magazines, found her to be an interesting subject. Gwen hated the notoriety. She enjoyed a small amount of freedom from the pests during her work week on the north slope. She wished they'd just go away.

During her weeks off, she spent a lot of time with Roger. They enjoyed the same things and were comfortable in each other's company. She suspected Roger was about to ask her to marry him. She spent time searching her own soul for answers to that question. She had been happily married once, but the years of pain, suffered after her loss, were not balanced by the memories of her late husband. Roger was engaged in a dangerous profession, she could lose him, too. She loved Roger with all her being, but what would she be like if something happened to him?

Roger was extremely busy. He barely had time for meals and he was losing weight. Preparation for the trials ahead was mind boggling. He worked long hours while Gwen was on the slope, in order to relax enough to be with her while she was home. His mind kept drifting back to her. All his life had been dedicated to the job. Now, after all these years, something was more important. He was deeply in love with this beautiful blond.

Dan was delighted when the office in Anchorage asked him if, on his first week back at the pump station, he'd fly into Fairbanks, pick up the little plane he had borrowed from his friend on the north slope, and return it to the Deadhorse airport. In Fairbanks, he stopped at an electronics store and purchased a portable compact disc player. With it, he bought several country and western discs. He tucked the package into his bag before taking off for the far north.

His only stop on the way to Deadhorse was in Bettles. The young native girl came out of the cabin to put gas in the small craft.

"You can get cinnamon roll and coffee inside," she said. "Hey, I remember you. Steve let you use his airplane."

"Yes, that's right. I have something for you. You did such a good job the last time I was here, I brought you a gift." Dan reached into his bag and brought out the disc player and the discs. "Here, I hope you enjoy the music."

She looked at the gift in disbelief.

"This is for me?"

"All for you."

"Shouldn't you give this to the pretty lady with you last time?"

"She'd like you to have it, too."

Dan went inside to drink coffee. He rested and visited with the family about an hour, then returned to his plane to drain the fuel tanks of water and check the oil before taking off into the afternoon sun. The voice on the radio was the same one he had talked with on his trip south.

"Have a good flight; you made my daughter very happy. Come again when you can stay with us for a while."

"Thanks," Dan responded, "I'll do that."

His work was interrupted often, as was that of Gwen and Roger, to fly "outside," the lower 48, for depositions and pretrial hearings. It had been three months of confusion and courts, lawyers, and press. Would it ever end? This week, however, he was going to be off work and he was going fishing with Roger and Gwen, and for a barbecue. Dan, an avid salmon fisherman, preferred a flyrod to more traditional bait or spin casting methods. Four species of salmon return to the Kenai River each summer. Dan fished for them all, and used whatever method worked best: flies for reds, silvers, and pinks; trolling and drifting for kings.

It was late afternoon on this, the last Friday of September. The silver salmon were running in the river and Dan was looking forward to giving exercise to a few of them. The days were getting shorter, but it was still daylight until 10 at night. His tackle box was a mess with hooks and lures tangled. He sat at the kitchen table sorting the tangle and teasing Beth.

"You claim to be a good housekeeper, but just look at the mess you left in this tacklebox.

left in this tackle box. And you've had all summer to straighten it out."

She turned, wiping her left hand on her apron, shaking a large kitchen knife at him with her right. "I'll straighten it out for you, mister," she said, laughing. It was good to have her life returning to normal. The memories were still very painful, but being home, in familiar surroundings, made them bearable.

The ringing telephone interrupted them. Dan reached for the receiver.

"Hello."

"Hello, my name is Wilson Carson. I'm from New York and I have some papers for you. I'd like to come to your home to talk with you, if you don't mind."

"Are you a reporter?" Dan asked skeptically.

"No Sir. I'm an attorney."

"An attorney! Does this have to do with the Government case I'm involved in?"

"No Sir, it doesn't. This is a separate matter all together. I'd like to speak with you personally. I promise, this will bring no harm to you, or your family."

"Okay, but I reserve the right to throw you out if I don't like what you're peddling." Dan gave the lawyer directions to his home, and hung up the phone.

"What's that all about?" Beth asked.

"I don't know. Some attorney from New York. He wouldn't say what it was about. He's coming out here, though. I think I should find my little tape recorder. Just in case."

Beth was more than a little upset.

"Why won't they leave us alone, Dan? When will all this be over?"

"Take it easy, honey. He said it didn't have anything to do with the Government cases. Let's just wait and see what he has to say."

They didn't have long to wait. It was less than 10 minutes until the rental car pulled into the drive. Dan and Beth were home alone; the two boys were at the river, fishing. They waited at the door. Dan had his arm around Beth's waist.

The car opened, a small, neatly dressed young man stepped out.

"Are you Dan and Elizabeth Webster?"

"That's right. And you must be Mr. Carson. Come in."

They sat in the living room, Beth brought coffee, while Lawyer Carson sorted through his papers and arranged them in proper order. He reached into his brief case one more time and retrieved a large document with a blue cover. He handed it to Dan.

"Mr. Webster, there is no need to read all this now, but this is your copy of, that portion of the will, which concerns you," he began.

"Wait a minute. Whose will? Who died?"

"Let me start at the beginning. You have been named as a beneficiary in the estate of Nels Bergstrom. Did you know him personally?"

"Bergstrom's dead?" Dan asked with surprise in his voice.

"Yes, Mr. Webster. He died of a heart attack 3 months ago while on a flight to Venezuela. The estate has kept it quiet, as most of the holdings are either held by the Bergstrom Enterprises Corporation or are outside the United States.

"Here's a letter of introduction," Carson took the top sheet from his brief case, "which will explain that our firm has been employed by Mr. Bergstrom for many years. We now represent his estate in the matter of his will."

"I can't believe it, Bergstrom is really dead?" Dan asked again.

"Yes, Sir, he is really dead."

"I wonder why Roger hasn't found out?" Dan asked himself, aloud.

"It's like I said," Carson explained again. "Not many people, outside the executive board, know about this."

"I'm sorry. I don't mean to keep interrupting you, but this is extremely hard to believe. So what did old Bergstrom leave me in his will? Another bomb?"

"No Sir. There is a letter in the document I gave you. Mr. Bergstrom admired you. You were the most honest and dedicated man he'd ever met. Although the two of you were on opposite sides of some issues, Mr. Bergstrom had great respect for you. You must have had contact with him, some 20 years ago, where you lost your job. He felt you had been treated unjustly, and, like I said, he admired and respected you.

"He had been involved in financing a wildcat oil operation at that time," Carson continued, "and acquired a very large block of stock in the new company. He set up a trust, in a Bahamian bank, in your name. The trust has been managed by the bank since then. The original trust was a holding of 25,000 shares of TexWest Oil Company. The history of the trust is contained in this folder." Carson handed another sheaf of papers to Dan. "TexWest no longer exists. It merged with some other company a short time after the trust was established. The bank in the Bahamas did well with your investment.

"I suggest you contact your lawyer to make certain everything is in proper order." He handed Dan one more folder filled with legal documents. "Then, if you are satisfied, you can sign this release and the trust will be turned over to you."

Dan was thumbing through the papers. They seemed to be genuine. "I can't imagine Bergstrom doing anything for me, after all, he got me shot twice. Just how much is this trust worth anyway."

"The total changes constantly, but as of the close of business in the Bahamas on Wednesday, it was," Carson spoke while looking at a ledger sheet in his brief case, "1,585,000 shares of assorted stock, mostly oil, and $3,621,911"

Beth looked at the man in disbelief. "Are you saying we have over three and a half million dollars in the bank?"

"Yes, ma'am. That is exactly what I'm saying. And since the holdings are outside the U.S., there are special tax considerations. I can recommend a good tax attorney with our firm if you're interested."

Dan was still looking through the papers when Mr. Carson closed his brief case and stood. "Are you leaving town right away or will you be staying until we sign the release?"

"I will be here as long as you want me to stay. You can have your lawyer contact me at this number," he said, giving Dan the business card of the local Best Western Motel. "Congratulations on your good fortune. I'll be seeing you next week. In the mean time I am going to try to catch a fish. I've dreamed, for years, of fishing the Kenai River. I plan to take advantage of this trip."

The couple was escorting the young man to the door when a car pulled into the drive. It was Roger and Gwen. Roger nodded a greeting to the lawyer as he passed the man.

"Hello, you two," they greeted as they climbed the steps to the porch. "We have news for you."

"Come in and tell us all about it," Beth said, smiling at her friends.

Inside the house, Roger turned to Gwen. "Go ahead and tell them, since this is all your idea."

"You are such a liar," Gwen laughed. "Pay no attention to him," she said. "He is just nervous because he'll soon have a wife to support."

"He finally asked you, did he?" Beth teased. "When's the day?"

"That depends on you two. We were sort of hoping we could be married here."

The friends talked and made plans for the wedding. They relived old times. Beth told Gwen about the man she was going to marry. After moving to Alaska, she relied a great deal on her friendship with Roger to help her and Dan through some tough times. They were reminded about the time Roger was the last one on an elevator. As a joke, he just stood and faced the other passengers. It had the effect of backing them to the rear of the car. He just smiled and stared over their heads. Roger liked to think he was sophisticated, but his impish humor betrayed him. He liked good wine, but preferred an ice cream cone to a beer. This kind of talk continued and it was several hours before Dan got around to mentioning that he and Beth were about to become wealthy. Beth and Gwen stayed in the kitchen while Dan and Roger went into the living room to look at the papers the lawyer had left.

Dan was reading the ledger sheet when Roger exclaimed, "Holy smoke, I almost forgot. I got a message on the Fax today, from Washington; it was about you. You will be getting an official letter from the White House in a few days. It seems the President wants you and Gwen to come to Washington, so he can present you with the President's Freedom Medal. That's the highest civilian award in this country. The last person to receive it was Ex-President Ronald Reagan."

"You're kidding."

"No, I'm not kidding. It looks like you will become rich and famous all the same day. Congratulations, Dan, you deserve it."

The rest of the evening was spent making plans and speculating about the future. The boys came home and became caught up in the excitement. Finally, after all the danger, the friends were relaxed.

The telephone rang and young son Tim went to answer it. When he returned he told his father, "That was Sam DeGrosso. He is coming down tomorrow to go fishing and wanted to know if you were going to be home. He'll be here sometime in the afternoon."

Everyone had gone to bed when Dan opened the refrigerator and poured milk into his favorite cup. He couldn't sleep for thinking about the events of the day. A lot had happened. He reflected on the past several months and on the early days of his career in California. He felt good about his life. He'd never done the things he was being honored for out of greed or a need for medals. He did them because they were right. Or at least he thought they were right at the time. Dan knew he couldn't change everything that was wrong in this country, but, he thought, if he could make his own little corner of the world a better place—then he had done his part. Life seemed simple to Dan.

If each individual would just do his part to stay within the rules of society, help his neighbor when he was down and keep his own family strong, then the social ills plaguing America would all but disappear. Before the government can be strong, the individual must be strong.

There will always be someone attempting to take unfair advantage, using the system. But if the public, John Q. Average, voices his objections, the lawless cannot survive for long. When the individual surrenders to corruption, when he says, "That's just the way it is," then he loses his country and his life to the lawless.

Freedom is a precious commodity. But as long as the individual is strong, the lawless, the manipulators cannot take it from us. So far, most Americans are winning.

It was going to be difficult to erase the hate for Nels Bergstrom, which he had nurtured for so long. Bergstrom had cheated him of revenge. John Sutter, one of the finest men Dan had ever known, died because of Nels Bergstrom. Dan had lived, the past 20 years, for the day Bergstrom would face justice for the crimes he had committed. But, justice would now have to come from Divine Retribution. Dan would have to change this hate to something positive. "I'll use Bergstrom's money to help John's family. The least I can do is see to it his family never wants for anything. Brother, it hurts to lose a friend."

He looked at the cup in his hand. He could still see the picture of the giant Redwood tree and could still read the faded lettering which read, "The Enchanted Forest." He rinsed the milk from the cup and went back bed.